Satyavati

Satyavati

The Queen Who Shaped the Destiny of the Kurus

RUPEEN POPAT

JAICO PUBLISHING HOUSE
Ahmedabad Bangalore Chennai
Delhi Hyderabad Kolkata Mumbai

Published by Jaico Publishing House
A-2 Jash Chambers, 7-A Sir Phirozshah Mehta Road
Fort, Mumbai - 400 001
jaicopub@jaicobooks.com
www.jaicobooks.com

SATYAVATI
ISBN 978-93-48098-09-2

First Jaico Impression: 2025

Page design and layout by Jojy Philip, Delhi

Printed by
Thomson Press India Limited, New Delhi

Satyavati

◂ The author with his spiritual guru Morari Bapu.
▾ Morari Bapu's Foreword in Gujarati.

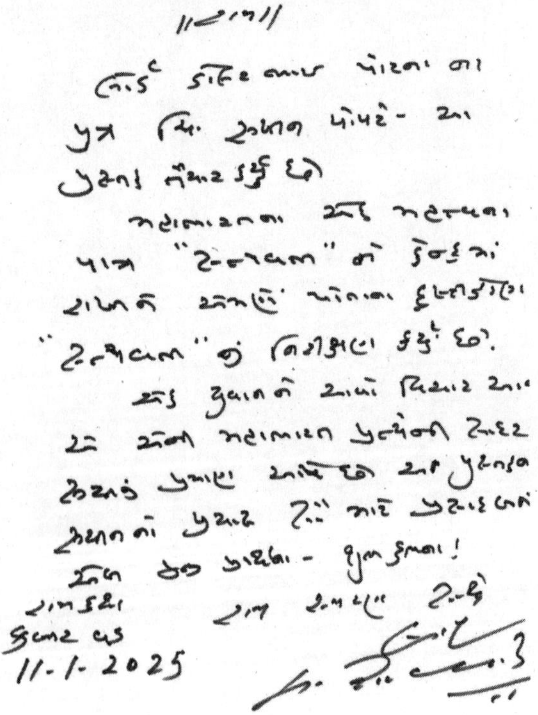
11-1-2025

Foreword

|| RAM ||

Lord Dolarbhai Popat's son, Rupeen Popat, has prepared this book. He has taken Satyavati's character and has expressed his views and analysis. Rupeen is a young man who has the Mahabharata in his heart, and shows his respect and love for the epic. Through his books, Rupeen will be able to spread the *prasad* of his understanding. With my best wishes and prayers to God.

With the remembrance of Lord Ram,
Morari Bapu
Kabirvad
11.1.2025

Prologue

The day had started well as the eight Vasus enjoyed themselves in the forest. The deities had few cares. Dhara (earth), Apa (water), Anala (hot fire), Anila (wind), Pratyusha (sun), Prabhasa (sky), Soma (moon) and Dhruva (stars) were brothers, born to Brahma Prajapati. They usually followed Dhara's lead, but today, it was not Dhara who dictated the activities of the group. Prabhasa had a request. His wife had spotted a beautiful cow and she wanted it.

'Please steal it for me,' she had asked Prabhasa with a flirtatious giggle.

Was it a test of his love, or did she really want it? Prabhasa couldn't tell, but he couldn't resist the challenge either. He gathered his brothers around him.

'It will be fun,' he said. 'Can you imagine what a game it will be?'

The group agreed. It would be an interesting diversion on this hot, still day. They gathered around the beast in a semicircle and herded it away from the spot where it grazed in the green pasture. The cow did not protest. No doubt it had eaten its fill of the lush, green grass. They left it outside their dwelling, tethered loosely with a rope, where it continued to thoughtfully chew the wild geraniums which grew through the cracks in the parched soil.

It wasn't until the following day that the Vasus realised their horrendous mistake, when Sage Vashishta arrived in a terrible rage. It was *his* cow. Why had they stolen it? It was an outrage.

No pleadings or apologies could assuage the sage's anger. He refused to listen to the eight brothers. Reparations had to be made. Raising himself to his full height and his arms to the heavens, Sage Vashishta issued a curse. The eight brothers would each live one life on earth as mortals, the most awful dishonour for any god. They would be subject to unimaginable suffering every day they spent as men. The eight fell to their knees and pleaded that the sage take back his curse, but he refused. 'Once a curse is cast, it cannot be taken back,' he said.

Yet, seeing the genuine sadness and remorse among the group cowering in front of him, the sage had a slight change of heart. He advised them that the goddess Ganga, who purifies sin, may be persuaded to help them reduce their suffering and perhaps even the time they lived on earth. However, Prabhasa, who had instigated the crime, would pay the full penalty. He would remain on earth for his entire lifetime as a man and suffer greatly every day.

Chapter One

The reeds, scratching lightly as they knocked against my small boat, were my constant companions. Each day, we were chased by the twin trails of water splitting either side of the well-worn hull as we gently made our way from one side of the Yamuna to the other. Those tiny waves never caught us, though. They always gave up quickly, flattening themselves into the smooth, sage-green waters of the river behind us.

My father, Dasharaj, had built this boat many years ago, using the teak from the trees that once stood sentinel along this very river. The rich red varnish, together with the intricate green and gold patterns adorning the sides, was once vibrant and magnificent. It has all faded now. Even so, it is clear that much care was put into my vessel's construction. Building this boat cost my father many weeks' wages. He sourced his paints and tools from passing tradesmen, sometimes waiting weeks for the next arrival. Yet, he had been patient and dedicated when it came to completing his grand design, even when his fellow fishermen teased him and said I would not need such an important boat. Surely, a simple raft could do the job? He batted away their jibes, saying again and again that he had to have something regal for me. He gifted it to me before I could first stand. It was, he said, my own floating carriage. Fit for a queen.

These lofty aspirations seemed at odds with my life. Each day, for as far back as I could remember, had been like this one. The world around me remained the same as I plied my trade, ferrying passengers back and forth. There had only been one day in my life when things were very different. My mind did not want to explore that now. That remained deeply hidden in the furthest corners of my thoughts.

The birds chatted with one another as they returned to their nests for the night. Some were quiet, though, the last of the day's food for their young ones clasped in their beaks, carried with stoic determination. A small gadwall swooped in low over my boat. For a brief moment, it appeared to pause in mid-air, its wings outstretched and head tilted, taking a look at me lying still in the hull, a small bag as my pillow. The bird squawked a quick greeting, but perhaps I didn't respond quickly enough for its liking. It flew away quickly, its cry unanswered. In the near distance, I heard the distinctive sound of two gharials stealthily sinking into the darkening waters of the river, their day's vicious hunting complete. Now that their bellies were full, they sought a perfect place to sleep. This ritual, where the gharials' long snouts and armies of teeth disappeared into the depths, was always followed by a discernible sigh of relief from the surrounding wildlife. Those hideous predators were gone for the night.

'Some queen,' I said out loud to no one in particular. My life could not have been further from the prophecy that my father had regaled to me more times than I believed possible to count. I'd never stopped him telling the story. I knew it gave him great pleasure. His face would light up as he described the reading of my horoscope when I was born. It was as though he was still in the room with the sage, entranced by his orange robes wrapped around my new-born body, fresh to the world. He could almost hear it all over again—the revered sage looking down at me and pronouncing that one day, I, Satyavati, would be the greatest queen in all the land and that my children would rule after me.

As a young girl, after hearing this story over and over, I used to enjoy fantasising about my future kingdom. I'd vividly imagine what it would be like to have wealth beyond the comprehension of mere mortals. There would be lavish feasts given in my honour, with tables groaning with enough food to feed the world and the stars too. I'd have an army ready to fight and die for me. They would carry great silken flags before them, bearing my crest as they marched to their fate. As I grew into a young woman, though, my royal dreamland began to fade. I was not a queen. Most of the people whom I ferried from one side of the Yamuna to the other barely looked at me. If they did, they didn't even seem to see me as a fellow human being. Often, my only interaction with them would be when they pressed a few coins into my palm. At other times, they would fill the time of the crossing by reciting endless tales about themselves. I did not mind hearing about the outside world. It was nice to know about growing cities in faraway places and the ebb and flow of rival kingdoms as they fought endless bitter wars. It was all the news of the world I could get; otherwise, the borders of my reality stretched just from my hut to the other side of the shore.

I shook my head irritably. What use were these pathetic musings? I had already relived this story a thousand times this year and a thousand times the year before that. There was no doubt tomorrow would be the same too. Sitting up, I looked out across the water towards the setting sun.

The bright yellow light had already turned to deep orange as it came into contact with the shifting sands and patchy vegetation of the landscape beyond. The fading light was reflected off the wings of the thousands of insects that had emerged to dance with abandon above the water's surface. Like the wildlife celebrating the departure of the gharials, the insects were letting loose now that the orchestra of birds was leaving them in peace for the night. It was time for me to return home before it became too dark.

Settling into my familiar seat, I grabbed the oars and gently pushed the boat away from the shore. The keel kissed the reeds goodbye as it passed over them one final time, and I ducked low to avoid the vibrating cloud of insects. Most of them obligingly shifted out of the way. The little creatures were in no hurry to meet a sudden teakwood demise.

The journey didn't take long. As the boat approached the jetty, I didn't even need to look for the familiar smooth post where I tied her up each night. I put out my hand and it was there, as always. I hooked the rope into place and stepped onto the shore, ready to take the last few steps of my routine.

Our house was pleasant enough. In fact, by the standard of most houses, or at least the ones I knew in my limited experience, it was quite large. My father, despite his grumbles, earned good money from fishing. We each had our own room, as did our small handful of servants. The dark-red paint covering the building blended seamlessly with the ochre sands of the river shore that the home loomed above, while the gold and green framing around each window and door worked hard to give it some stature. I'm not sure if the paint quite achieved that aim, but it did at least make each wall look as indifferent to the dust and dirt as possible. My favourite part of the design was the wooden veranda that ran the length of the house, overlooking the river. It would be easy to suppose that I'd have had enough of the view, but I could spend hours watching the water flow past. If I flowed with it, where would it take me? Would it transport me somewhere I could discover my supposed destiny?

I was doing it again. Shaking my head once again to flush the daydreams away, I headed to the kitchen. This was another ritual. The first stop of my homecoming each day was to check the large terracotta cooking pot. It would most likely contain some sort of fish—it always did—but the cook never failed to make an interesting feast. He had an intricate knowledge of where to find the tastiest and the most aromatic herbs and spices along the riverbank. Inhaling the rich scent would always ground me. I was home.

My next stop was always to seek out my father. Today, he was where he could be found most often, at the back of the house, counting the day's catch. This was his daily ritual before he went on to tie the fish to dry on the wooden rack.

'It looks like a good catch today', I said with a smile.

The last few months had not been good for fish. Perhaps today's good fishing fortune was a sign that our luck was turning for the better.

'Good evening, my little Queen,' my father said, turning to face me as he uttered his nightly greeting.

I smiled in response. If I was not mistaken, this would be the gentlest remark I could expect for the evening. My father was not a patient man and rarely curbed his emotions. If the fishing had not been good, he would be sharp and irritable with everyone, including me.

'A good day's haul, Father?' I pressed, trying to disguise the hopeful note in my voice.

'A few more golden fish this week than the last, which seems like a good-luck sign,' he said, turning back to his neat line of fish. Then, he shrugged. 'But still, my buckets are never quite full at the moment.'

I stayed silent. It was best that way, but my toes were already curling into the sand of the backyard as I braced for what would come next.

'And you, Satyavati, how was your work today? Or have you been sleeping again? If the fish won't come to me, perhaps we can swap. You do this, and I will bob about on the river all day, gossiping with customers.'

I smiled back, pretending he was teasing. We both knew he was not, though. He barely tried to hide his disappointment with me anymore.

'I'll check on supper,' I said softly, turning and walking away.

There was no way I would reproach him or raise the subject of why he was so angry. It was a lovely dream, but just a prophecy. Nothing more. No reasonable person could chastise their child for not becoming queen.

I had already checked on supper. As always, the cook had it all in hand. Instead, I turned my steps towards the veranda. It was almost dusk now, but even if I could barely see the river, I enjoyed the comfort of standing there, feeling the warm comfort of the wooden slats beneath my feet.

My moment of solitude was disturbed by the rhythmic sound of horses' hooves. It was barely discernible at first, but it rapidly became louder and louder. It was almost hypnotic, as though the greatest musician in all of Bharat had commanded the hooves of the horse to create a perfect drumbeat. How unusual it was, though, to hear horses on the road at this time of day.

Squinting into the gloom, I was surprised to see a bright ball of light in the direction of the noise. The last rays of the sun had long since melted into the sand, yet the light seemed golden. In the rapidly approaching oblong of gold were different patches of bright colours, which glinted as the brilliant vision rose up and down in perfect harmony with the drumbeat. It was a chariot, a golden chariot, bedecked with beautiful jewels. I was transfixed.

That this chariot belonged to no ordinary man was certain. It was the shape and size of a nobleman's chariot, and I had never seen anything like it in my life. The decorations were so ornate, so precise, so regal. It was priceless. This was no ordinary man.

The chariot was close enough now for me take a proper look at it. My gaze dwelled on the driver for a few seconds. He looked very ordinary, dressed in the simple robes most people wore when going about their business. The only thing that was remarkable about him was his intense concentration as he worked to keep the chariot steady and his master comfortable. My gaze switched to the man standing stiffly to his left.

The nobleman, whose thick, black hair fanned out behind him in the breeze, was tall, certainly taller than the men that usually passed this way. He was broad-shouldered, yet slim and muscular. This was clear to see, even though he was adorned in a robe of rich purple silk, edged with gold. What was by far the most noticeable about this mysterious man, though, was his expression. He looked distracted, melancholy, his thoughts far away in another world.

The chariot was almost alongside me now, and I prepared to step back into the shadows. I was too slow to slip away unnoticed, though.

'Sarathee!' the nobleman's voice boomed through the twilight. 'Stop the chariot at once!'

My heart beat faster and I began to feel breathless. I suddenly regretted not changing out of my sari, the one I had worn all day while working. I felt shabby in the presence of this great man and his golden chariot. I didn't want him to see me, but I had no choice. Sarathee did as he was bidden, and the chariot came to a halt directly in front of me, kicking up a cloud of sand in its wake.

For a few moments, the world lapsed into complete silence. Even the pangolins shuffling in the undergrowth of the forest behind me in their constant search for ants had abruptly stopped what they were doing.

I hardly dared look directly at this man, but felt compelled to do so. As the dust around us settled, the richness of his attire became more apparent. Draped around his body was a finely tailored blue *pashtush*, which settled around his shoulders now that the chariot had stopped moving. There were a dozen or more thick gold chains around his neck. In all my time working the river crossings, I had seen little golden clothing. Occasionally, a wealthy man might pass through with a small gold pin on his clothes, or perhaps a lady would wear a delicate golden ring, but never in my life had I seen this much gold.

This was not what held my attention, however. I could not tear my eyes away from the golden crown that sat atop this man's head. It was as if it were its own source of light, a thousand mirrors shining down on me, engulfing me in their aura. The sun itself was resting for the night on this man's head.

Mesmerised, I watched as the man leapt deftly down from the chariot.

'Good evening,' he said. His voice was like silk.

I stared at him, unable to answer.

'What is your name?' he said, pretending not to notice I had not returned his greeting.

I took a deep breath. No one had asked me this question in years. Resolving that I must reply, that I just had to, I took a step forward to force myself into a position where I had no choice.

'I … I am Satyavati,' I said quietly.

I felt embarrassed and foolish. This man, with his expertly groomed beard and fine clothes, must be toying with me. Yet, the smile that spread across his face and to his deep brown eyes didn't seem to echo that sentiment. He looked genuine.

'Well, good evening, Satyavati,' he said, giving a small bow of respect. 'I am King Shantanu and humbled to meet you.'

A very small part of me wanted to let out a small laugh. Or run to fetch my father. *You see, a king, he is here. The prophecy is true!* This was foolish on so many counts. First, this was hardly a declaration of love and away from a marriage proposal, which was, now I was confronted with a true king, the most ridiculous idea. How had I ever toyed with such fanciful daydreams? Second, I couldn't even bear to imagine how my father would react to a bona fide king standing on his doorstep. No, I would remain where I was and enjoy bathing in the glory of this fine man.

Without meaning to, I found myself smiling back at him. Somehow, he had the trick of making me feel at ease despite my nervousness. That was the talent of a true king, I supposed. They momentarily help you forget their power and status and instead make you feel like the most important person on earth.

'Would it be possible for you to take me across the river?' he asked, glancing behind him at my boat moored on the jetty. 'I can pay you, of course. I see you have finished for the day, and I feel a little bad about pulling you away from your supper. It does smell rather lovely.'

If the request surprised me, I hid it well. I would have given up one hundred grand feasts to spend just a few minutes with this charismatic man.

'Yes, your Majesty, of course, please follow me,' I said, keeping my voice low. My tone now was about not alerting my father, rather than out of awe of the king. My father would have almost certainly changed everything about the evening.

'Please, do not call me your Majesty. Call me Shantanu.'

I indicated the way to the jetty with a sweep of my arm, and the king began to walk towards my boat. I fell into step just behind him and snuck another look at this extraordinary man. As he walked, the *pashtush* had slipped away from his shoulders, revealing his bare arms. Being this close, I could see that his muscles were adorned with the occasional scar, spoils from what must have been years of warfare.

It was difficult not to speculate why he wanted to cross the river at this late hour. He wouldn't have his chariot with him when he reached the other side, so he'd have to make his way from there on foot. Perhaps he merely wanted to see, out of curiosity, what was on the other side, an eagerness to see every corner of his kingdom. I wondered if he had passed through here before and I had not seen him, or, whether this part of his kingdom was new to him.

Once we arrived at the boat, I untied it, and gestured for him to please board the small craft. After entering the boat, instead of sitting straight down, the king turned to me and held out his hand, gesturing that he would like to help me into the boat. This had never happened to me before, and this time, I could not hide my shock. Yet, without speaking, I reached out to him and he guided me to my seat.

If the king noticed my reaction, he did not comment on it.

'This is a fine boat,' he said, stroking the top ridge of the side where he sat while gazing out over the now-dark emerald waters. 'How grand my rivers would look if they were filled with these boats!'

I pushed away from the shore with an oar and began the short journey across the water. The king started to hum a beautiful tune to himself, one that I did not recognise but was quite mesmerising, nonetheless. My oars hitting the water were the only other sound, and I watched his gaze straining through the gloom to see the few birds that hadn't made it back to their nests yet. To our surprise, a perfectly coloured great hornbill flapped its way past us, just a few feet from the boat. The gaze of my royal passenger followed the course of the bird, and he gave an approving nod as it disappeared from view.

'A fine bird,' he said, turning back to me as if to gain my agreement.

The silence returned, save for the light splash of the oars. When we looked at one another, though, I felt that we were somehow having a conversation of a thousand words, without uttering a single one.

When we reached the opposite bank, the king climbed out of the boat and once again gave me his hand, this time to help me to the shore. I took it and stepped onto the cool, damp sand, realising with a start that I had forgotten to put my slippers on. If the king noticed too, he did not mention it. Instead, he turned away from me and walked a few steps, his hands clasped behind his back, his eyes searching the trees ahead of him and then the darkening sky.

I found myself strangely at ease around this man, despite his noble lineage. Yet, something deep inside me was telling me to stay away from him. My instincts told me that he had a secret, just as I did, a secret that he could not bring himself to reveal. What lay behind that sadness I could see in his eyes? There seemed to be a deep pain that scorched his insides.

Whatever my foreboding, I ignored it. The compulsion to strike up a conversation was too strong.

'Have you been to the Yamuna before?' I asked tentatively.

He swung around to look at me, as if awoken from a deep sleep, and smiled.

'Far further upstream, where the waters are a lot narrower. They run close to my palace, in fact.'

'Is it a grand palace?'

His smile grew larger and he took a small step back towards me, his hands stretched wide, 'It is the largest and finest in Bharat.'

How strange this conversation was! I had dreamt about palaces every day for my whole life, and this was the first time I had ever spoken to someone who lived in one.

After a few more minutes, Shantanu asked politely if I would return him to the other side of the river. I was a little surprised that he had stayed for such a short time, but it was almost dark now. As the boat eased its way across the still river, we made small talk, but something felt different, almost like a spell had been broken. Once we reached the bank, he extended a hand as before. As my feet touched the shore, he gave a small bow and said he had to be on his way. Before stepping into his chariot, he checked himself and returned to press a number of gold coins into my palm.

'Thank you,' he said, with a respectful nod of his head.

And then, he was back on the chariot. Sarathee touched the horses with the whip to make them move. I watched as they picked up speed and disappeared into the distance. Soon, the only evidence that the king was ever there was a distant rumble of hooves.

'Who was that?'

I swung around to see my father standing at the door.

'What did he want?'

I took a moment to formulate my response. What should I tell my father? How would he behave if he knew that a king had come to his doorstep, a king who had flattered me?

'How long have you been standing there?' I said cautiously.

'Just now,' he said, his voice beginning to harden. My answering his question with one of my own irritated him.

'It was no one, Father,' I said hurriedly. 'Just a few hunters looking for directions.'

To my relief, it was enough to satisfy him.

'That's mighty irresponsible, being out lost whilst hunting at this time of day!' he grumbled as he headed back through the door. 'Making us late for supper ...'

Chapter Two

The following day passed like any other, with a steady, if not overwhelming, flow of customers waiting to cross the river. When I arrived at my usual position, I found a few hunters impatient to make their way into the forest to get a head start on their quest. They were followed by a salesman, who spent the whole journey across the river aggressively trying to sell me his wares. I much preferred listening to the stories of my next customers, a young woman and her child who were searching for new lands. Their eyes shone with excitement at the adventure that lay ahead. I could relate to that. But as one customer blurred into the next, I became distracted, my thoughts constantly returning to Shantanu. Had my adventure ended before it had truly begun? Would he return?

That evening, without really thinking about it, I changed into my finest clothes when I got home. I chose a delicate red sari with an elegant silk embroidery detail that snaked around the neck and hem in a darker shade. It was the one my father had purchased from a wandering trader many years before, at a time when he was convinced that it was only a matter of time before such finery would be needed every day. I had rarely worn it, so it was still in pristine condition.

As I sat on the steps to the veranda, ostensibly practising my braiding with fresh green reeds still oozing their sap, I kept telling myself not to be so silly. I had allowed my imagination to run away with itself. If my father had not gone on and on about that stupid prophecy, I would have put the previous night down to what it was, just a remarkable experience. I would have barely thought about it again.

Letting out an impatient sigh, I told myself to focus on the here and now. Then, fearing I had spoken aloud, I glanced nervously around me. The servants were wandering in and out of the house, going about their daily business, and if they'd heard me, they didn't react. The youngest of them was tending to the plants around the entrance, humming as he did so, but he seemed oblivious to my presence. I shifted a little on the wooden step, enjoying its warm embrace after its long day bathed in the sunlight that always lit up the front of the house. The smooth boards were always soothing to the tired soles of my feet. The sky had, by now, turned from a pale blue to a misty grey as the sun prepared to depart for the day, its work complete. My day was also complete. It was time for me to go indoors and forget my fantasies.

I had barely stood up when I heard the sound of hooves in the distance. Thinking quickly, I turned to the servant tending the plants and asked him to check on the ones at the back of the house. The last thing I needed was a curious servant reporting back to my father.

Smoothing down my sari self-consciously, I watched in anticipation as the golden chariot thundered ever closer. I could tell almost the moment it hove into view that something was different this time. The king was standing proud and tall at the front of the chariot, just as before, but he was alone.

It didn't take long for the chariot to arrive at my door, whereupon it stopped abruptly in a familiar cloud of sand. As the sand settled and the king lightly jumped from the chariot with a broad smile, it was difficult not to feel awkward. He had clearly taken extra care with his appearance. While his clothes were just as grand as on the previous day, they were cleaner, more polished. What was most noticeable was that his crown shone. Someone had been tasked with working that gold and its brightly coloured embedded jewels to a high shine.

'Good evening, Satyavati,' he said, giving a low bow. 'May I once again trouble you for your services in crossing the Yamuna?'

If I found the request surprising, I was determined not to let it show.

'Of course,' I replied. Everything within me wanted to add that I had been hoping he would visit. But I stayed silent. That would be too forward. Instead, I motioned for him to follow me to the jetty.

Once again, the king helped me into my boat, only settling into his seat once I was in mine. He was a little quieter this evening, seemingly lost in thought, perhaps grappling with some inner demon. It was not until we were halfway across the river that he suddenly cried out.

'Where is my hornbill?' he said, in mock exasperation. 'I had hoped he would come to pay his respects to me once again.'

I couldn't help but laugh.

'That bird, it has a mind of its own. Sometimes, even I don't see it for months, and I cross this river a dozen times a day!'

Now, it was the king's turn to laugh.

'Ah, well, in that case, perhaps I will have to stay here for months in wait,' he said, throwing his hands in the air. 'Then, when it does deign to pay me homage, I will capture it and take it. It will make a fine pet.'

By now, my curiosity was getting the better of me. All hopes of propriety had melted away in the silly exchange about the hornbill.

'Sir …' I began and then giggled at my customer's look of feigned outrage at my form of address. 'Sorry, Shantanu, you … are not … do not behave in the way I'd expect a king to behave.'

The king settled back in his seat, one arm slung carelessly over the side of the boat, his fingers almost trailing in the dark water. He scrutinised my face with interest.

'Did you expect an old warrior, too occupied with thoughts of conflict and politics to take notice of the birds in the sky, the fish in the water, and the perfect woman I have met working the Yamuna?'

Feeling embarrassed, I looked away. I had not expected that answer, nor did I understand how I was supposed to react.

By now, we had reached the opposite bank. As before, he climbed out and helped me out before walking a few paces away, his hands clasped behind his back. I watched in silence and then I saw him nod, as though he has finished his musings and come to a conclusion.

'You are, without a doubt, the greatest beauty in all of my kingdom, and the kingdoms beyond it, and even across all of the stars,' he said walking towards me with a determined air, his eyes never leaving mine. 'If you lived within the walls of my city, then you would have no shortage of suitors courting you. But you are here. And it is my greatest pleasure to have found you.'

A great part of me wanted to tear myself away from his gaze, but I could not. My legs would not carry me away either. This was beyond my comprehension. The king immediately sensed it too.

'Don't worry,' he said, holding out his hand to guide me back into the boat. 'It does seem like a lot to take in. I can barely understand it myself. I thought I would never feel like this aga…'

The king seemed to check himself.

'Please, if you will, take me back to the other side. With your permission, I will return tomorrow.'

I wanted to say that I was in no position to grant permission to a king, but I could not speak. Instead, I took the oars and began to row.

The king spoke little on the return journey. He seemed as preoccupied as I felt. When we reached our destination, he thanked me, paid me for the crossing and said farewell. Within a few moments, he and his golden chariot were gone. The only sign that they had been there and that this had not been a vivid dream was the small cloud of dust kicked up by the horses and the distant rhythmic thunder of their hooves.

I began to worry about stepping into the house. Surely, my father had heard our visitor this time or wandered to the front of the house and seen the golden chariot outside, a chariot which spoke so clearly of our royal guest's patronage. I needn't have been concerned, however. As I walked into the kitchen, he didn't even look up to acknowledge me. He was too busy berating the cook over how he'd like his dinner prepared.

The next day was different from the last. I now knew the king would arrive later, so I was both impatient and nervous. I was also concerned that it wouldn't be long before my father learned my secret. When he did, he would almost certainly intervene in a way that neither I nor the king would want him to. It was quite likely that he would gloat, or announce that the prophecy had been right after all, and scare my royal friend away for good. Otherwise, the day was the same as any other, save for the thousands of phuti fish which mysteriously surrounded my boat in the afternoon. I swear they'd come en masse to pluck my boat clean from all its algae and prepare it for events ahead.

Somehow, by the time Shantanu arrived, I felt more relaxed than I had expected to feel. I had so looked forward to seeing him that I could not help grinning broadly as he leapt off his chariot. He was once again alone and, once again, even more handsome and well groomed than the day before.

As we began the crossing, he was much more talkative too. He seemed to have much to say, his words almost tripping over one another.

'Satyavati, I have to tell you that for the whole day, all I could think about was seeing you again. The politics within the palace walls did not interest me one bit. The feasts prepared by my cooks could not satisfy me. I feel whole only when I am in your presence.'

Whatever had strengthened my resolve to look forward to the arrival of my royal suitor, for I was almost certain now that a suitor was what he was, gave me the fortitude to reply in a way that was not meant to discourage.

'You are far too flattering to me, Shantanu,' I said quietly, stealing a glance at him as I rowed. 'I would hate to think that I am a distraction to you in looking after your grand kingdom.'

My brief glance showed me that he was staring at me, waiting for this reply. He clearly approved of my boldness because he gave a low and appreciative chuckle.

'You are not a distraction. I hope that you will soon be part of it.'

That response stopped my daring in its tracks. Was he asking me to return with him? Would that be as his wife? Or was he just teasing me? It seemed incredible that this could happen, and so quickly.

'I … I saw your hornbill today,' I said quickly. 'It was a little early. I did, I, well, I told it to come back later.'

Shantanu did not press the point. He was a sensitive man. Instead, he followed my lead and asked about the other wildlife I'd seen that day. He did not, however, hurry the routine we had established, spending an equal period on the opposite bank before it was time to return and be on his way.

Thus the pattern continued. As if playing an elaborate game of cat and mouse, he arrived each evening, full of compliments. For my part, I would try to be welcoming, but fearful where this might be going, I would always pull back. He, in turn, would take my lead and change the subject when I did. He was always charming, though, and would speak to me of many things.

Ferrying people across the river seemed far less important than it had ever been before. I did not even attempt any conversation with my passengers and hardly cared when they pressed money into my hands. Each day, I was only focussed on one thing: Shantanu's next visit. Some customers may have noticed my distant mood, but few said anything about it. The most that was said was by a regular, a hunter who lived close by and who liked to imagine he knew everything about everyone.

'You have so little concern in your life,' he said, sounding irritated. 'You have a wonderful house and a brilliant father; what could possibly be haunting your thoughts so much that you barely acknowledge your customers?'

I did not respond in words, but mustered a smile so as not to appear rude.

The truth was that I did have concerns. I enjoyed every moment with Shantanu, but there always seemed to be a barrier between us. Something saddened the king, something that every time he smiled, or laughed, would see him check himself as though he should not show joy. He had the look of a man haunted by eternal grief. I did not want to pry, and I know some secrets are best left untold. When they are buried so deep, it can take a lot of effort and will to dig them out. Some secrets are better left alone.

But I wanted to ease this man's obvious pain.

Some days were worse than others, and this was one of them. After Shantanu had arrived, alone in his chariot, he looked sadder than ever, a million *aratni* away from the man who had once joked about the hornbill. He was silent as we wandered over to my boat, which was moored in its usual place. After helping me in, he sat down, and I began to slowly paddle across the water. This time, he paid little attention to the wildlife, the waters, or the goings-on of the world around him.

I stopped rowing as something deep within me stirred. I was a nobody, I could not challenge a king, but I needed to help him. *That* was my purpose. Perhaps even the prophecy had been a little bit right. My life on this earth was to support the king and help him do what was right.

'What in your life has caused you this pain?' I said, hardly believing I could be so bold.

The king tore his gaze away from me and looked towards the far horizon. One hand was over the side of the boat, absent-mindedly caressing the calm surface of the water.

'Satyavati, I wish to share … it … with you. I will do so soon. I am not ready yet. It is still … a most difficult thing.'

What else could I do other than tell him I understood?

I picked up my oar to resume my trajectory to the opposite shore. For the first time, though, the king laid his hand on it and asked quietly if we could return to his chariot. I nodded to show I understood, even though I did not. My mind raced with questions, but the king's countenance was resolute. My heart felt like it might break in two. I had gone too far. I was now certain this was the last time I would see this man.

Shantanu was as kind and gentle as ever as he helped me from the boat, but I hardly noticed it. I was bracing myself for his last words to bid me goodbye forever. I began to prepare my facial expression into one of well-meaning friendship. *Please stay in touch. Drop by whenever you need to be taken across the Yamuna. I'll be here.*

After he helped me from the boat, I took longer than usual in tying it to its post. I couldn't bear to follow him to the carriage. I was just straightening up when I became aware that he was back, standing just beside me.

'I would like to return to you tomorrow if you will accept my presence?' he said, his eyes searching my face to read my reaction.

I smiled, and this time, I took a step forward and accepted his outstretched hands.

'Of course, please return to me tomorrow. I shall be waiting.'

He nodded, but neither of us said anything more. He then turned and headed to the chariot, and I watched as he flicked the reins to signal to the horses to depart. I stood by the jetty for a few moments, watching him disappear over the horizon. *What was it that pained the king so greatly?*

The next day, and for the next week, the king arrived promptly each afternoon, and I ferried him back and forth. On some days, he would discuss his kingdom and several of its problems; on other days, he would ask endless questions about my family and me. Happily, my father was away for long periods, the absence of fish forcing him to go further afield.

Each day, I asked Shantanu, 'Do you feel ready to speak to me about the pain you harbour?'

And each day, the answer was the same, 'No, not yet.'

My yearning to know the truth grew stronger and stronger, building to almost the point of bursting. It was not simply because I was curious. I knew that I could help him. Yet, how could I get it out of him? What would be the right combination of words to unlock the box in which he kept that truth hidden away? I wondered too if he felt the same way as I did, his pain boiling to the surface, a pin poke away from overflowing.

I could not sleep at night. I lay wide awake, trying to piece it all together, trying to seek some sort of answer or at least something that might prompt him to finally confide in me.

On the seventh day, my curiosity was overwhelming. As we reached the halfway point across the river, I prepared to ask my question once more. The second my words began to form, though, Shantanu sprang to his feet, his expression resolute.

'Satyavati, I have hoped since the day that I met you that you would be my second chance, that you would be willing to receive all the love in the world that I have to offer, and I would be able to give you all that I have in my heart. But you must first know my story.'

As he finished speaking, he looked exhausted, almost like he was about to pass out. I sensed there was more, though, so I stayed silent.

'Satyavati, I … will tell you everything, but it is very painful, so forgive me if I do not deliver it as I should.'

I smiled softly but remained silent. The moment had finally come. I would give him all the time in the world.

'I must begin by telling you that I have been in love before,' he said, staring out across the river. 'It was a long time ago. It began in a place not dissimilar to this. I would walk beside this river every day to clear my head. I enjoyed listening to the birds and watching the fish dart about. There was something so peaceful about spending time in a world so different to the one within the walls of the kingdom of Hastinapur.'

His gaze returned to me, and he settled back in his seat.

'On one evening as warm as this one, after a trying day in the courts, arguing over a conflict I can scarcely remember, I wandered down the banks of the river. As I pondered the events of the day, I heard a splash beside me, close to the river's edge. I turned to see whether an animal or a fish had made the noise. Instead, I was greeted with the sight of the most beautiful woman I had ever laid eyes on.'

By the way he stared at the shore of the Yamuna, it was clear he could see this vision right then, as clear as day. Tears began to form in his eyes.

'She rose from the water, yet her skin, her clothes, her hair … they were all completely dry. Her perfect red and gold dress was completely unblemished by the green waters that she emerged from. I was entranced, and my body was no longer in my brain's control. I almost sleepwalked towards her and she towards me.

'After a moment of standing in silence facing one another, as close as you and I are right now, she revealed her name. I have not uttered this name in a very long time, so please excuse my difficulty in saying it, but her name was Ganga. She is a goddess. An extremely powerful, divine goddess.'

The king looked down at his golden slippers and shook his head before letting out a low chuckle.

'Strange though it might sound, she revealed that we had known one another in a past life. I have little recollection of that life, only that I must have loved her then as much as I did in this one. She was impossible not to fall in love with. She could make the coldest of men melt.

'I dropped to my knees and pleaded with her to marry me. She smiled and accepted. But she had just one condition. It was that I would never question her. When I readily agreed to it, I had no idea that it would soon come to torment me for every living moment of my life.'

My head filled with questions, but I knew I must stay quiet and let him tell me his story in his own time. If I interrupted, he might stop.

'We celebrated our nuptials in the most lavish of fashions. Everyone in Hastinapur drank and partied. We were loved by all. They saw us as a perfect, powerful husband and his beautiful wife, ruling the kingdom with compassion.'

This was the first time I had seen Shantanu smile properly since he began his story. But that smile instantly evaporated. This was it. We were coming to the part that had caused him so much pain.

'Soon, she gave birth to my first son. He was a strong child, who would have grown into the greatest prince any kingdom in India would ever see.'

The king's expression became even darker, and a single tear escaped and fell down his cheek.

'For a few days after the birth, my wife behaved as any other mother would. She was, of course, in recovery, but being who she was, with her incredible strength, it was very quick for her. She cradled our son throughout every day and every night, nurturing him and loving him. I spent every possible waking hour by their side, trying to be the best father I could. I was as loving and as grateful to Ganga as I had ever been.

'But in the darkest hours of the fourth night, I felt the bed move as Ganga rose from it. At first, I thought nothing of it, assuming she was rising to go refresh herself or see to the baby's needs. I slumbered for a few moments more, but a deep feeling of foreboding began to grow in my heart.

'I went to look for my Ganga, but I could not find her anywhere. I searched the palace from top to bottom until eventually a guard pointed me in the direction of the river …'

Shantanu's breath was coming in short gasps as he spoke. He was reliving those moments.

'I remember asking myself: What could she be doing? I hoped that she may just have been unable to sleep and had taken the baby outside for a walk. But somehow, I knew this was not true.

'I ran towards the river, faster than I had ever run even in the heat of the most ferocious battle. When I got there, though, I was greeted by a sight far more horrifying than the grisliest of battles I have witnessed.'

I too was breathing hard by now. Despite my eagerness to hear the king's story, I no longer felt as ready to do so. There was no going back, however.

'I watched helplessly, unable to do or say anything, as my wife, the woman I loved, the mother of my child … I watched as she carried my newborn son to the river and drowned him. I fell to my knees as I watched his body, so fresh and innocent, plunge into the forsaken river.'

Tears flowed down my cheeks. This was worse than I could have ever imagined.

'I fell to my knees, every single part of me aching to call out, to dive into the waters and to save my son. But I couldn't. My vow to Ganga could not be broken; I could never question her.'

What pain for a man to bear! I sensed that there was more to come, but I could no longer bear to see him relive it.

'Please, Shantanu, stop, I do not want you to tell me anymore if it will bring more suffering upon you.'

His eyes darted back to look into mine, and he shook his head. No, he was resolute on this path.

'I hoped that this was only a test. Despite the horror that I had just witnessed, I still had a deep love for her in my heart and trusted that this would never happen again.

'After the birth of our second child, we slept in different chambers. She had requested it, and I relented. This time, it happened on the night of the child's birth. My son had only seen the light of one day.

'I never truly slept well after … what happened. When I heard the sound of movement in the middle of the night, I felt a great sickness in my heart. But I told myself I had to be wrong. Alas, though, I was not!

'I knew where she'd be and went down to the river. My heart was in my mouth as I watched her walk towards it, my second born wrapped in her arms. Was it worse that time, knowing what I was about to witness? I don't know. I can only say the pain of watching my son being drowned like his brother was immeasurable. I would not wish that agony on my worst enemy. Again, though, I did not cry out. I could not break my vow.'

Shantanu's head slumped into his hands, and he did not move. I wanted to step forward and fold him into my embrace, but his demeanour showed he did not want to be approached. He had not finished. He had much more to say.

'I hoped, really hoped, that this was the end of it. But no, my third son, and the fourth, both met a watery death at the hands of the person who was supposed to love them the most.

'After the fourth child had been taken from me, I was delivered some hope in form of news that two babies had been found alive and well, a little way down the river. I wondered whether they could be two of my children who had somehow survived. Was it possible? It was not. They were two strangers, but at least we were able to give them a decent life. Kripa and Kripi have been raised by sages.

'My story did not have such a happy ending, though. I lost three more children. Each time, I saw it happen, and the pain was just as intense. I was powerless to stop it because of my vow.'

The king paused, his eyes closed.

'When it came to my eighth child, I could take it no more. When I saw that it was happening all over again, I followed my wife to the river's edge. The moment she began to slowly lower our son into the water, I cried out. I told her she had to stop.

'I broke my vow.'

I caught my breath. Had she stopped? I could hardly imagine how this goddess would react to this act of defiance.

'She lifted my son far above the waters … he was saved.'

Shantanu's eyes were open now, and his gaze had reverted to the riverbank as he relived the conversation he'd had with his wife.

'I told her that I had spent the last few years watching the lives of our sons, and the future generation of Hastinapur's kings, being snuffed out for reasons I could never understand. But I could take it no more, even though I had to break my vow.

'Ganga listened and said nothing at first. Then, with a slight smile, she promised me that my son would live, but since I had broken my vow, I would not see her again. And I did not.'

His story over, Shantanu was silent. Now, everything became clear. Although he felt he had found happiness with me, there would be a pain deep within him that would never go away. He had watched as seven of his sons were drowned and his goddess had left him after he broke his vow. It was an impossible situation, and he had lost everything.

'What of your son?' I asked. 'The boy you saved?'

'His name is Devavrata, and he is every bit the greatest man I have ever come across,' he said, his face lighting up with pride. 'Through all my pain, he has made my life worth living, and every day, he makes me yearn to do the right thing, not only for the people of Hastinapur, but also for the people who surround me in life.

'His mother raised him and taught him the ways of the gods. She took him away to train him, to perfect him, to allow him to be everything he could ever possibly be, and she did a fine job. She taught him how to use every weapon imaginable. He is strong and powerful and the most accomplished fighter you ever saw. You should see him in battle—the way he fights and the mercy he shows. I truly believe that if he weren't my son and I had to face him in war, I would command my army to surrender on the spot. She also schooled him in politics, ethics and philosophy. His abilities and knowledge go far beyond the realms of reality into a place of power that I have never seen. The world, the elements, all bend for him. Anyone with that much power should be a terrifying prospect, but that power is safe in his hands. He wields it out of kindness. He may be only half-human, but he is far more human than anyone I have ever met. He is pure perfection in human form.'

As Shantanu spoke with such pride about his son, everything became clear. I understood his pain, but I also bathed in the pride he felt for his most magnificent son. How glad he must be that the kingdom of Hastinapur would one day be led by the demigod Devavrata! It would be the most powerful in all of India.

Chapter Three

The next evening, I sensed something was different from the moment Shantanu arrived. He steered the chariot to the house in his usual confident fashion, but as he jumped onto the ground, he suddenly seemed a little less sure of himself, perhaps even a little nervous. The moment I had heard the chariot approaching, I had already got to my feet and hurried towards the jetty, eager to get the boat untied before my father could appear. We'd been playing with fire. My father had no idea of my daily visitor, but it was only a matter of time. I could not rely forever on him being away, being distracted by his nightly *pachisi* game, or by ordering the servants about.

Turning to see if the king was on his way down to the jetty, I froze, the boat's rope still held tightly in my hand. Standing at our front door, looking at Shantanu, was my father. I knew that expression only too well. It was one of greed and anticipation. My father had never been one to miss an opportunity, and he saw one before him in a golden, bejewelled chariot. My only hope was that somehow, he would not learn of the true status of the man standing in front of him.

I began to rapidly re-tie the boat so I could make my way back towards the house as quickly as possible. In my haste, I was all fingers and thumbs and kept dropping the rope. I couldn't make out the words between them yet, but when I turned and looked back, I saw my father greet Shantanu and the king give a low bow. My father's expression was fixed to look friendly; his body language was anything but. His legs were planted in a wide stance, his arms folded across his chest and shoulders thrown back. Strangely, Shantanu did not have the usual confident swagger I had grown to admire so much. His body language looked unsure, almost apologetic.

I tied the boat and hurried to join them. I was close enough to see clearly that the expressions on both their faces had changed. My father's gloating had transformed into pure anger, while Shantanu seemed hurt. Was my father really rebuking the king? Did he have any idea? I could not, for the life of me, imagine what the disagreement could be about. Then, abruptly, they both turned to face me.

Shantanu was the first to step forward. His face was etched with concern, and his hands outstretched towards me, palms upwards.

'Satyavati, I am so sorry,' he began. 'I had no ...'

'... idea that you had not told me what was going on,' my father interrupted.

'I ... I meant to tell you ...'

'Except that you did not. And then this man, this king, arrives to ask me for your hand.'

For a moment, I could hardly breathe. This should have been my dream, but it was unfolding like the worst nightmare. Everything was happening at such speed that I could not process it.

'Satyavati, I will say again, I am so sorry. I have got this completely wrong.'

Shantanu looked heartbroken as he said this. I wanted to tell him that I too was sorry, that I had made a terrible mistake. I had no idea why I had not told my father sooner. Of course, he was always going to find out, and he had done so in the most terrible circumstances. His desire to control every aspect of his life, and mine, would take precedence over everything. It always did. He would be blind to all else.

'Father, I am so sorry,' I said, turning to him. 'This is King Shantanu. I was going to tell you about him when the time was right.'

'The time was right?' he said slowly. 'Right for what? How long has this been going on? When were you going to mention about this king visiting our home every night?'

A silence grew between us. My father's anger consumed him as much as sorrow and shame consumed me. Shantanu looked shattered.

It was my father who broke the silence in the most unexpected way.

'Satyavati, you are the most beautiful woman in all the land, destined for great things,' he said, his voice icily calm. 'Marrying a king would be the realisation of a life's dream for both of us. But I gave this royal my conditions, and I will not move from them.'

'Conditions?'

I looked from my father to Shantanu. The king was staring at the sand beneath our feet, avoiding eye contact.

'That if I give my consent, your children must rule.'

I stared at my father uncomprehendingly. Why had he asked this? It didn't seem to make sense. It had been his life's dream that I should fulfil the prophecy and now, when it had come to pass, he was creating obstacles.

'... he has refused this request, so I cannot let the union go ahead.'

Once again, I was unable to speak. Deep within me, there was something that wanted to cry out and launch myself at my father, beating against his chest, demanding to know why he was standing so firmly in my way. But I couldn't do that. That was not how a daughter behaved. And it would do nothing to change his decree. Once my father had made up his mind, that was it.

I turned my gaze to Shantanu and realised he was staring at me.

'I am sorry, Satyavati,' he said. 'Please do not blame yourself. I have gone about this all wrong. I was so swept away the first time I saw you that I have not been thinking straight. It has been so long since I have known happiness that I wanted to keep you all to myself.

'That was wrong. I know that now. Do not be angry with your father. He is right to protect you and your interests. I would do the same.'

He took a deep breath.

'I cannot agree to this request, however much my heart wishes I would do so. I have promised the throne to my son, Devavrata, and I can never go back on that.'

I nodded. I understood completely. What father would betray his son like this? It wasn't even just that. If Devarata did not become king, it would be to the detriment of the entire kingdom. Replace a demigod with the child of a mere mortal? It did not make sense. There was no chance at all that I would challenge this.

My whole life had been about ferrying people who wanted to go away from the only place I had ever known, while I dreamt of a fantasy that, deep down, I had doubted from the start. For a few weeks, I had dared to believe I had been wrong, that the prophecy would be fulfilled. A wonderful king had arrived, and I had fallen for him. He'd come to me offering to take me away from it all, carrying me away to his kingdom to share his fortune and power. But what he offered wasn't in his gift to give, certainly not on my father's terms. I had to accept this. I could not add to the king's pain.

Taking a step forward, I took both the king's hands and held them in mine.

'I understand, and I accept your reasoning,' I said. 'I am so sorry this cannot be so.'

Shantanu looked shattered, but he understood. Our situation was hopeless. With one last squeeze of my hands, he turned to my father and gave a small bow before returning to his chariot, his shoulders slumped.

As the chariot clattered away, I wondered if he would ever return. I doubted it. The encounter with my father had shamed him so much that it was unlikely he had any desire to pass this way again. I had to ask myself too: Did I even want that? It was impossible to imagine how any future encounter would be. There was no way of knowing if he'd be friendly or upset. In my wildest imaginings, I could hardly think that he'd be in love with me after this. Perhaps he would even send an army to arrest my father and I for insulting him. I put a stop to that train of thought. No, he was not cruel. I sensed a kindness in him.

The king did not appear the next night, nor the next. I would sit on the veranda night after night, straining my ears to hear horses' hooves, but there was nothing. Occasionally, my heart would leap as I thought I detected the sound of an approaching chariot, but it was always something else.

By the end of the first week, I gave up hope.

That evening, I sat on the veranda more out of habit than anything else. The sun had set an hour earlier, but the earth outside the house was still warm. I swear it groaned a little as it settled, gradually becoming consumed by the chill cloak of darkness. Curled up deep in my usual seat on the wooden bench, I listened hard, waiting for the cicadas, crickets and katydids to begin their nightly symphony. Right now, they were just warming up, and the odd click and buzz would pierce the night air. But in an hour or so, this seemingly million-strong orchestra would reach its pinnacle with an almost deafening, yet quite beautiful, song, a song that would continue unabated until morning. When the symphony finally died down at dawn, that would be the signal for me to return to the river.

I closed my eyes and rubbed my forefingers over my temples. I wanted to shut out the feeling of dread that seemed to plague me every day now. The air around me felt permanently heavy, dragging at the folds of fabric in my sari and overwhelming me with tiredness. Without warning, my stomach would turn over and my heart pound against my chest. I had no idea what was happening. I was worried about Shantanu, but I had also completely accepted the hopelessness of the prospect of any sort of future with the king. Hard though it was to bear, it was right and proper. His son, the Crown Prince Devavrata, was not just the rightful heir to the throne; he was also the greatest and most accomplished hero of his generation. It was inconceivable that he would give that up and put Hastinapur at such a great disadvantage. No sane person would even ask for that.

A distant rumble interrupted my dark thoughts. My eyes flew open, and I stared ahead with a growing sense of disbelief. A chariot, a golden chariot, was approaching, drawn by a powerful white horse. But it was not Shantanu's chariot. I already knew that despite the gloom of the night. And even from the distance,

I could tell that it was not Shantanu standing proudly beneath the white silk canopy. I had watched his approach to the house so many times that I could describe every inch of his gait.

I squinted to get a better look. Now that the chariot was a little closer, I could see that the man driving it was alone. He was tall and wore a richly embroidered cloak, which flowed behind his broad shoulders as the light wind whispered through his thick, dark hair. His gait was bold and unshakable, the master of a thousand wild adventures. He was undoubtedly a prince.

'Crown Prince Devavrata,' I said, realising with a start I had spoken out loud into the night air.

Rising to my feet, I moved to the edge of the veranda. I felt almost childlike as I watched the chariot cover the last hundred yards or so, the toes of my bare feet curled over the wooden boards. Not once did I take my eyes off the approaching figure.

The carriage was close enough now, and I could take a proper look at Devavrata. He was, without doubt, the most perfect man I had ever seen. His skin was so golden that it glowed like fire, and even though it was nearly dark now, his tousled hair shone with the light of a thousand jewels. He wore a close-fitting armour of white leather over his lean, muscular body, the edges decorated in rich gold. What was most noticeable, though, was his face, and in particular, his eyes. They shone with raw power and self-assurance.

The carriage was now within a few yards of the house and drew to a halt, the leather reins creaking. Then, as if sensing me there for the first time, Devavrata's gaze turned towards me. I had to stop myself crying out in shock. That gaze seemed to penetrate my soul, looking right through me. For the briefest of moments, we locked eyes, but then I had to look away.

Breathing hard, I forced myself to look up once again and watched Devavrata deftly dismount from his carriage. *How was I to address this prince?* A thousand greetings ran through my mind, but none of them seemed to fit. What I really wanted to say is: Why are you here? But somehow, I already knew why.

Devavrata was closer now. I could feel the heat of his body after the exertions of the chariot ride and smell a sweet scent of amber and vanilla that surrounded him like a soft cloud. Not knowing what else to do, I bowed low, reaching forward as if to touch his feet.

'Sir,' I began, but the words dried on my lips.

Devavrata had taken a step back. Straightening, I saw he had a gentle, yet intense, expression, which also seemed to radiate reassurance.

'That is not necessary,' he said. 'It is I who should be touching your feet.'

Every gesture, every syllable uttered by his powerful voice, told of Devavrata's nobility and status as a demigod. Yet, he also had a kindness about him, as though he understood the frailty of men and felt it his duty to put them at ease. Sensing my confusion, he smiled once again.

'We have time to greet one another properly,' he said quietly, 'and I look forward to that. Now, though, I would very much like to speak with your father.'

He pretended not to see my eyes widen with concern, but I did not get a chance to respond. We were interrupted by the sound of the door opening behind me. My father, Dasharaj, had heard the approaching carriage too.

'I am here,' he announced.

The fisherman's voice didn't give away anything of his feelings about the arrival of our noble visitor, nor that the visitor was not Shantanu, as he had most likely expected. As far as my father's demeanour seemed to show, the Crown Prince could have been a common peddler going from door to door to sell his wares. A frown crossed my brow as I looked between my father and Devavrata. *Why wasn't my father showing any respect?*

Devavrata stepped forward and bowed deeply, as though he was greeting a fellow nobleman or a sage.

'It is my pleasure to meet you, Sir,' he said, straightening up and giving a warm smile.

For a moment, everything was silent, save for the chorus of insects which, without my noticing, had already reached the full force of that evening's orchestration. Even though I had my back to my father, I could imagine the expression on his face. I'd seen it a hundred times as he played *pachisi* each night. It didn't matter who his opponent was—his expression was always the same as he stared at them over the complex cross and circle board game, the cowrie shells they used seemingly strewn at random across it, though each had been so carefully placed. He would stare intently, as though about to bring down his rival with the blink of an eye. He wanted to win. *He had to win.* Always. If ever he lost, which was rare, he would shout and kick out in fury and throw cowries on the floor from such a height they'd scatter to the four corners of the room. The servants would wait until he'd stalked out, his expression grim, before scrambling around to recover each one.

'Go inside,' my father said.

It was not a request. It was a command. Deep inside, the slight burnt. I wanted to stay, but I would never ever have dreamt of disobeying my father. I stole a last look at Devavrata and saw that he was once again staring at me. For the past few minutes, his expression had been fixed and intense, resolute even, but just for a moment, as we locked eyes once more, it softened. He tilted his head in a barely discernible nod of reassurance before reverting his gaze to Dasharaj. *It will be okay,* the nod seemed to say.

Reluctantly, I turned and stepped back onto the veranda from the ground below. The familiar feeling of the smooth wood below my bare feet was usually a comfort because it spelt home, but not this time. Tonight, the boards felt cold and inhospitable. I glanced at my father as I walked past, but he was staring ahead and didn't acknowledge my presence. I'd been right, though. His expression was exactly as I'd anticipated. My father was clear that he was embarking on the greatest game of his life, and he was obviously confident of his chances of victory.

Almost the second after I closed the door behind me, I heard my father speak.

'Your Grace honours our home with his presence,' he said.

I winced as I crouched low and crept towards the open window, concealing myself behind the heavy drapes. My father's voice was stiff and laced with sarcasm. He could be charming when he wanted to be, when he wanted to wheedle a little extra from the visiting merchants. He could even be pleasant enough to the servants, as long as he had not lost his game of *pachisi.* But this evening, his voice dripped with contempt and Devavrata could not help but know it. Even the most unobservant fool would know it.

'Why can this not wait until sunrise?' Dasharaj went on. 'Is this great warrior afraid of the wild creatures that roam these woods?'

I watched as my father threw his head back and laughed at his own joke. Devavrata smiled politely but did not take the bait. He simply continued to watch the older man intently.

'Sir, I came to your house because I have a question to ask you.'

From my position behind the window, I was sure I saw my father's tongue greedily dart across his lips as he edged closer to Devavrata. The game had begun.

'Could you tell me, please, why the king has spent his time between our camp and your house? We have barely seen him during the daylight hours for many days, and when he is with us, he seems upset and distracted. Now, though, he has not been here for days and is deeply troubled.'

My father shifted from one foot to the other, seemingly almost unable to contain his excitement. His face broke into a broad smile.

'Won't you come inside?' he said with a broad sweep of his arm as he indicated the door. 'We will take a seat and have some refreshment, and then we will talk.'

Devavrata did not move. He stared at the fisherman with the watchfulness of a father weighing up a son who he knows has already let him down but who refuses to admit it. He did not look angry, though, only a little weary. I was sure he already knew the answers to his questions, indeed to all questions mortal man might pose, but he felt the need to give this man a chance to respond on his own terms.

'I would be more than happy to sit down and drink your tea, Dasharaj,' he said softly. 'But I would be grateful if you would do me the honour of answering my question before I take you up on your kind offer. Please tell me what has happened to my father.'

The fisherman smiled as he took another step towards Devavrata. They were standing close together now, and the differences in their height and stature were almost comical. Devavrata was tall, and every line of his body was beautiful and perfect with strength and grace. My father, on the other hand, was short and stooped, the rich folds of his robe unable to hide his portliness, the result of years of excess and lack of restraint. Even so, my father drew himself up to his full height.

'He wants to marry my daughter, Satyavati,' he said, his voice rasping with the sheer joy of the attack. It was obvious that, in his mind, the complex game was all but won. He'd always prided himself upon his opening attack.

To my father's evident surprise, Devavrata nodded. *I was right; he had already known.*

'Then, what is the problem?' the Crown Prince said calmly. 'Do you not approve of the match?'

My father looked confused at Devavrata's measured response. He had not anticipated this move. As far as he was concerned, he'd had the upper hand in this contest ever since the first dice was thrown. The composure of his interlocutor unnerved him.

'What … what … are you saying?' he stammered.

Then, he checked himself. This was not his style. He had not lost. It was merely a temporary setback. Just one cowrie shell put in the wrong place, but it was recoverable. There was always another strategy.

My father broke into a broad smile. Had Devavrata noticed that that smile did not reach the fisherman's dark eyes? I had.

'Of course, the match is suitable,' my father soothed. 'Eminently suitable. There is just one problem.'

Devavrata had not taken his eyes off my father's face, but he remained silent. He merely shifted his stance a little, his legs planted slightly apart, arms folded across his broad chest. The searching cleverness of his gaze spoke more than any words.

'Satyavati's horoscope said it was her destiny to be queen and that her son would rule one day,' my father pronounced proudly. 'The king refused to promise that it would be so when he proposed marriage. He said there was no question of it.'

He was speaking a little faster than usual. He had more than met his match and he knew that now, but he had gone too far and invested too much in this game to back out. And this was not the sort of contest where you could scatter your cowries on the ground in a rage and stalk out. Devavrata had come here with a purpose; anyone could see that.

Devavrata's hands fell to his sides, and his eyes narrowed a little. If he had not known before, he was now certain of the type of man my father was. He was avaricious and only concerned with material gain, yet too selfish to think through the consequences of what he had asked for.

The Crown Prince turned and took a few steps away. He had his back to us as he began to speak, so it was not certain whether he was addressing my father at all. His voice, though low, was forceful. When he spoke, it echoed through the forest behind us and seemed to bounce back from the river in front of us.

'It is not in the king's power to give you this reassurance anymore,' Devavrata began. 'He was entirely right about that. He has already exercised this right by making me the Crown Prince, and no king can promise the same thing to two people, can he?'

My father stepped forward, apparently about to try to swing Devavrata around to face him. He instantly checked himself, though, perhaps thinking better of the extravagant gesture. Looking more closely, I could see the fisherman was sweating now. His shoulders were taut and tense, as though he anticipated a physical blow. I was certain that he was squirming inside, wondering if he had overplayed his hand.

The silence between them grew. At last, Devavrata turned around to face my father. He drew a deep breath and bowed his head slightly in my father's direction. *Was he giving in? Admitting defeat?*

'I understand my father's moral predicament,' he said steadily. 'It is not in his gift to promise to another what he has already promised to me. That would be unjust.'

He paused and leaned in towards my father, his loose, dark hair falling forward. His face was a picture of purity and honesty, and his stare so piercing that my father had to look away.

'However, if I want to, *I* can give away the throne,' he paused to let the words sink in and then added, 'I pledge to stand aside as Crown Prince, so my father is free to marry Satyavati. She will fulfil the prophecy and be queen.'

I caught my breath as I watched my father lean in greedily—he already seemed to anticipate there was more to come. The very sky seemed to be cracking with electricity and tension at the Crown Prince's momentous declaration. However, I didn't want to hear any more. This was too much. I didn't want this honour, and I knew for certain that Shantanu would be as devastated as I was to hear these words spoken by his beloved son.

We were right, though—there was more.

'The child that ensues from this union will be king,' Devavrata declared. As he said these words, a flash of lightning split the clear night sky into two, and a loud peal of thunder reverberated around us.

'I give you my word,' Devavrata announced, raising his voice to be heard above the cacophony.

Devavrata's words fell on me like boulders from above. I could scarcely bear the enormous weight of any of them. This demigod, the child Shantanu adored so much and who had brought joy back to his life, was prepared to give it all up so that his father could be happy. I had heard the pride in Shantanu's voice as he spoke of Devavrata's brave exploits and his skills, each one far above anything a mortal man could achieve. The king's face had been aglow with happiness when he spoke of his son. His delight that the kingdom of Hastinapur would be in such good hands had been unparalleled and rightly so. This could not be happening. Devavrata had bestowed the greatest gift of all to his father, yet nothing about his demeanour gave anything away of the emotions he must surely have felt about giving up his destiny.

I glanced at my father, fully expecting him to be grinning in triumph. He had won the greatest game of his life. His eyes were indeed shining, but his expression was blank.

'It's not enough,' he said flatly.

I had to stop myself from crying out with rage by clasping a hand firmly across my mouth. I could not stop the hot tears that began to spill down my cheeks, though. Not enough? Not enough to put the entire kingdom in danger and to destroy Shantanu's dream? With Devavrata out of the picture, Hastinapur would always be vulnerable, and no king would wish that to be his legacy.

Devavrata showed no signs of puzzlement. He'd anticipated this too. I knew that now. My father's next move had always been written in the stars for him. The fisherman simply had to say it out loud to make it so. How I wanted to leap to the door, throw it open and stop my father from saying what he was about to say next! I wanted to shout, beat his chest and spin him around, forcing him back into the house. I would keep him there until the Crown Prince's chariot clattered away. However, this was not how things were done. One had to honour one's parents, no matter what they said or did, however reckless and destructive they might be, whatever consequences their actions might lead to. My rage could have been the sharpest *asi*, but it had to be kept sheathed.

And then, my father said the words—the words I didn't want him to say, but the words Devavrata had clearly come to hear.

'What is to stop your heirs from coming back to claim the throne?' my father asked.

Devavrata stood still, waiting. He knew my father had not finished.

'You have given up your right to the throne for your father's happiness,' the fisherman went on. 'You have kindly allowed Satyavati to fulfil her destiny and her children to rule. But, just as your father was unable to speak for you, you cannot speak for your own children. What if your future children lay claim to the throne of Hastinapur, son of Ganga? My grandchildren would be in constant danger from your heirs.'

My father's expression was triumphant now. This was his winning move.

I didn't know what I expected to see when I turned to look at Devavrata. Sadness, perhaps, or resignation to what he was being asked for. He already seemed to know why he was there. I was surprised to find that his eyes were closed. He seemed to be bracing himself, almost like a mortal man would behave when summoning up the strength to go into battle. But he was never fearful of battle—his father had told me that. He had taken on many hundreds of men alone. Confronting my father did not bother him.

What was his dilemma? How would he answer my father's request? I could hardly imagine his response. I supposed he'd give his word, which was more than any mere mortal's word. How difficult it would be for him, though, when he would meet and marry his princess one day but be forced to tell their children that they must never break his promise.

My mind was forced away from its calculations as Devavrata began to speak. He was not speaking in the calm, measured manner as before. His voice boomed forth, even louder now, loud enough to reach the very heavens.

'Dasharaj, you are correct. I cannot speak for my children. Once again, though, I have the right to do as I please.'

The statement invited no response. I watched with growing alarm as an aura appeared to grow around Devavrata's body, building in intensity with each second that passed. His whole body shone as brightly as the sun, and it was difficult to look at him without blinking. The expression on his face seemed trance-like, yet I sensed he was in complete control of every movement he made. Moving slowly and deliberately, he drew himself up to his full height, his arms stretched wide. The aura around him grew even more intense, casting a brilliant light on everything around us, sharply illuminating the trees and the house as though they were bathed in the brightest beams cast by the midday sun. Devavrata's whole body had risen into the air and appeared to be effortlessly hovering above the earth, his feet barely skimming the bare soil. The gentle breeze from earlier had disappeared, and the cicada orchestra had abruptly halted its symphony. I was certain that the whole world had stopped turning on its axis. Everything had led up to this moment, and the air itself crackled and fizzed with anticipation. When Devavrata began to speak at last, his voice was even louder and more potent than before.

'I, son of Ganga, in the presence of the four cardinal points and the Earth and the sky, take this oath. I will remain celibate throughout my life. I will live childless, and I will die childless.'

Spreading his arms even wider, Devavrata raised his eyes heavenwards for his final devastating declaration.

'This is my eternal oath,' he boomed.

Devavrata had barely uttered the final word of his pledge before the sky cracked open with the brightest flash of lightning I had ever seen, followed by the loudest clap of thunder I had ever heard. Rain began to hammer angrily against the parched soil, but Devavrata did not move. He remained, arms outstretched, sealing his oath into history. Then, as slowly and deliberately as he had begun his oath, his arms returned to his sides and his feet to the ground.

He did not look at my father. He had made his oath. He had done what he had come to do. Perhaps, like me, he knew the expression he would find there, one of extreme gloating over the audacious victory. But Devavrata did pause to stare at the window which I was crouched behind. I was certain he couldn't see me because I was wrapped up tightly in the drapes and had kept to the shadows. Yet, he did see me. I know he did because he smiled and bowed.

I was too ashamed to come out of my hiding place. This demigod had given up everything for the happiness of his father and me, and the entire kingdom of Hastinapur would suffer because of it. Wave after ugly wave of guilt and despair washed over me. I wanted to vanish forever.

Chapter Four

From my position, curled up in my bed, I watched with a growing sense of sadness as the sun slowly rose over the river and cast its brilliant, warm glow. This had always been such a perfect spot to view the dawn of each new day, and the sight had never failed to fill me with optimism. Today, though, all I could think was that this would be my last sunrise in this home. Rising out of bed for the final time was an equally odd sensation. I had grown up in this room and slumbered every night of my life in this bed. What would happen to it now? Would the room be closed up, left to gather dust? Perhaps one of the servants would claim it. For a fleeting moment, I kidded myself that my father was far more sentimental than I credited him for and my room would be left untouched to return to as I wished. I knew this was not true. This was not part of his grand plan. Not now that he had finally claimed his prize.

As I began to reluctantly dress myself, I listened to the birds that carefully built their nests in the eaves outside my window each year. I swear their songs were melancholier today. In the distance, I could hear the fish beginning to leap in and out of the river, their best insect-catching tricks on display. Usually, this would make me smile. This was my alarm call, telling me to get to my boat. *Half the day is over, come on!* But my pretty little boat would stay in its moorings now. I wished I had treasured my time alone on my boat more, as I realised now that I may never have that time again. I hoped that, at the very least, my father could find a use for my boat when he was out fishing and the boat wouldn't rot away in the river, forgotten.

And what of my regular customers? Perhaps the next time they would hear of me would be when word had spread that I was the new queen of Hastinapur. What a strange thought that was! Would they have treated me more kindly all these years if they could have known that this would be my future?

My finest sari was ready for me, cleaned and pressed to perfection. Once I was fully dressed, I made my way out of the room, rehearsing in my mind how to say a quiet farewell to the servants. The first one I encountered, though, a maid sweeping just outside my room, avoided eye contact and instead dropped into a deep curtsy. Was this my life now? Just yesterday, I would have bidden her a cheerful good morning and she would have replied with a smile. We might even have exchanged some pleasantries.

Tarran, the head servant, was waiting for me as I reached the kitchen. This man had been with the family since before I was born and had cared for my father and me with deep loyalty. He was kind and patient and was perhaps the only person who could talk my father out of his fits of rage when he lost his *pachisi* game. Tarran, at least, seemed to be behaving normally.

'I wish you well, my new queen,' he said with the warmest smile.

'Thank you, Tarran, and thank you for everything you have done, and everything you are yet to do for my father.'

I wanted to say so much more, but found myself tongue-tied. I hoped Tarran realised that I had the best of intentions but was just too overwhelmed.

My appetite was not up to much that morning. The cooks had prepared a large feast for my breakfast to help prepare me for my long journey ahead to my new kingdom. (My new kingdom!) Instead, I asked for the only thing I could bear, a *kamrakh*, freshly picked from our garden. Even the mild, sour taste of the fruit that I usually enjoyed so much brought me no pleasure. I made myself finish it, though, and when I had done so, I wrapped a few of its seeds in a small piece of fabric. I hoped that one day soon, I would plant them in the grounds of my new palace. In many years' time, I would eat the fruit that it bore so that the taste would lift my heart with a little hope.

My possessions had already been packed into several small sacks. It was strange to see one's whole life compressed into such little space. I'd thought I owned a lot more. I imagined that when I lived in a palace, surrounded by riches, my modest belongings would seem quite meagre and pointless in comparison. Perhaps I shouldn't burden the horses and just leave them here.

I was so absorbed in my farewells that I hadn't noticed the arrival of the chariot. The knock at the door startled me, and I watched as the servant hurried to answer it. The loud and clear voice announcing his presence was unmistakable. It was Devavrata.

'I have come to collect the queen,' he said. 'Please tell her to take her time, though. I do not wish to interrupt her farewells.'

Tears pricked the corners of my eyes, and I blinked hard to keep them in. *Why was I sad?* There was nothing for me here. Not really. I knew why I was sad, though. I was sad because of what had happened—what this great man, Devavrata, had felt he had to give up for his father's happiness. I could not change what had been done, but the guilt would live with me until my dying day.

I got to my feet from my seat at the table and turned to take a last look at the house, breathing in its familiar smells. I spun around slowly, taking in all the little details that I had seen every day, but never really noticed. There was that dent in the wall where I had once dropped my father's tools after slipping on some spilt mango juice. On the table in front of me was a chipped bowl, broken when he had flung it on the floor in a rage, about what, I could no longer remember. How long would it be before I forgot this place too?

As I stepped towards the door, I realised that I hadn't even thought of my farewell to my father. I knew where he would be. In the backyard, in his fishing clothes, preparing for his day. No doubt, he'd have a piece of rope in each hand as he skilfully tied the knots. I had never thought of it, but my father may have been the finest fisherman in all of Bharat. I didn't believe anyone knew more about the fish and the waters than he did.

As I walked towards him, there were a thousand things I could have said. While he had his faults, and he was an impatient man, he had been a good father and had only ever wanted what was best for me. In some ways, he was not that different from Devavrata. He loved one person so much that nothing else could stand in the way. The big difference, though, was that he had been doing this for me, a nobody with nothing to sacrifice, whereas Devavrata had given up everything. A whole kingdom would suffer as a result.

There was no point going over it again. What was done was done. Without a word, I embraced my father and whispered 'goodbye'. In return, he muttered something so softly that I could barely make out the words. I think I heard the words 'daughter' and 'love', but I could not be sure.

When I reached the front of the house, Devavrata was waiting in the chariot, my few sacks arranged at his feet. As soon as he saw me, he stepped down and offered me his hand to help me up. Despite my nerves and misgivings, I could not help but laugh. His stance was almost identical to that of his father when he used to help me into my boat. Seeing my reaction, he too broke into a broad grin.

'I am so pleased that you are at ease with me,' he said.

For the first time, I noticed how hypnotic his deep voice sounded. There was a nobility and confidence about him that could not fail to put one at ease, even if I had not reacted to the coincidence of him holding out his hand to help me.

I nodded, but averted my gaze. Even though the tension had been broken, I still didn't feel ready to speak with him. I was just too much in awe of this demigod, whose presence seemed to fill the space around us. Part of me was also worried that if I did say anything, I would embarrass myself. I would not be able to stop apologising for what had happened at my father's house.

Again, Devavrata seemed to sense exactly what I was thinking and feeling and did not push for a response. Instead, with the gentlest flick of the leather reins, he spurred the horses. I watched my home receding into the distance, surrounded by a halo of sand and dust kicked up by the chariot.

My mind went blank as we moved on. I had so much to say that I was unable to make sense of it, my thoughts collapsing into one another to create a void. However much I wanted to snap out of it, I was simply unable to do so. I was feeling hugely self-conscious, standing beside this great man—a man who had given up everything for his father and me.

It was a grand chariot, the grandest, but even then, we were forced to stand quite close to one another. Occasionally, when the chariot jostled just so, Devavrata's arm would brush against my shoulder, causing me to jump just a little. He had no need to do so, but every time he accidentally knocked into me, he uttered the humblest of apologies. What an extraordinary and polite soul he was! Did he take that from his father? Or could it have been his mother's training? I thought it was the former. I could certainly see a lot of Shantanu in this person standing ramrod straight beside me.

The chariot was travelling at speed now. Devavrata, after asking my permission, gently guided my arms with his hand, indicating the rail I should hold to remain steady. I still didn't feel comfortable enough to look him in the eye, so I nodded, staring hard at my hands on the chariot rail ahead of me. To my horror, I realised I was beginning to feel queasy at the constant motion. Perhaps I should have eaten properly earlier, but it was too late.

Strangely, having something else to focus on seemed to help clear the fog in my head. In some ways, I wished it hadn't because a long list of questions began to form, none of which I had immediate answers to. Was I truly to be queen? What qualified me, since I knew nothing of politics, or war, or even court life? Just as important, I knew nothing about Hastinapur other than what I had heard from Shantanu during his time with me. Perhaps other travellers had mentioned it when I ferried them across the river, but I had not really paid attention at the time. How could I have foreseen this situation?

My legs were beginning to feel weak, and I was gripping the rail of the chariot so hard that my knuckles had gone pale.

'Would you like me to slow down?' Devavrata said, pulling gently on the reins. He'd sensed my discomfort.

I shook my head. I did not want to be a burden and put him to any more trouble. I did not want to be there at all. Whatever the prophecy, whatever the monumental oath that had been taken, I did not want to be queen. What I wanted was for this chariot to turn around. No, I wanted to turn the clock back and stop all of this before it began. How could one ever rule justly and fairly with a burden like this? What kind of person did it make me, to accept the throne knowing what I knew about how my power was gained and what sacrifices were made for it? Wasn't I already a traitor to a land I had never set foot in?

I could stand it no longer. Tears began to stream down my cheeks, and I opened my mouth to shriek 'Stop'. This had to end. It had to. The desire to cry out, though, was tempered by my thoughts of Shantanu. What would he say? He didn't even know what had transpired at my father's house. Shouldn't he have some say in what we did next?

Without realising it, I clasped a hand over my mouth.

Devavrata said nothing. He simply stared ahead, steering the chariot. But he had noticed. Of course he had.

The chariot continued apace for some minutes before I managed to collect myself and breathe calmly. I even began to become more used to the rocking movement of the chariot and relax my grip on the rail just a little. In time, as the chariot crashed on, I became confident enough to steal a glance at my companion. From his smooth facial features, it was clear that he was still young. In fact, if I had to guess, I'd have said he must have been around the same age as I. Yet, he had the body of a man much older and more mature than men of his age. His arms, in particular, were sculpted and muscular. He had the stature of a warrior, yet he bore no scars as other fighting men did. I supposed a demigod could not be harmed in such a mortal way.

Everything about Devavrata was groomed to perfection. His hair was clean, the long locks expertly trimmed to sit carelessly on his lean shoulders, his short beard cropped close to his angular jawline. Even amid all the dust being kicked up around us, his leather uniform, which had seemingly been melted onto his taut body, was spotless, the golden buckles shining as much as they would have been on the day they were forged. What was perhaps most noticeable, though, was the slight smile that had played across his face since he first helped me onto the chariot. Was this confidence? Anticipation of his father's happiness? Or simply joy for life itself?

I wondered how much he knew of the story of his childhood that Shantanu had told me—that he had come so close to dying at the hands of the woman who had brought him into this world. Then, I checked myself. Of course he knew. This was a man who knew everything.

The chariot had picked up quite some speed and the horses were kicking up so much dust that my eyes were becoming irritated. I risked taking one hand off the rail to rub them, but quickly found that it just made it worse. Once more, I stole a glance at my companion and saw that he was not bothered one bit by the dust.

Tiredness began to sweep over me. I had no idea of how long I had spent standing at the rail of this chariot. I closed my eyes to get some relief from the dust, and amazingly, found myself drifting off. Somewhere between being half-asleep, or was it half-awake, I began to dream about the story of King Bharat. It was a story my father had told me over and over when I was a young girl.

King Bharat had been faced with deciding which of his children would rule after him. Among his sons were many great men, any of whom could have grown into great rulers and warriors. Yet, instead of choosing one of them, he had shocked his kingdom by choosing to pass his crown to someone outside of the family.

Nobody could understand this choice. Every person in the court was baffled that someone with such great power would choose to hand his throne to someone not of his blood. They were so shocked that they forgot royal protocol and questioned his decision. His sons, advisors, army and even passers-by wanted to know why he had done so. Each time, his answer was the same:

'All my subjects are my children, and the king must look after all of his children.'

What he was saying, my father explained over and over, was that responsibility to the kingdom had to come first. No matter how intense King Bharat's affection was towards his family, or how deep the ambitions of his children, he had to make the right choice. Oh, how crushed his children must have been to have their life's work taken from them!

My eyes flew open. Was I thinking about this now because of what Shantanu had done? Like King Bharat, he had put kingdom before family. Except that he had not. He didn't yet know of what his son had done. Nor could Devavrata be as crushed as the children of King Bharat. It had been *his* decision to take the oath. Did his status as a demigod give him an understanding that we as mere mortals would never know? None of this thinking, however, made what lay ahead any easier.

I pictured Shantanu seated in my little boat before me. His kind eyes were always so filled with sadness. Despite his power and wealth, he had perhaps been the saddest man I had ever met, and now I knew why. In my years of crossing back and forth on the Yamuna, I had met many grieving people, some of whom had just buried their entire families. Even then, none seemed to carry such a burden of sadness as Shantanu. I couldn't bear to think of how he would react once news of his son's sacrifice reached him.

My hands begin to shake against the golden rail and my knees begin to give way. I couldn't do this …

I felt myself sinking towards the hard wooden floor of the chariot, but suddenly, I was scooped up to my feet by an unseen hand. At the same time, the horses were brought to a gentle stop, the chariot rocking slightly from side to side. Devavrata had caught me in mid-faint and had also been able to skilfully stop the horses, which had been running at full pelt. Without turning to thank him, I jumped from the side of the chariot and staggered a few steps away from it. My head was still spinning. I had no idea what I was doing or where I was going.

The situation was hopeless. I couldn't run away from my destiny. My future was written in the stars the moment Devavrata took his oath. As I sank to my knees in the dirt, I heard Devavrata stepping down from the chariot behind me and his approaching footsteps.

When I steeled myself to finally look at him, he was smiling reassuringly. The late afternoon sun behind him was low and bathed him in its light. The aura around him was reminiscent of the glow that had surrounded him when he had taken his terrible oath, but now it was softer, almost joyful. He looked every inch the celestial being that he was. The realisation hit me; I was kneeling in the shadow of a man more powerful than anyone on this earth. Why had I not been showing him the respect that a man of his power deserved?

'I … I apologise for the sudden stop; the sickness of this journey is beginning to overwhelm me,' I said with a rising sense of embarrassment.

Devavrata shook his head.

'You are far from your home for the first time in your life,' he said, holding his hand out to help me to my feet. 'But you are coping very well and will continue to do so. I already know that you have more presence of mind and inner strength than the most experienced warriors.'

I frowned. Me? Strong? How could he not know that I had been quietly falling apart? He seemed to know everything else I'd been thinking.

We stood facing one another in silence. Once again, I felt tears beginning to form, but this time, I fought hard to stop them flowing. I did not agree with this man's assessment of my qualities, but I knew I would need every ounce of what strength I did have to support Shantanu in the coming days and weeks. If there was one thing that I knew about being queen, it was that duty came first. I had a duty to my king and our kingdom. I also had a duty to show my greatest respect to the demigod standing before me.

'Please, Devavrata, forgive me,' I began haltingly. 'All of this has happened so quickly; I feel as if I have not shown you true respect. Allow me to kneel before you and kiss your feet.'

I took a step backwards, preparing to drop to my knees, but Devavrata echoed the move. At the same time, he put up his hands, palms outwards, entreating me to stop.

'Satyavati, you are now my mother,' he said, his voice strong and unwavering. 'Although we are still new to one another, you are the bride of my father and therefore now my family. To allow you to kiss my feet would be a perversion of the concept of family and an insult to my father.

'Please, do not see me as anything but your son. If any respects are to be paid, it should be from me to you.'

Now, it was my turn to protest. It would be unthinkable that this powerful man should kneel before me. Instead, I took both his hands in mine.

'Our interests are aligned,' I said, never once removing my gaze from his. 'We both love and care for your father and must work together to ensure he is happy and his kingdom is well cared for.'

Suddenly, it had all become clear. It was my role to be like King Bharat. I must serve the best I could and not allow myself to be distracted by regret or by trying to change things I could not change. My role in life was to do the right thing and, with the help of Devavrata, protect Shantanu and Hastinapur.

Chapter Five

My knowledge about weddings ran shallow. I had never attended one, and all I knew of them came from two sources. First, several times a year, I would ferry people over the Yamuna to weddings, or on their way back from them. Sometimes, they would barely mention the events, but mostly they would share every detail they could recall with unabated enthusiasm. Occasionally, someone would come along who had taken little enjoyment in the ceremony, and who looked back upon it with regret, declaring it wasted time. This was rare, though. Everyone seemed to think weddings to be the most wonderful way to pass the time. My second source of reference was my father. His stories were told in the context of the prophecy and centred around tales of opulent royal weddings which would go on for days and days. At these events, the feasts were so extravagant that the tables groaning with food abounded in the corridors and grounds of palaces, feeding everyone from nobles to farmers, with no belly left unsatisfied. Each day, the lavish feast ended with mountains of treats, pure and sickly sweet, made in every joyous colour of the rainbow. Then, it would all resume the following day. No one who attended a royal wedding ever wanted it to stop.

My father, who was usually not the least bit interested in clothes, would be in raptures about the outfits worn by kings and queens for their celebrations. There would be a new outfit for each day of the wedding celebration. Each garment would be made from the finest silk sourced from all over the land, skilfully stitched by the greatest seamstresses in each kingdom, who would have worked on them for months in the run-up to the event.

My own wedding was not anything like those tales that were fed to me.

It was not that my wardrobe was not magnificent. In fact, my wedding dress was the finest piece of clothing I had ever seen, a flowing yellow silk sari with pure gold embroidery delicately sewn into it by dozens of nimble-fingered craftsmen. The imposing hall in the grand palace of Hastinapur was exquisitely decorated, with the freshest and greenest of shrubbery expertly woven around every white marble column and window frame. The cool stone floors had been cleaned and polished so thoroughly that they perfectly reflected the whole wedding.

It was neither the clothes nor the palace that did not match my expectations of a royal wedding. These were as lavish, perhaps even more so, than I could ever have imagined. No, what changed everything was the response of the courtiers. This was not a celebration which attracted everyone in the land to share in the union of their king and his new queen. It was as muted as it was possible to get. The number of guests who witnessed our union barely filled a dozen rows of seats. Nobody wanted the celebration to continue for days and days.

Devavrata was, of course, there, seated in the centre of the room, his ever-present smile radiating warmth and encouragement to his father and me. Beside him were a smattering of Shantanu's military advisors and closest friends, and behind them rows of courtiers who knew their place. Sarathee, the charioteer, was there, but took a respectful place at the back of the hall, not wishing to intrude on the gathering of noblemen and their wives. There was no one there for me. I didn't invite my father.

Everyone was quiet as we made our vows, only cheering or uttering the required responses when encouraged to do so by the sage performing the ceremony. Out of the corner of my eye, I had seen three of the commanders of the king's army talking quietly to one another during the service, their expressions grave. Each one shook his head slowly from side to side. I was quite sure Shantanu had seen what I had seen. Certainly, at almost the same time, his facial expression had slipped from sadness to despair.

I didn't need the wisdom of a sage to understand what was happening. These same people had been at the union of Shantanu and Ganga two decades or more earlier. Shantanu had told me about that wedding and the joy throughout Hastinapur as he married this goddess. Everyone had celebrated their wedding, rejoicing at the prospect of a powerful lineage of demigods, warriors so strong in body and heart that they could protect Hastinapur from anything and everything. Of course, it had not worked out that way.

But out of the despair, Shantanu had managed to rebuild the hopes of his kingdom. While he had broken his own heart by breaking his promise to Ganga, he had brought his people Devavrata and ensured the future prosperity of Hastinapur. That powerful lineage of demigods promised by that grand wedding was assured, albeit it was just one demigod. Even so, Hastinapur's future was assured: This kingdom would be stronger than any other.

In that very hall, a few years before this wedding, Shantanu had introduced his grown-up son to an eager crowd. After eighteen years with his mother, Ganga, being trained in all the arts he would need as a future king, he had returned. The celebrations, as Shantanu declared his son his true heir, had gone on for days and were more lavish than any wedding. Moreover, the loyalty and affection for Devavrata ran so deep that his bond with the people of Hastinapur was seemingly unbreakable. This man was so powerful that he would protect them from anything.

Shantanu had done his best to be upbeat for our own ceremony. He wanted to do right by me, but as we stood before the sage, it was clear his heart was breaking. As we sat side by side on our thrones, listening as the sage addressed the small crowd, I drifted off, reliving, once again, the dreadful moment when I had revealed to him the promise Devavrata had made.

When we had arrived on Devavrata's chariot a few weeks ago, he had led me into the grand hall where the king was talking with his closest counsellors. I was so overwhelmed by the conversation I was about to have that I hadn't paused to look at the palace or take in its splendour. The king had jumped to his feet when he caught sight of me and began to race towards me, his arms outstretched. Then, suddenly, he'd stopped, his face a picture of concern and confusion. His mind had begun to piece together that something was not right: Why had his son brought me here, and how much did he know?

Devavrata had taken charge and had gently led his father to a room to one side of the opulent grand hall. Once again, as I followed them, I barely had a chance to register my surroundings. I was too caught up with what we had to say.

'Shantanu ...' I began, but the words dried on my lips. *How could I do this?*

Devavrata had stepped forward and taken his father's hands. Shantanu's eyes had been wide. Instinctively, he had known what was about to be said would change everything.

'I have been to speak with Dasharaj,' Devavrata said, his voice steady. 'I have told him your marriage to Satyavati should go ahead, and he has given it his blessing.'

'But … but …' Shantanu stammered.

'The conditions?' Devavrata said. 'I have given him my word.'

'Your word?'

The son stared at his father. We all knew what he said next would come as a shock to the older man.

'I have taken an oath. My oath is that I, Devavrata, will remain celibate and will live and die childless. You are now free to marry Satyavati, and the children you have together will rule, safe forever more in the knowledge there will be no challenge from me or anyone of my lineage.'

Shantanu cried out, then dropped to his knees, collapsing into a crumpled heap of misery. I raced forward, dropping to my knees, scooping the king into my arms.

'I am so sorry,' I whispered. 'This was not something either of us wanted.'

Devavrata gave me a polite yet insistent look. He wanted me to stop speaking.

'This was my choice, and I wanted to do it,' he said. 'No one forced me, and even if they had tried, they would not have been able to make me do anything I did not want to do.'

For as long as I live, I will never forget the howl of despair that came from the king as he knelt, his head hung low.

Had Shantanu accepted Devavrata's decision? The fact that we were here, in our wedding finery, seemed to say as much, at least to those in the kingdom. But we both knew that it was Devavrata who had made this happen. He had convinced Shantanu that the king must honour the oath Devavrata had made to my father and go ahead with the wedding.

'It will make me happy,' he had reassured his father. 'In fact, nothing could make me happier.'

Looking at Shantanu as he listlessly watched the sage go through the wedding rituals, a faraway look in his eyes, I wondered if he would ever be happy again. I suspected not. He was too consumed with guilt at how much his son had sacrificed.

In the days following the wedding, Shantanu's mood did not change. He was polite and attentive to me when we were together, but he spent much of his time wandering around the palace in deep contemplation. There was little pattern to his meandering walks, but he stopped at every balcony and would stare out across his kingdom, seemingly examining each different view of Hastinapur. He was searching the horizon for a solution, when there was none to be found.

On some days, I would find it too heartbreaking to watch Shantanu's helplessness and I would retreat to my room. The palace had a rich library of books, and I would attempt to distract myself by reading ones which told the history of Hastinapur. The books were works of art in themselves, with rich hand-drawn illustrations finished with gold leaf. Yet, most of the time, the words swam before my eyes. I found it too difficult to concentrate.

I was in my usual spot, staring blankly at another page, when I heard a faint knock on the door. When I opened it, I was surprised to see my husband standing there and even more so when I saw that he was smiling a little. Had the hills around Hastinapur presented him with an answer after all?

'Good evening, my Satyavati,' he said, giving me a polite bow in greeting. 'If possible, I would like to take a moment to speak to both you and my son.'

It was only then that I noticed that Devavrata was standing behind his father in the shadows.

'Of course,' I said, stepping back to let them into the chamber.

'Forgive me for the intrusion, Mother,' Devavrata said as he walked in. 'My father deemed this as the most relaxed location for our meeting. I must confess, though, that I don't know what it is about.'

Trying not to give away the unease I was feeling, I did my best to keep my tone light and welcoming.

'This is no intrusion at all, quite the opposite,' I said. 'Please make yourself comfortable.'

With a sweep of my arm, I indicated that they might like to sit on one of the elaborate plump cushions arranged in a colourful circle on the floor in the middle of the room. While the past week or so had been difficult, I always felt at ease sitting there. After ascertaining that my visitors did not require refreshments, I dismissed my maid and joined them on the cushions.

'I have spent the past few days trying to convince my son to change the vow he made to you, my queen,' Shantanu began.

I noticed he was avoiding eye contact, but the gaze of his son was firmly upon me. With the slightest motion of his hand, Devavrata bade me to be patient and to hear out his father.

'I know that my doing so goes against what was promised to you, but I felt that it was in the best interests of the kingdom,' Shantanu went on, addressing his son. Then he turned to me and added, 'I had to at least try and discuss it with him. But, Devavrata, he is a stubborn man, almost as stubborn as his father.

He will not shift from his stance in the slightest. This has ... upset me, but now I must accept and be grateful for the fact that he is doing it out of the kindness of his heart.'

The king closed his eyes and sighed heavily.

'My son does have a good heart. While I have found it difficult, as you know, I can see that this vow was taken for us, to ensure that the king of Hastinapur has a beautiful and perfect queen, the queen Hastinapur deserves, no matter the cost to my son.'

Shantanu was looking at me now, his expression urging me to agree with this sentiment. I nodded slowly to show that I understood, even though my heart and soul were broken. It was as I had realised on the journey to Hastinapur. All we could do was to make the best of a terrible situation. My penance for this terrible thing that had been done on my behalf would be to protect and serve my kingdom and do whatever it took to ensure its survival.

'I realise that I cannot change his mind and can only thank my son for his sacrifice,' Shantanu continued. 'But my thanks alone are not worth what this has cost him.'

His gaze shifted back to Devavrata, who smiled at his father with a warmth so genuine that it was all the more heartbreaking for the circumstances in which it was given.

'For the gift he has given to me, to us, I would like to grant him a boon,' Shantanu went on. 'That boon is that he will be allowed to choose the time of his own death.'

This was an almighty gift to bestow upon anyone, something that is given very rarely and in the most extreme of circumstances. The prince, for once, looked unsure of how to respond. His hand was clasped to his heart, but he was speechless, his gaze wandering around the room as he desperately tried to think of a response to what his father had said. Before he could do so, Shantanu began to speak once again.

'Also, after the promise that you have made, I have decided that the name Devavrata no longer befits you. From now on, you will be known as Bhishma, "the one who has taken a terrible oath".'

Silence befell the room.

There were so many things I wanted to say, but each one felt intrusive. I was grateful that my husband had shared this moment with me, but I felt unworthy to be part of it. They had both given up everything for me. I wanted to throw myself at their feet and beg forgiveness. But this was not what was required. Even if I did not think or feel like a queen, I had to act the part. Self-doubt was a selfish emotion. I had to give myself, all of myself, to my kingdom.

Mustering all my strength, I got to my feet, indicating to my two visitors that they should do the same. *This conversation was over. We would no longer look backwards. We would only look forward now.*

Both men followed my lead. I glanced at Devavrata and saw he was looking at me before giving the smallest nod of approval. If I hadn't been looking straight at him, I wouldn't have noticed it. He always seemed to see right through me, and somehow, on this occasion, I sensed his thoughts too. With the merest of looks, we had the deepest connection.

Then, he turned to his father.

'You have been too generous to me today, when there was really no need,' he said, his voice firm and steady. 'I thank you for the boon. I would also like to assure you that I will be here for as long as it takes to do right for the kingdom. You can be assured of that.'

Shantanu clasped his hands together and smiled, but it was a regretful smile. His countenance was still dejected and gloomy, as much as he tried to mask it.

Bhishma, as I had to get used to calling him now, remained resolutely upbeat. He knew we were all actors, playing a part in this charade, but he was not going to break character. He understood, as I did, that we must work together, and the task of protecting the kingdom did not allow time for melancholy.

'I must also thank you, Mother Satyavati,' he said, turning to me, his eyes shining with warmth and affection. 'You make a fine queen and an even finer mother.'

'Thank you,' I said, stepping forward to clasp both his hands. 'Thank you for everything.'

Something passed between us at that moment. Wordlessly, we both fully understood our future roles. We were bound together to support the king and Hastinapur. Nothing else mattered.

Chapter Six

While I had hoped the discussion that day would put the king's mind at rest, it soon became obvious this was not the case, although he did behave a little differently than before. His moods became strangely erratic. He swung between being overly jovial, laughing and joking with everyone in court uproariously, and then withdrawing to his room to be alone for hours at a time. At other times, he would return to pacing the corridors silently in the early hours, lost in deep contemplation. It was lovely to spend time with him when he was the life and soul of the party, but I could tell that, deep down, he was gradually becoming consumed by despair. No one but Bhishma and I saw this, and we were both sure to carefully and enthusiastically play the parts we'd accepted. *Everything was going to be alright now.*

We must have been the most accomplished actors because the court seemed to gradually recover from the shock of recent events. Those who had shunned the wedding began to drift back. We were sure to provide regular feasts and events, and few people could bear to miss out on the extravagant spreads the palace servants would provide. Those who were not entirely convinced by these worldly pleasures were tempted back by Bhishma's regular hunting parties. Who could resist spending time in the presence of this magnificent and powerful man? He was the most accomplished hunter, and just watching him at his art was reward enough for those who committed to the early morning rise to pursue the rich quarry offered by the forests around the palace.

Fulfilling my own vow, I devoted myself as much to Shantanu's happiness as to seeing to the well-being of the kingdom. In some ways, he responded well and reverted to being the same man who was so enraptured by me as I rowed him across the Yamuna. He still looked at me with that same intense love and pride. He also enjoyed spending time speaking to me about the needs of his kingdom, increasingly seeking out my opinion on what course of action to take with this problem or that. I was pleased about this. It helped serve my other purpose, training me in what it took to ensure that Hastinapur functioned well and making sure that there were no dangers I did not understand because I was too inexperienced to recognise them. Yet, late at night, I would wake up and find he was also wide awake and restless. Each time, when I asked what ailed him, the answer was the same.

'Do my people think less of me now?'

My response was the same each time too. I gave the king the same assurances that they did not think less of him. They loved their king and trusted his decision-making wholeheartedly. Choosing my words carefully, so as not to point out how few people had attended our wedding, I reminded him how many courtiers were always there now. Everyone wanted to be close to their king, I told him. But in the depths of the night, I could see my words had little meaning.

In my own darkest moments, I would tell myself that time would be our greatest ally. Shantanu would see how much the people of his kingdom loved him and that Bhishma and I were by his side, supporting him in everything. I wanted to reassure him that despite all the upheaval, nothing had really changed. But now, I knew I was wrong. There was a new hurdle to face, one that might send my husband into a further downward spiral.

I was pregnant.

Normally, such joyous news would be celebrated all over the kingdom. The festivities would have gone on for days. The throne was secured for another generation; the longed-for heir was on its way. But our child would surely symbolise all that the kingdom had lost. It would not be a powerful and skilled demigod, but a mere mortal with all the fallibilities that went with that status. I hardly knew how to tell even my husband the news, so I kept it to myself.

Over the past few months, I had found myself increasingly straying away from the palace grounds on my daily walks and heading further afield into the city beyond. I enjoyed the rhythmic hum and vibrations of the city as everyone went about their business. Seeing the market stalls piled high with the brightest and most aromatic of foods was a sensory delight. The children would scamper amongst the stallholders, oblivious to their shouts of frustration lest their carefully stacked produce was disturbed. The little ones didn't care, for they were having too much fun playing chase. Often, the sheer variety of the city's daily life would overwhelm me. It was very different from my former existence on the river, and the distraction was what I needed.

One late afternoon, I was wandering back from my walk in the markets, going over and over in my mind how to tell Shantanu my news. My belly was beginning to swell now. I would not be able to hide my pregnancy in the folds of my sari for much longer. Besides, Bhishma always seemed to know things about me before I did. It didn't seem fair that he should know before his father.

Glancing behind me, I saw that the sun had almost set. What harm would it do to sit a while and watch the end of the day? I thought, as I sank onto the warm stones of a low wall. Since my childhood, I had always loved the rising and setting of the sun. Perhaps it would give me the strength I needed to say what I needed to say.

The warmth of those last rays on my face afforded a sense of calm and well-being. It was so important to appreciate the wonders of nature, though too few people paused long enough to do so. I thought about the *kamrakh* seeds I had brought with me from home. It would soon be time to plant them. The tree would grow alongside my child, and I would one day tell him or her the story of my own childhood, which was so different from theirs.

'Haven't you all heard the story about the King of Shelva?'

Without wanting to, I found myself tuning into the conversation of a group of men standing nearby. I was not particularly interested in them, but I did always enjoy a good story. A quick glance at their robes told me they must be fairly well-off, perhaps visiting merchants. They were certainly not courtiers, whom I would have recognised. If they were travellers, they'd have fine stories to tell, just like the people I used to meet on the river. I stared ahead of me at the sunset, pretending I had not noticed them, but in reality, I was listening keenly.

'My, well, this is quite a story,' the merchant continued.

I couldn't resist another peek at the man who was talking and saw he was leaning in conspiratorially towards his companions. So, a *good* story then.

'It involves Devavrata …'

Now, he had my complete attention.

'Bhishma,' corrected one of the other three.

'Bhishma,' repeated the first merchant. 'When he was just 18 years old, he took on the entirety of King Shalva's army.'

The man who had corrected the speaker scoffed, 'He's a demigod, but a *whole* army?'

'Do not laugh. It is the truth! On the gods, I promise it. There was a war, a Great War between Hastinapur and Shalva. Both armies had been fighting for as long as anyone can remember. Then, Devavrata ...'

'Bhishma.'

'Bhishma,' the first man almost growled after being interrupted and corrected again. 'Bhishma returned to the kingdom after his training with his mother. The first thing he did was to take his chariot and head to Shalva, while here in Hastinapur, they'd barely finished their celebrations at his return.'

The two companions were silent now, hanging on to his every word, like me.

'He fought that Shalva army, all by himself, and defeated them within minutes. A *whole* army. By himself. Rank after rank of soldiers fell, no match for this fearless warrior. Then, the returned prince found the King of Shalva's son.'

I held my breath.

'The rules of engagement state that Dev ... Bhishma ... had the right to execute the Shalva prince right then, to punish the whole kingdom for their prolonged war against Hastinapur. But he did not do so.'

The merchant paused for effect. This man was a born storyteller. His companions didn't interject, though, or ask any questions. They were, no doubt, used to this, or perhaps the man who had interrupted earlier was fearful of irritating the storyteller so much that he would storm away without finishing his tale. Either way, silence ensued and the tension was palpable as we waited.

'The Shalva army was stunned by the sight of their ruler's son in Bhishma's grip. They all stood back as the young man picked up the rival prince and put him on his chariot.'

I snuck another look at the merchant and saw him miming throwing a man onto a chariot, his eyebrows raised to add to the drama.

'The prince of Shalva was carried all the way back here, to Hastinapur, whereupon he was thrown at the feet of King Shantanu, who was seated on his throne. By all rights, it was up to the king to decide the fate of the captive, and it is, of course, customary to execute such people. But De … Bhishma had other plans. He persuaded his father that sparing the young man and returning him to his father was the only way to stop the bitter war with Shalva. The king was not sure, believing it to be a disservice to his own kingdom, and considering that it might even shore up problems for later. But his son convinced him. Besides, King Shantanu was so happy about the return of his son that he'd have granted him any wish.'

I looked across once more to see the other two nodding with approval.

'He is astute, that one,' said the interrupting man. 'An asset to any kingdom.'

'If he were allowed to rule …'

The conversation stopped abruptly. One of the merchants had spotted me on my perch on the wall and nudged the others. *How many conversations like this were going on every day?*

Getting to my feet, I hurried past the group. I didn't look at them, fearful of catching their looks of embarrassment, or worse, humility, because they knew they had to bow to me. I had been responsible for removing their kingdom's greatest warrior, and yet, they had to revere me as their queen.

As I walked, I asked myself the same question I had asked over and over: Could I change this? Yes, I had vowed to accept it and do what I could to protect the kingdom. Yet, this baby changed things. We had a matter of months left before the birth. Maybe this was our very last chance to persuade Bhishma that he must reverse his oath before a living, breathing heir to the throne came into the palace.

Was this irrational? I didn't care. All that mattered was that Hastinapur had its greatest asset in its rightful place. By the time I reached the palace steps, I was like a woman possessed. I needed to speak with the king, break my news and implore him to help me try again to persuade Bhishma.

It took a little while to find Shantanu. He was in none of his usual places. Finally, after what must have been close to an hour of searching for him, I tried the stables, and to my surprise, spied him grooming his horse. He'd been doing it for a while too, since the beast's black coat shone in the lantern light. I couldn't dwell on the sudden thought that this was a blessing and he was at last finding some new interests. This could not wait.

'Good evening, Satyavati. How has this day been for you?' he said quietly.

After all the urgency in locating my husband, I was briefly lost for words.

'It's been a lovely day,' I managed at last.

Walking towards my husband, I took a deep breath and held out my hands. I waited as he put the brush down and then took my hands, a small smile playing on his face.

'I need to tell you something and make a request,' I said.

A look of fear and uncertainty flickered across Shantanu's face, but he assented.

'You know I would do anything for you, my love,' he said, his eyes searching my face for clues.

'I am pregnant,' I said, letting go of one of his hands to reach up and tenderly push back a strand of hair from his face. My hand moved down and I put a finger over his mouth so he could not reply yet. 'I am well and couldn't be happier. What I do want is for you to join me in speaking with Bhishma. I feel like time is running out. We're on a path neither of us wants ...'

The king nodded. I didn't need to say anything else. Instead, he reached up and took my hand and began to walk towards the door to the stables.

'You are right,' he said simply.

It didn't take long to find Bhishma, who was in his chambers, reading. I noted, not for the first time, how the room exuded an air of quiet dignity, reflecting the wisdom and valour of its venerable occupant. The walls were adorned with tapestries that told tales of battles fought and victories won, each thread a testament to the epic journey of this man. The ambient glow of flickering oil lamps cast a warm, golden hue upon the chamber, revealing intricate carvings that adorned the wooden furniture. A massive, ornately carved bed dominated the room, its polished wood gleaming with age. Bhishma's personal arms and armour, a silent witness to the countless conflicts he had weathered, were displayed with pride on stands near the bed. The air carried a faint scent of sandalwood, a soothing fragrance that seemed to linger in reverence to the great warrior's presence. As moonlight filtered through the latticed windows, it gently caressed the room, highlighting the subtle lines etched on Bhishma's face as he stood to greet us, a living legend in his sanctuary.

'Good evening, Mother Satyavati and Father! What has brought you to me this evening?' he said.

He was looking at me as he spoke and, once more, I was certain he knew exactly what I was about to say next.

'Bhishma, I know that we have spoken about and debated your vow more times than we can count,' I began. 'Today, when I was in the city, I heard again how much pain it is causing the people of this kingdom. They need you to protect the throne. You are what Hastinapur wants and needs.'

Bhishma opened his mouth to respond, but I didn't give him a chance to give us the familiar response.

'I … I am pregnant.'

Bhishma broke into a warm smile and looked about to exclaim his congratulations, but once again, I did not give him time to utter a word.

'Please, now, as your new mother, I am imploring you, break this oath,' I said. 'I now feel it more than ever: You should be the next to rule Hastinapur, not my child.'

Shantanu was beside me, silently imploring his son to agree to my heartfelt request.

The smile on Bhishma's face had gone, replaced by a grave look of contemplation. He was weighing his words, but I already knew his answer. I could see it in his eyes.

'I thank you both for your honesty and congratulate you both on this momentous news,' he said. 'Satyavati, you are new to Hastinapur, but the care you show for its people is immense. It is clear that you care more than most politicians and soldiers who have spent their entire lives serving this place. You have earned respect far more than I believe you realise.

'But I have taken an oath, and that oath was for you, and my father, and for Hastinapur. The kingdom's next ruler should be born of Hastinapur, and the child of its current queen, not the child of a queen who is no longer here. Take this as my final answer. This vow cannot, and will not, be broken. I am sorry for the pain that may cause you both.

'Please know, though, that when your child is born, I will continue in my pledge to protect the kingdom. I will do everything in my power to train and raise him to be the greatest ruler Hastinapur has ever seen. That is my promise.'

An oppressive silence spread across the room. I was crushed, yet unsurprised at Bhishma's response. It was not the answer I'd hoped for, but his honesty and eternal support eased the blow a little.

I looked over at Shantanu, and I could see that the dark cloud had returned. His guilt was destroying him.

Chapter Seven

The last of the ministers said their goodbyes to Shantanu, rising from their seats fanning out from the dais where he sat, which ran the length of the main hall. I watched from my own throne at the back of the dais as they walked away. I heard whispered fragments of small talk as they readied themselves to head back to their own homes all over Hastinapur after their day's work. The king had been polite enough throughout the day, but all those who had tried to make conversation with him about anything over and above the business of the court had not managed to engage him. Most had abruptly stopped in their efforts. They, like I, could see his thoughts were elsewhere.

Once everyone had left, the only people who remained were Shantanu, I, and a handful of guards. The sun was beginning to set, and a few of the maids busied themselves lighting candles in case we wished to stay for a while longer. Certainly, Shantanu had made no sign of movement. He still sat deep in his golden throne, his head resting lightly on his hand, his eyes unfocused on the ground before him. I walked over and laid a hand on his.

'How was the day? Did it go as you expected?'

From my perspective, albeit inexperienced, the day's politics had seemed quite productive. A lot of time had been spent listening to the details of an ongoing dispute between two farmers. Neither party could agree on whose land belonged to whom. Shantanu had listened carefully and then ordered each man to give up a little land to the other, parcelling it out so it was fair and advantageous to both. To the farmers and those in the court, it may have seemed quick and decisive, but in reality, I sensed the decision was more driven by disinterest and a desire to swiftly resolve the case.

Shantanu dipped his head, acknowledging my question, but did not look up. He was in no rush to expand on his response. Should I push him and try to engage him? I knew from experience that I would struggle. He was never rude or impolite; he was just not really present.

My attention was taken by the sound of the door opening at the end of the hall, followed by the sound of tiny footsteps scampering towards us. It was our children, Chitrangada and Vichitravirya, escorted by their nurse. I smiled as they called out to me and braced myself for the inevitable jolt as the two little ones crashed into me. They may be small, but the enthusiastic bodies of toddlers can generate some force.

'Hello, my children!' I said, enveloping them both in my arms and inhaling their scent as I kissed their heads. 'What trouble have you been up to today? Are the streets of Hastinapur safe now that you are inside here with me?'

'Yes, Mama!' they replied in perfect sync, followed by a hail of giggles.

The elder one, Chitrangada, climbed up my leg to plant himself in my arms. It was his new trick, and I did my best not to wince as he found handholds on my flesh. At last, he reached his goal and placed his head on my shoulder, his arms wrapped tightly around my neck. I did my best to adjust my balance, but it was not easy with my elder son wriggling around and the younger circling my feet. It was made even more challenging when Chitrangada leaned out far to the right to let lose a grin at his father.

Rapid action was needed to make sure I did not topple over, but I managed it somehow. When I had recovered my stance, I glanced at Shantanu to see how he had reacted to the cheeky greeting from his firstborn.

He had not moved. The only sign that he had even noticed the two boys was that he had lifted his head and given a small wave of acknowledgement.

'Please do excuse me, Satyavati. It has just occurred to me that there is something I need to attend to,' he said, rising from his throne. 'I must … must retreat to my quarters. I do hope you and the boys have the most pleasant of evenings.'

He did not wait for a response as he began to walk towards the door. The room was silent save for the sound of his leather slippers clacking against the polished stone floor. Even the usually boisterous boys were quiet. They sensed something was not as it should be. For a second, my gaze helplessly followed Shantanu's receding figure, but then, I had an urge to intervene. Handing the wriggling form of Chitrangada to his nurse, I hurried after the king.

'Shantanu, are you sure you cannot stay for a little while?' I said, breathing hard. Was it the exertion of trying to catch up with him or nerves at seeming to question the king? I could not be sure. I had been so unsettled for so long now. 'Your sons have been with the nurse all day and are eager to see you.'

Shantanu stopped and swung around to face me. For a moment, I was startled, as it dawned on me how little time we had spent with each other of late. It felt like forever since I had looked into his dark eyes. Before, when we'd been on my boat what seemed like a thousand years ago, they had been softened by laughter and sheer joy at the world around him. Now, his eyes were cold and the pain behind them all too evident. I doubted even the appearance of his beloved hornbill would make him break into a smile.

'I am sorry, my queen,' he said, his voice as flat as his expression. 'I … I …'

He could not finish, but he didn't need to. His sense of lost hope was there for all to see. I did not stop him when he turned to walk away. There was no point.

Shantanu had been growing more and more distant from me since Chitrangada had been born. He had checked on me quite regularly in the time leading up to the birth, but when the time came for him to meet his son, it took a long while for him to appear. Eventually, hours and hours after Chitrangada had been brought into the world, Shantanu arrived in the room, but he could hardly look at the baby in my arms. I believed he thought that I wouldn't notice it, as he spoke to me and made a great show of ensuring I was comfortable, but it was quite obvious that he was avoiding gazing upon his son.

I had asked him to hold the newborn because I knew no better back then. Shantanu was a great warrior and a fierce politician, capable of making decisions that could change a kingdom in less than a second. Yet, when I said those words to him, I watched him freeze, his mouth half-open, gaping like a fool. I had taken charge and pressed his son into his arms. He hadn't looked at the baby, though. He had just looked straight up towards the ceiling, desperately trying to hide his tears from me.

Over time, he had tried to get to know Chitrangada. He really had. Some days, he was much better than others. He'd break out into a smile, laughing at the small child's antics. After all, who could ever resist the joy of watching a child take his first steps or uttering his first words? Each time, though, he would check himself. It was almost as if an inner voice questioned whether he had any right to enjoy his son. He kept returning to the same thing in his mind. *This was the boy who would one day be king, usurping Bhishma, the person more suited to the throne than any mortal.*

Those inner voices won the battle for my husband's soul. The smiles and laughs grew fewer and fewer until, eventually, they disappeared altogether. Shantanu himself seemed to disappear too. If he did not need to be in the court, he would absent himself, spending long hours in his room by himself. When the time came for Vichitravirya to enter this world, he did not appear at all after the birth. It was left to me to bring the baby to court to present him to his father some weeks later.

My heart went out to my youngest. As a baby, he would lie in the nursery all day, with me and the sweet nurse by his side, waiting for his father's arrival, but it never happened. Vichitravirya would grow up barely knowing his father. For now, he was still too young to question it, but I was certain that Chitrangada was aware that something was amiss and yearned for attention from the king.

I had turned to go back to the boys when I heard the sound of the door opening once again. For a brief second, I wondered if Shantanu had had a change of heart, but when I swung around, I saw it was Bhishma. I had barely smiled in greeting before I felt the two small boys rushing past me, racing to embrace Bhishma. Bhishma had always been their favourite and never seemed to begrudge spending time with Chitrangada and Vichitravirya.

Bhishma dropped to his knees, his arms outstretched, a broad grin on his face. His stance remained solid, even as the pair barrelled into him. In one deft movement, the great man scooped up his half-brothers and rose to his feet before spinning them both around. This was what the youngsters loved. I had seen him doing this for hours, and he would never even break into a sweat.

'Hello, my children,' Bhishma said, laughing. 'Has today been a fine day?'

The only response from the boys was a shower of giggles. They had both stretched their arms wide, so they soared like birds in the sky as they went round and round.

'That's enough! The poor things will get dizzy,' I laughed.

'We won't,' Chitrangada shouted as he sped by. 'We never do.'

Bhishma shrugged as if to confirm this was the case, but he did relent after a few more turns. He placed them back on the ground, where they rocked a little from side to side.

'You see!' I said.

'They're fine,' Bhishma said. 'It's great training.'

The words 'for what' began to form in my mind, but Bhishma was on his knees addressing the children.

'Now, you two, as you have been so good today, I have a special present for you,' he said, reaching inside the folds of his robe. The boys gasped as he produced a golden arrowhead. It was a little damaged, but the small, shiny piece was still magnificent to behold. Normally, I would not have wanted such dangerous weaponry around my children, yet it was so beautiful I could not help but be drawn to it. It glinted in the light like the finest jewellery I had ever seen.

Chitrangada had already reached out to take it, but Bhishma retracted it quickly.

'Before I give you this, you must both give me your word that you will be very careful with it. It is very dangerous.'

The boys' eyes widened—beautiful and dangerous ... It was almost impossible to resist.

'It is fine, though, isn't it?' Bhishma went on. 'I found it today while out on patrol with our soldiers. By the looks of it, it may have been from a great battle many years ago. Perhaps it was owned by a king or a great warrior. Now, can I trust you to be careful with it and take good care of it?'

'Yes, Brother!' the children chorused.

'Good boys, I knew you would be sensible. Now, go along to your mother! I am sure she will want to see it too!'

Chitrangada took the arrowhead as carefully as though it was a freshly laid egg and carried it in both hands as he walked towards me, Vichitravirya following closely behind.

'Look, Mama! Look what our big brother has brought us. Isn't it fine?' Vichitravirya said, unable to stop smiling.

I knelt down to examine their prize. It was even more entrancing up close. I would have loved to know its story.

'Yes, my beautiful children, it is wonderful. But please do as your brother says and take care, or else I will feed you to the gharials!'

They both nodded and ran off to examine the arrowhead at their leisure, their nurse trailing in their wake.

'Thank you,' I said, turning back to Bhishma. 'You are always so thoughtful.'

'It's nothing,' he said, 'although one cannot help but appreciate its beauty.'

Bhishma and I had seen a lot of each other over the last few months. Whenever the children seemed to feel their father's absence most acutely, Bhishma would always appear and step in. He seemed to be able to read their thoughts, just as he could read mine. He had an endless supply of jokes, activities and curious gifts, which had an almost hypnotic power of distraction. Their sad faces would instantly transform to sheer joy. What a gift Bhishma had! He had also taken them to the forest to shadow a hunting party, and had recently started to teach them the basics of sword-fighting and archery. On some days, he would take them on long walks through the town and countryside, describing the flora and fauna. No wonder they adored him and constantly wanted to be with him.

I could never say it out loud, but I often felt embarrassed by Chitrangada and Vichitravirya. My imagination would haunt me, thinking about what Bhishma was like as a boy being raised by Ganga. There was no doubt that he would have been a strong, determined and intelligent child. He was a demigod after all. My children were merely human, and the difference must surely be noticeable already. I was convinced this explained why the king showed no interest in the boys, even though, in fairness, he had yet to give them any chance to prove themselves. Did Bhishma judge them in the same way? If he did, I could not blame him.

However, Bhishma had given me no cause to think he judged the boys harshly. In fact, it was quite the opposite. Whenever we met, he would regale me with tales of time spent with the children and say over and over how wonderful they were. To begin with, I believed that my joy at hearing Bhishma speak was merely a mother's happiness in seeing her children thrive. As time passed, though, I realised that I found great reassurance in simply hearing his voice. When I was in his presence, my fears for Shantanu would fade for a short time, as did my worries that the children would grow up to be a disappointment. When Bhishma was near, the clouds that gathered around me and cloaked my spirit would lift. What a tremendous gift he had! I felt honoured that he was willing to spend so much time with me.

Bhishma had never once voiced any resentment at the situation in which he had found himself. When I had first arrived, it had taken me months to accept that he bore me no ill-will for the fact that my children would take the throne from him. Even after Chitrangada's birth, I feared that every conversation with Bhishma would turn into a confrontation about the situation that we had put him in. But those words never came. He was not even thinking along those lines. His eyes shone with love and kindness, and there was no sign of anger in them. He was pure of heart.

Our conversations were never one-sided either. I would sometimes worry that I was a burden on his time, but he consulted with me almost daily on the decisions he made, even on subjects I knew barely anything about. The other week, we'd had a long talk about a solider in Hastinapur's garrison who had been caught stealing food to feed his sick family. Bhishma told me he had been torn between wanting to be firm and understanding. After we'd spoken about it, he resolved to make sure that the soldier's family would be fed every day for as long as the solider served Hastinapur. I was quite sure that he would have come to that decision without my input, but it was kind of him to include me. It seemed important to him that I learned about the day-to-day running of Hastinapur.

Almost out of nowhere, a thought struck me. *What if Bhishma was preparing me to run the kingdom?* He could not have failed to notice how depressed and disengaged his father had become. Did he foresee a time when I would need to take over? He always seemed to know so much more than us mere mortals.

'I hope court has not been too tedious today?' Bhishma said.

Pushing the negative thoughts away, I smiled brightly.

'Not at all. Your father met the farmers to speak about the upcoming harvest. There are fears that the rains might come early and drown the crops. They wanted his advice on whether they should bring the crops in now and store them somewhere dry.'

Bhishma looked thoughtful.

'It's a difficult matter. Too soon and …'

He was interrupted by a messenger appearing at the door. The man glided silently across the stone floor towards us and then addressed us both. Two sages had come to visit and were eager to pay their respects. This was not unusual. Bhishma always welcomed these holy men and ensured they were given refreshment. He had spent much time training with sages and always viewed them with the utmost respect.

'Please show them in,' Bhishma said right away, 'and then go to the kitchens and ask them to prepare some food and drink.'

One elderly and one young man were ushered into the room, and within minutes, a table was laid with *khichdi*, *dahi bade*, and *dosaka*, as well as a jug of chilled mango juice. The younger sage waited respectfully until the older one was served before helping himself. They were both silent as they worked their way through their first plates of food and then reached for more. It looked like neither of them had eaten for days.

'You have travelled far?' Bhishma asked the older sage as he began to slow down in his meal.

Our guest glanced at his feet and shrugged. His orange robe was slightly frayed and torn at the base, giving away the fact that he had been on a long journey.

'We have many people to visit,' he said simply. 'I have much to teach this young man.'

We both sensed he had more to stay, so we let him speak. The sage settled back in his seat, folding his robe around himself, one hand absent-mindedly stroking his beard.

'Do you recall the story of the two babies found on the riverbank?' he said.

I was transported back to my home and my little boat, as I remembered how Shantanu had heard about the babies and hoped that they might be his.

'Kripi and Kripa,' I said. "They were brought up by a sage.'

The older man smiled with approval.

'Correct, Sage Shardavan. Well, I would like you to meet Kripa.'

The young man shifted in his chair awkwardly.

'What a pleasure,' Bhishma said. 'I can see he has grown into a fine young man.'

'The pleasure is mine,' Kripa said, 'and your hospitality is very generous.'

Despite his initial embarrassment, Kripa was a confident man and spoke in a strong, steady voice. His unfortunate beginnings did not seem to have inflicted any lasting harm.

'We wanted to visit because Kripa is to become a royal priest and would like to pay his respects to the king,' the older sage went on. 'It was King Shantanu who arranged for his and his sister's upbringing and who ensured they had the best start. Kripi is now married after a very auspicious match.'

Even as he spoke, I was already feeling alarmed. Once Shantanu retired to his quarters each day, he did not like to be disturbed. He would not return downstairs, however much I asked.

'I … I am sure the king would be very happy to meet you,' I said. 'He has spoken fondly of you and your sister …'

I felt suddenly awkward and glanced at Bhishma.

'It is late,' he said, taking the cue. 'Perhaps you will do us the honour of spending the night, and we can present you to the king in the morning.'

The older sage had barely opened his mouth to speak when a commotion behind the door distracted him. The large door was flung open and two servants hurried in. From the expressions on their faces, it was clear something awful had happened.

'My lord, my queen, you must come right away,' one of the servants said, his voice cracking with emotion. 'Something has happened to the king. I think he is … dead.'

Chapter Eight

Clasping the cool rail of the chariot, I closed my eyes, trying with all my heart to cast my mind back to happier times. With effort, I summoned up a vision of my little teak boat, but as I saw it in front of me, a vision of my husband appeared alongside. I forced my eyes open. The sadness of this memory was just too much to bear. If he and I had stayed where we were and Bhishma had never taken his oath, or perhaps if Shantanu had never passed by and asked me to take him across the river, none of this would have happened. In both scenarios, I would still have been ferrying passengers in my boat, listening to my father's nightly grumbles about his fishing.

When I had lost Shantanu, I would not have believed that anything else in my life could cause me such pain. Then, seemingly just a few years later, my eldest son, Chitrangada, was gone too. It had happened so fast. The coronation of Chitrangada had been a muted affair. The kingdom was still reeling from the loss of Shantanu. Despite everything, my husband had been a popular king, well respected by his courtiers. Crowning his successor, though, one who was still a young boy, laid bare the vulnerability of Hastinapur. Even with the unquestioned love of a mother, I knew that my son was not a worthy king and would never grow to become one. Stand him beside Bhishma, and there was no contest. Bhishma was a mighty demigod. The kingdom, any kingdom, would have been safe with this man. There was not a single thing that he could not do one thousand times better than mortal man, whether it was fighting or keeping the peace with his wise counsel.

Bhishma had done his best. He had worked and worked with Chitrangada as he grew into his teens. And to be fair, Chitrangada was an accomplished swordsman under the great man's direction, but he would never be a fraction of the warrior that Bhishma was. Chitrangada was a mortal man, after all. When it came to matters of the court, he was completely out of his depth. Again, this was not his fault. He was his father's son, so he would one day be just as respected and adored by his courtiers, but right then, he was too young and inexperienced to make a mark.

Did my son know this? I hoped not. I did not want that to be the thought he took to the grave with him. But how could he not know?

I stared at the far horizon as the chariot rattled on, finding the smallest crumb of comfort in the familiar sound of stones being flung off the wheels in our wake. It reminded me of the twin trails of water that I used to imagine chased my boat. Sarathee, Shantanu's charioteer and now mine, stood silently by my side. In the past few weeks, I had called upon him almost every day. I told myself I needed to tour Hastinapur to show my face and let people know that things were under control. *Everything is fine, the queen is always out taking some air. She must be relaxed.* If only they knew how hard I had to bite my tongue to stop myself instructing Sarathee to keep going, to take me all the way back to my father's house.

I had started these daily chariot escapes the day after Chitrangada had been killed in the duel. I wanted to clear my head and understand what had happened. Yet, it was impossible. Just days after the coronation, a *gandharva* had arrived unexpectedly at the palace. We were welcoming to the demigod, and we felt sure that the dancing and musical skills of his ilk would bring much-needed lightness to the court. But there was no gaiety about this *gandharva*. He was angry and cruel. Upon arriving at the palace, he had announced that he was also called Chitrangada and only one of them could lay claim to this name. Bhishma had tried to intervene when the *gandharva* had challenged my son to a duel. He knew more than anyone that the young man was ill-prepared for such a contest. The *gandharva* sealed my son's fate by mocking him, offering to let him live if he changed his name. My son, my Chitrangada, was full of pride and would not be persuaded to back down.

Chitrangada had proven himself well. The air in court had been charged with anticipation as the two opponents circled each other, their eyes locked in a silent exchange of determination. Chitrangada, clad in regal armour adorned with its intricate designs, wielded a finely crafted sword that gleamed in the soft moonlight. The *gandharva*, on the other hand, possessed a slender and ethereal appearance, his wings shimmering like delicate jewels as he gracefully unsheathed a celestial blade with an other worldly glow.

The rhythmic clash of steel echoed through the night as the prince and the *gandharva* had engaged in a dance of blades, each movement a testament to their skill and finesse. Chitrangada's swordsmanship had been honed through years of rigorous training with Bhishma, but the *gandharva*'s agility and supernatural grace made him a formidable adversary. Each of Chitrangada's powerful strikes were met with the *gandharva*'s swift parries. The court seemed to come alive with the dance of their weapons. As the battle unfolded, however, it became evident to even the most ardent supporter of Chitrangada that he was no match for the *gandharva*. Despite his passion, sword stroke by sword stroke, he became progressively weaker. He fought and fought though, right to the very end.

When the *gandharva* killed his opponent, he simply left the palace without even a backward glance, the gasps of the courtiers and the broken-hearted sobs of a mother ringing in his ears. Whenever I thought of it, a vision of the crumpled, bloodied heap of my brave son would flood my mind, and the pain would return, as fresh and raw as when it first happened.

'Do you think our luck will ever change?' I asked Sarathee.

The charioteer stared ahead, the reins clasped in his hands, his face a picture of concentration. I was used to this. Ordinarily, it would be unheard of for a king or queen to seek the counsel of their charioteer. Over time, though, I had formed a bond with Sarathee. We spoke to one another as equals, even though in everyone's eyes, this was far from the reality. I welcomed it too. The only other person in the kingdom whom I could count on to give me an honest answer was Bhishma. Everyone else couched their conversations in terms they thought I wanted to hear. What I had learned about Sarathee, though, was that he always considered his responses carefully. He'd never just blurt out an answer.

'I think it will,' he said, at last, 'But ...'

'But what?'

It was unlike Sarathee to hesitate before he completed what he had to say. My heart began to beat faster. *Had he heard something? Was there still more bad news to come?*

'People are worried,' he said quietly.

'In the court?'

'Yes, certainly, but further afield too.'

I stayed silent. Something else I had learned from living at the palace was that people told me what they thought I wanted to hear. Any news I gleaned in any other way was usually quite different. I'd catch snippets of conversation as I wandered around the corridors in my slippers. It was only once I was right beside these huddled, gossiping groups and they noticed I was there that they'd break apart with a start. Their expressions, which were often grave before they saw me, would instantly transform onto ones of happiness and cheer. These days, their whispered conversations were almost always about the threat from neighbouring kingdoms. The loss of Bhishma as heir was still keenly felt, and even more so now that Vichitravirya had taken over the throne. He, like his brother, was young and inexperienced, in fact, even more so. The courtiers felt our vulnerability keenly. What would happen if he too was challenged by a passing *gandharva*, or if any number of disasters befell him? What would happen to the kingdom then? Would Bhishma break his oath and step in? I think they suspected that he would not, and I agreed with them. There was no chance he'd break his oath.

'I … I would like to know what people are saying around the kingdom,' I said, trying and failing to sound less concerned. 'I get told so little.'

Sarathee nodded.

'It is not different from what you have picked up in your walks around the palace,' he said with a shrug. 'People are concerned about the future. They hear things …'

'Hear things?'

'... from people who travel more widely. To other kingdoms.'

For a moment, I was transported back to my youth, to a time when I would listen to stories about intrigues between various kingdoms. Back then, they were just good stories. Now, these rumours represented a great danger to Hastinapur.

To my surprise, Sarathee brought the carriage to a halt and turned to face me, the reins now dangling loosely in his hand.

'There is talk that there are armies amassing in at least one, possibly two, neighbouring kingdoms,' he said, his expression grave. 'They see the weakness in ...'

Sarathee checked himself as he tried to find the right form of words.

'They see an opportunity in a kingdom being run by such a young king.'

'But Bhishma ...' I interrupted.

Sarathee nodded again.

'... can only fight one army at a time,' he said, 'however accomplished he is as a warrior. Even with his divine status, he cannot be in two places at once. If more than one enemy attacks, or they coordinate their attacks, Hastinapur is vulnerable. The people whom I meet in the markets and on the streets, they know this and they are fearful.'

My mind raced. Deep down, I already knew this to be true, but now I had proof that it was unsettling the people of my kingdom. I had to act and act quickly before full-scale panic broke out and things got out of hand.

'We need to show strength,' I said, voicing my thoughts out loud before they were fully formed. 'To show everyone that we have a plan to strengthen our position.'

As I spoke, I stepped off the chariot and began to pace up and down. Somehow, the warmth of the sand beneath my feet helped me to think better, perhaps because it reminded me a little of my old life in the fisherman's house. Sarathee stayed at his post in the chariot, watching in silence as I formulated my plan.

'The most obvious point of vulnerability is … is …,' I paused and swallowed hard. This was difficult to say. '… is what happened to Chitrangada. People will worry that if something like this happened again, the bloodline will be lost.'

I stopped pacing and looked back at Sarathee. We were both thinking the same thing.

'And Bhishma won't break his oath,' I went on. 'So, we need to strengthen the bloodline. We must find a bride for Vichitravirya.'

As I said this, my mind flashed back to one of those whispered conversations I had overheard just a few days ago. Kshyksi, the king of Kashi, was apparently planning a lavish event where his three daughters, Amba, Ambika and Ambalika, would be invited to choose their husbands. I had not thought much of it at the time. If anything, I had dismissed it as the idlest form of palace gossip, for the palace staff spent far too much time swapping news of who was hosting what lavish event here or there. It didn't interest me. Perhaps I did not think it of any interest because Vichitravirya was so young, and the time when we needed to choose his bride seemed so far away. I had been wrong. This was urgent.

My mind made up, I walked back to the chariot at a determined pace.

'Please take me back to the palace as quickly as you can,' I told Sarathee.

It took half an hour or so to retrace our steps. Even though I was consumed by a sense of urgency, I was grateful for this time to organise my thoughts. We needed a strategy to make sure Vichitravirya was chosen by one of the Kashi daughters, and there was only one person for this important job: Bhishma.

It didn't take me long to find Bhishma. He was in the main hall of the palace issuing instructions to a small group of ministers. This was where he spent most of his days, ensuring, as per his vow, that the kingdom ran smoothly. Vichitravirya was too young to take this role, but I was ashamed of the next thought that popped into my head. How I wished that Bhishma would continue to run the kingdom even once my son came of age! The rest of his day was usually spent in training Vichitravirya to hunt and fight. He was a diligent and patient teacher.

As soon as he saw me, Bhishma excused himself from the group and hurried forward to greet me. Despite all my worries, my heart always beat a little faster in the presence of this great man. It was impossible not to be overwhelmed by his charisma.

'May we speak privately?' I said, after we had greeted one another.

'Of course, Mother Satyavati.'

Bhishma indicated for me to follow, and we walked together towards the smaller chamber to the side of the main hall. It was one of my favourite rooms in the palace. The ministers in charge of the judiciary used it for confidential talks about legal disputes brought before them by the citizens of Hastinapur. Perhaps in keeping with the gravity of its purpose, it was not decorated with the colourful, rich opulence of the rest of the palace. In fact, it was remarkably plain. No pictures hung from the walls, and the only furniture was a long wooden table with seats on either side. A small splash of colour was added by the red cushions on each seat, but other than that, it could have been the living quarters of any moderately well-off person in Hastinapur. Perhaps that was why I liked it so much. It reminded me a little of home.

'What is it that troubles you?' Bhishma asked, waiting until I had settled into a chair and he had done the same.

I didn't comment that, once again, he could read my mood exactly. I had already marvelled at this too many times. Where to begin, though?

'I've … I've been thinking about the future.'

Bhishma nodded but stayed silent.

'Vichitravirya. I think we need to find his bride. To secure the bloodline. He's young, I know, but I don't think it is too soon.'

Bhishma stretched his arms in front of him and put his hands down on the table. He looked thoughtful.

'You think this will help the people to feel calmer about the future of the kingdom?'

I inclined my head to indicate 'yes'.

'There are rumours …'

'… there are always rumours,' he interrupted. 'Don't listen to the palace gossip. A lot has happened over the past few months. Things will settle down.'

'It's not just in the palace. There is talk out there that enemies are circling us. We may be vulnerable.'

The smallest hint of a frown passed Bhishma's brow.

'I have sworn to protect Hastinapur. Do you doubt my abilities?'

'No, of course not! I just want to show everyone that we are planning for a stronger future.'

I never wanted Bhishma to think I was anything but eternally grateful for his support. I admired his skills more than I could ever express. Stumbling over my words, I pressed on.

'I have heard that Kshyksi, the king of Kashi, is planning to ask his three daughters, Amba, Ambika and Ambalika, to choose husbands. One of the girls would be perfect for Vichitravirya.'

Bhishma's expression changed. A dark cloud seemed to descend upon him and he leapt to his feet, his hands balled into fists at his side. In a matter of seconds, the atmosphere in the room had become heavy and tense. I had rarely, if ever, seen him rattled. Was he angry about my earlier comments when he mistakenly thought I doubted his abilities?

'I … I want to ask you to go to Kashi on my behalf,' I said, watching in growing alarm as he began to pace to and fro. He seemed to be deliberately avoiding meeting my gaze.

I got to my feet and walked to the other side of the table, planting myself in the path of his pacing. Bhishma had no choice but to stop directly in front of me and look me in the eyes. How I wished I could read his thoughts as he could seemingly read mine! All I could see when I looked into his deep brown eyes were wells of sadness. But there was anger there too.

'What is it?' I asked, reaching out. As I did so, he stepped back, shaking his head.

'It is not something I wished to bother you with.'

Bhishma checked himself and his expression softened. Whatever private battle he had been fighting in his head appeared to have found a resolution.

'I knew about this selection from the kingdom of Kashi,' he said. 'I too had the same thought as you, about Vichitravirya.'

'But?'

'But the kingdom of Hastinapur has been excluded from this ceremony.'

'Excluded? Surely Vichitravirya is the perfect match? Any king with an eye to the future would know that. And isn't it protocol to invite your neighbouring kingdoms to such events? That is how we secure some semblance of peace between us.'

Bhishma watched as I worked it through in my mind.

'Is it because Hastinapur is in a more weakened position than I imagined?'

'No!' Bhishma almost shouted. 'Don't think that way. It is because of me.'

'You?'

This was so confusing. We seemed to be going round in circles. I had thought this was such a simple request for something that could greatly help our circumstances.

Bhishma pulled out a chair and bade me sit in it before settling in the one beside me. He began to speak quietly.

'King Kshyksi approached me about a match with his sister. She is very beautiful and accomplished but, well … it was after I took my oath.'

Now I understood. The king of Kashi had been furious at what he saw as a snub from Bhishma. Out of pique, he had excluded us from the ceremony to find husbands for his daughters. I wanted to be angry with this vain king, but I knew he was not really to blame. It was my fault. By forcing Bhishma into the oath, I had once more reduced the prospects of the kingdom.

There was something else, though. Something that irked me. Bhishma had always promised to do everything that he could to protect Hastinapur. When Shantanu had withdrawn into himself in the depths of despair, the two of us had forged an unspoken alliance. We would work together to make sure what had been done would never be to the detriment of the kingdom. And we had. Every action in the past had been with full consultation of the other. We spoke every day, sometimes several times a day. I'm sure I flattered myself that Bhishma would ever need my advice, but he was always sure to ask my opinion about significant decisions. Why, then, had he kept this from me?

'It would have been helpful to have known this, so I could have managed expectations,' I said, my face became hot as I spoke. Who was I to ever rebuke this great man?

For a moment, Bhishma looked stricken.

'I am so sorry, forgive me. The last thing I would ever do is hurt you or allow you to think badly of me. I should have said something.'

Seeing his look of remorse, my brief flash of anger vanished. I was embarrassed to have said anything and wanted us both to forget the conversation had ever taken place.

'Let's just forget it,' I said. 'Hastinapur does not need these Kashi princesses. If they are anything like their father, so easily offended ...'

'I'll go,' Bhishma said, jumping to his feet. 'Let me put this right.'

'There is nothing to put right,' I said.

I fixed my expression into a soothing smile. Something was wrong. Bhishma was always so calm and measured. Now, he was irrational and distracted. How I wished I had never started this! I needed to use all my powers of diplomacy to defuse the situation.

'I will leave right away.'

He was already heading to the door, but then paused and turned back to me, giving the briefest of bows to show his respect. I could not stop him. He was determined to go.

'Bhishma,' I called since he was almost out of the door. 'Please take my chariot.'

He turned around, looking confused.

'What is wrong with my own?'

I forced myself to give a broad smile to show this was a light-hearted remark.

'Well, if you are going to be bringing back a bride, mine seems a little more luxurious,' I said. 'It's far better than your chariot, which is more suited for scaring opponents in war.'

Bhishma did not return my smile, but tilted his head to show he would do so. He did not say anything as he left, closing the door behind him.

Chapter Nine

During my time in the palace of Hastinapur, I had noticed that the trees, plants, animals and weather, all seemed to reflect upcoming events. When there was a wedding, flowers bloomed, the sun shone and the clouds disappeared. When there was death, the sky turned grey, the gardens wilted and birdsong was temporarily silenced. That was why I was alarmed the evening when Bhishma was expected to return. At sundown, the skies of Hastinapur turned a vicious red. Animals scuttled away early to their resting places. The sambar deer that always came to the river for an evening drink were nowhere to be seen. Was the entire ecosystem of Hastinapur preparing me for what would come next?

For days now, I had not been able to shake the vision of Bhishma leaving with Sarathee. He'd been standing ramrod straight in the chariot, his expression a tangle of anger and frustration. I was desperate to know what had happened in Kashi. Was King Kshyksi dead? Injured? Had someone managed to do the impossible and harm Bhishma? I barely wanted to allow myself to imagine what the cause of all this disruption could truly be. I also doubted I could be the only one with this fear. Many who had been in Hastinapur far longer than I could not fail to notice the changes in the atmosphere, just as I had done. But they didn't know what had passed before Bhishma had left on his quest.

I passed the time by impatiently wandering through the palace. Walking past Bhishma's quarters, I stopped and then entered his room. It always struck me how it was another of the plainest rooms in the palace. Like the room for the justices, there were no real signs of opulence aside from the tapestries on the walls. There were a few spoils of war, swords and shields, casually propped against the walls, a shelf of books and two deep couches. It had a transitory air about it, like the room of someone who didn't expect to be staying for too long. Or, perhaps, that was my innermost fear talking.

Re-emerging into the corridor outside, I directed my steps towards the balcony and peered into the dimly lit courtyard below. The moon's efforts at lighting the courtyard were in vain that evening. The dense clouds were moving rapidly, shrouding the moon's hard work. But even in this light, I could see the courtyard was still empty.

Then, the silence of dusk was broken. The grand doors at one end of the courtyard swung open, revealing torchlight from the flares either side of the door. There, in the middle was a tall, well-built figure. It was unmistakably Bhishma, moving at an aggressive speed, and trailing in his wake were three other figures. While I could not quite make out their faces, I could tell from their gait and dress that they were young women. Were these the Kashi princesses? Surely not. If Bhishma had been successful in his quest, he would have brought back just one, not three. And why were they cowering behind him?

Even as I raced back along the corridor, the echo of my slippers bouncing along the stone walls, I was filled with dread. My heart beat harder in my chest as I heard sobs from the grand hall. I could not bear to imagine what had happened.

After turning the last corner and bursting through the doors into the hall, I stopped dead in my tracks. Bhishma was directly in front of me, his face still the same picture of fury I'd seen when he'd left for Kashi. Cowering behind him were three figures. Even though their saris looked dusty and crumpled from the journey, I could tell they were made of the most expensive silk. These girls were of noble blood. The worst part of what lay before me was that these princesses looked distraught. Their faces were pale, drained with shock, and tear-stained.

My heart was sinking into depths that I didn't know it could reach. I turned to Bhishma, desperate for an answer or explanation, but I was thwarted. For the first time ever, he was avoiding eye contact. He looked distracted, confused even. Stepping forward, I placed a hand gently on his shoulders and turned him to face me. He flinched in surprise, almost as if he hadn't registered that he was in the palace.

'What has happened?' I asked gently.

Silence. Bhishma was staring straight ahead.

'Is … is the king dead?'

For the first time, Bhishma caught my gaze and shook his head.

'King Kshyksi is very much alive, but I have taken everything from him.'

Raising his hand, he took my hand from his shoulder and gently let it drop before clasping his palms together in front of his chest.

'I am sorry,' he said.

Then, he turned and began to walk away, shaking his head as he did so.

'Sorry for what?' I called after him.

He didn't turn back. It was devastating. The strong bond between us seemed shattered. The worst part of it was that I had no idea why, and without this knowledge, how could I seek to repair it?

This was not a question for now. I had become acutely aware of three pairs of eyes staring at me. The princesses were waiting for me to speak. Waiting for me to behave like a queen. The pressure that I had to get what happened next right caught at my throat. If I could not rely on Bhishma, what did I have?

'Are you all okay?' I said, composing myself as I turned to the girls. 'Are any of you injured?'

The girls were silent, but all three shook their heads to indicate that they were not injured. But it was clear that they were very unhappy and did not wish to be here.

I needed to get to the bottom of what was happening, but I couldn't ask the princesses. They were in shock. What, then, was I to do with them? Bhishma had herded them into the palace as though they were his prisoners. I couldn't possibly prevent princesses from another kingdom from leaving if they wanted to go. Whatever had gone on, that would surely make it worse.

'You must all be thirsty and desperate to clean up after your long journey,' I said. 'It is very late, so I will prepare some quarters for you all to rest. Then, in the morning, we can talk and ...'

My voice trailed off. *Talk and ...? Find out what has happened? Arrange to get you home?*

To my relief, the young women did not question me, nor did they seem to notice that I was unsure of what would happen next. I instructed one of the maids to lead them to the guest quarters. The rooms were always kept spotless by the servants, ready for any esteemed visitors. The girls all clung together, whispering that they wanted to share a room. I couldn't help noticing that one of them seemed surer of herself than the others. From what little I knew about the Kashi princesses, Amba was said to be the most confident, and she had clearly taken charge. As I instructed the maid to grant their wish and let them stay together, she was the only one of the three who looked me straight in the eye before they left to follow the maid. Her own eyes smouldered with anger and indignation. Whatever had happened, it would not be easy to resolve.

There was only one person who could help me now. I turned my steps towards the stables, ignoring the questioning glances of the courtiers who always hung around the palace corridors. They'd seen and heard the loud arrivals and were eager to know what it meant. Let them gossip and speculate, I thought. I needed to know the facts.

I found Sarathee exactly where I'd expected him to be. He was tending to his horses, brushing down their coats after the long ride back from Kashi. He did not need to do this. We had grooms for that. But loyal Sarathee always saw to it that his horses were properly groomed and fed before he himself settled down for the night.

The night chill clung to the folds of my sari, and I shivered as I walked towards Sarathee. He looked up at me and waved, and as I closed the distance between us, I became suddenly aware of how exhausted I felt. I was compelled to speak to Sarathee, yet a big part of me also wanted to return to my quarters. Who knew, if I slept well, I might awake to discover this had all been a terrible dream. Silently, I chided myself. That was how a girl would think, not a queen.

As I got closer, I could see that Sarathee looked as tired as I felt. He was still wearing his dust-covered riding clothes, his usually beautifully polished armour dulled with dust. They must have been riding at a tremendous speed to kick up that much dirt. Now that I was almost upon him, I could see his expression. It was one I had not seen on him before. He looked afraid.

'Sarathee, I have just met the three princesses. What has happened? What did you see? Why are they all here?'

My charioteer dropped his gaze and shuffled his feet awkwardly.

'You know I have always trusted you to speak freely with me,' I reminded him. 'I really need you to do so now.'

Sarathee looked up.

'Did … did Bhishma not speak to you?' he asked.

Part of me wanted to retort that I would not be asking if he had, but I stopped myself. As far as I knew, none of this was Sarathee's fault. It would not be right to take my impatience out on him.

Sarathee picked up a cloth which had been slung over the stable door and began to wipe his hands. It was a slow, deliberate action typical of the charioteer. I knew why he did it too. He was working out how to tell me what had happened.

'I should warn you, this story will be … uncomfortable.'

I indicated that I understood, but would like him to continue anyhow. With great care, Sarathee folded the cloth into two and returned it to its place on the door. He then took a deep breath.

'You saw us leave. Bhishma was quiet during the entire journey to King Kshyksi's court. It was strange because he's usually such good company. Typically, any journey with him goes by in a flash because of his non-stop tales of politics and intrigue. Truly, riding with him is usually a joy and an honour.'

He paused before adding, 'I must make it clear that despite what I'm about to tell you, I would still ride with him until the day I die. That is a promise.'

It didn't need saying, but I was glad that he had done so.

'Bhishma made us ride right through the night. We didn't even stop for a meal or drink. The horses are more exhausted than they have ever been after any cavalry charge. I hope they can forgive me for their ill-treatment.'

I wanted to interrupt. That my charioteer cared for his horses was never in dispute. I needed to know what happened at the palace. This was his character, though. He was a thoughtful man, not to be rushed. I stayed silent.

'When we arrived at King Kshyksi's court, our reception was … muted at first. There was whispering all around the road leading up to the palace gates. From noblemen to peasants, it felt as if we were on show for everyone. I could not make out what anyone had to say, but I knew that it was not good. When we entered the court, before we could even really begin to speak, King Kshyksi's voice boomed out. He condemned Bhishma for even coming to Kashi and claimed he was arrogant to even imagine he'd carry away one of his daughters. He said … terrible things about Hastinapur. He could not believe that our kingdom could even consider that Kashi would stoop to agree to a connection through a royal marriage …'

Sarathee's voice trailed away. He looked genuinely saddened.

'What insult could we have given them that would make humiliation like this suitable punishment?' he asked. 'The noblemen around him all joined in too … It was like some sort of sport. Even King Shalva, whose life he had spared all those years before. What gratitude is that?'

I racked my brains to recall the story behind the name. Shalva was our neighbouring kingdom, but we had some history, I was sure. Then, I remembered. King Shalva was the person I had overheard the merchants talking about when I had been walking close to the palace that day. Bhishma had defeated Shalva's army when he was just 15 and captured the prince of Shalva, but he had gone on to persuade Shantanu to be fair and spare the prince's life.

I now had a sense of where this story was going, however much I hoped that it hadn't ended how I already knew it had. While I prayed that those princesses came to Hastinapur on their own accord, I would have to accept that this was not the case.

Sarathee had a faraway look in his eyes. I had no doubt that he was reliving what had happened, moment by moment. His slumped shoulders told me we were not far from the worst part of the story.

'After a few minutes of standing in silence whilst the king and noblemen heckled us, Bhishma just … snapped. He drew his arrows from their quiver, lifted his bow and fired a volley of shots with greater speed and precision than I've ever seen him do, even in the heat of combat. The shots all met their targets dead centre.'

I gasped. Had he killed everyone in the palace? Was he lying when he told me the king was alive? Seeing my reaction and anticipating my thoughts, Sarathee held up his hands.

'He didn't hurt anyone. The arrows were strong and true, though, and went exactly where he directed them. They pierced the crowns of all the noblemen, ripping them from their heads. The crowns hurtled together in a group, before they were pinned against the walls, hanging there like a bizarre painting. The gasps of shock at this insult sucked the air from the room.'

My eyes widened as he told this story. I could hardly believe that Bhishma, a demigod, would lose his cool like this with mortal man and behave with such disrespect in a neighbouring kingdom. No matter what the provocation, and this was provocation without a doubt, this insult was not something we could easily recover from.

'What happened next?' I asked quietly, even though I was not sure I wanted to know any more.

'Bhishma did not move for a little while. He stood with rage in his eyes, the likes of which I have only seen in the wildest of tigers during the fiercest of hunts. Eventually, he spoke to the king, almost shouted really. He said he was there as his brother's representative, as a proxy, and asked how the Kashi king dared to insult him, the guardian of Hastinapur. His voice became calmer when he said he had only travelled to Kashi out of goodwill, with thoughts of peace, love and unity. How, he asked, could King Kshyksi run a court where insults were flung about like bread to the poor?

'I thought that was it. I was sure one of two things was about to happen. Bhishma would either return to the chariot and we'd come back to Hastinapur or he would challenge the king to a duel. He did neither.'

Sarathee paused and sighed deeply.

'He jumped forward like a jaguar, throwing to the ground the guards who were looking after the royal dais. Ignoring the shouts of protest from all around us, he instructed the three princesses to follow him, then dared anyone to try to stop him. It was pandemonium. Everyone was shouting, but even though the guards unsheathed their weapons, no one dared to attack after the marksmanship they had just seen, even the princesses' father. All that the king could do was to tell his men to stand down and let Bhishma leave.'

I closed my eyes as I pictured the scene. Bhishma with his charisma and other-worldly strength and presence. No wonder they were all too scared to respond.

'He took them?' I said slowly, even though I already knew the answer.

What had happened to Bhishma? This was so out of character. Had he finally succumbed to the pressure we'd both been feeling since Shantanu's death?

I glanced at Sarathee, readying to thank him for his candour. To my surprise, I saw that he wasn't finished. He was steeling himself to tell me something that had clearly pained him. I could hardly believe there was more to add to this terrible tale.

'What is it? What else?' I said, hearing the panic in my own voice.

'The journey back was chaos. Bhishma was silent, glowering in fury, but he treated the princesses with respect. Even so, to begin with, the princesses cried so loudly that the birds were startled from the trees. Then, they were quiet. I thought perhaps they had no more tears left, but then I became aware that they were all staring into the distance in terror.'

Terror? How could this situation have become even worse?

'To our left, atop a dark hill, a huge cloud had emerged. It just seemed to grow and grow. I knew what it was. Of course, so did Bhishma. We've both seen our share of approaching armies ...'

'... armies? How had King Kshyksi mobilised so quickly?'

'No, not King Kshyksi. King Shalva.'

King Shalva? But he was indebted to Bhishma. Sarathee interrupted my thoughts by continuing with his story.

'Soon, at the base of the cloud of dust, horses became visible. A few in number at first, then many, many more. We had to stop. Our chariot was overloaded, and we could not escape at speed.'

'... And Bhishma was never going to run away anyway.'

'That is true,' Sarathee shrugged. 'But, he was, as I have said, almost eager to be the aggressor. Normally, he is the statesman, looking for a fair solution.'

Sarathee began to explain, 'Bhishma knew King Shalva. He was just a prince when they last met and he …'

'… spared his life,' I confirmed. 'I know the story.'

I was impatient to know what had happened during this confrontation.

'The king rode a fine horse and was wearing golden armour that reflected the moonlight perfectly. Bhishma did not flinch. When the king was just a stone's throw away, Bhishma dismounted from the chariot and walked towards the cavalry line without fear. I wondered if Shalva would show any gratitude. After all, he had only ascended to the throne because of Bhishma's mercy.

'He did not. He leapt off his horse, ordering his men to remain where their horses stood and then swaggered forward. He was pointing at Bhishma, hurling insults at him. The insults were unoriginal, uncreative, not that different to what we had received at Kshyksi's court.'

My blood ran cold. All the world seemed united in mocking Hastinapur now. How quickly we had been diminished in the eyes of our neighbouring kingdoms!

'It was clear that King Shalva had not moved on from his previous defeat. The two walked close to one another and began to speak. Their voices were low. I am sorry that I could not hear what they said. I heard mention of Princess Amba in particular, but that was all.

'I could hardly believe what happened next. Without warning, King Shalva removed his sword from his belt and swung at Bhishma. What mortal man would do that? Of course, Bhishma, without even removing his arms from by his side, dodged it with ease.'

Sarathee looked incredulous as he recounted what had happened next.

'King Shalva swung his sword frantically, non-stop, and Bhishma continued to move with lightning speed. At some point, Bhishma had enough of this ridiculous dance. He reached out, grabbed the blade of Shalva's sword, and snapped it in two like it was the lightest twig. He then threw both pieces on the ground like darts.'

What a strange story! It didn't seem to make any sense that King Shalva had done this. He had already been humiliated by Bhishma once and knew he was no match for him. No mortal man could be that. There must have been something else that fuelled his courage, his stupidity.

'Bhishma drew his bow and fired a volley of arrows, pinning the king to the ground. I could see that King Shalva's men felt the embarrassment of his defeat keenly. Some even turned their heads away so that they wouldn't see their ruler's shame. A few loyal soldiers did manage to summon the courage to step forward, as though to help him to his feet, but Bhishma warned them off with a look. Bhishma returned to the chariot and told me to continue. That is what we did.'

Sarathee was at last quiet, his story fully told.

Thanking him and urging him to rest, I turned to walk back to the palace. I had many questions, but I knew enough of the story now. My mind was spinning, but I needed to think.

The main hall of the palace was quiet when I reached it. It was very late, and everyone had retired to bed by now. That was a relief. I could not bear to see the courtiers looking at me inquisitively, wondering about my next move. I was not ready to be the decisive queen they wanted me to be, not yet.

I had two problems. The first was that Bhishma had acted so out of character in this entire episode, and I needed to find out why. The second issue, though, was more pressing. I needed to work out how to put things right with my three royal guests. Part of me wanted to run to the guest room and set them all free, but I already knew that could make things worse, for doing so would humiliate Bhishma. I'd just heard what humiliation could do to a man. Shalva was the prime example of that.

As I returned to the court, I ran Sarathee's story through my mind once more. Were there any clues there for me? Perhaps there were. He had mentioned that Shalva may have been talking about Amba. Maybe they knew one another. From my brief encounter with the girls, I already knew she was the one who was not afraid.

Walking through the main doors, I stepped back in surprise. Amba was standing in the main hall. She'd clearly been waiting for me.

The princess was composed, staring back at me, her expression blank. Even in the half-light of the hall, I could see that she was a very beautiful woman. She had a delicate, neat, perfectly poised frame, and the glint of haughtiness in her large dark eyes spoke of complete self-assurance. Her glossy hair, which must have been in a neat plait before her journey, was long and hung loosely over her shoulders, which added to her air of soft femininity. However, this woman was no weak-willed bystander.

'I believe it's Amba, isn't it?' I began.

She inclined her head to indicate affirmation, but seemed in no rush to respond.

'I did not think you would know who I was,' she said at last.

'I have heard a little about you and the other princesses. It is a pleasure to finally meet you.'

This last statement was a mistake, but I realised my error too late.

'A pleasure to meet me?' she said slowly. Her tone was polite but could barely mask her anger. 'Was this how you wanted to meet me?'

I could not argue with her. She was absolutely right to be affronted.

'You are right, of course,' I said quickly. 'That was clumsy. I have only just heard a little of what has happened, and I am still trying to understand.'

Before she could respond, I added, 'I'm … I'm … concerned about the trouble this must have caused.'

I chose my words carefully so as to not undermine Bhishma by apologising on his behalf, or in any way condemning his actions. All I could do was to be kind and accommodating.

'It was unfortunate that you had to witness what was surely a very violent moment between King Shalva and my son-in-law.'

I was not in any way prepared for the explosion that followed these words.

'Unfortunate?' she said, trying and failing to keep her voice steady. 'Have you ever had your future husband humiliated before your eyes? The man you love pinned to the ground in front of you like he was nothing?'

How had I not known this? Amba had been promised to King Shalva. I had been told that she was one of the three potential brides of Kashi. I had got it all wrong. The bad situation we found ourselves in had just become even worse. The woman before me was the future kin of a man twice humiliated by Bhishma.

Hastinapur's armies must be notified, for this could be a trigger for war.

I took a long moment to consider my next words. Finally, I made my choice.

'I would like you to leave for King Shalva as soon as you are able to travel,' I told Amba. 'I will arrange the transport, provide you with an entourage to accompany you and gifts to show our respect. Go to him and be with him. Please, let's put these events behind us.'

Amba gave a low bow, but said nothing. Her eyes said it all, though. This was not over. Not ever.

I felt a rising sense of panic. Had I done the right thing for the sake of peace? I had a strong feeling that I had made things a whole lot worse.

Chapter Ten

Bhishma's mood remained unchanged. Not angry, but not calm or secure either. He was unsettled, restless, strangely oblivious to the world around him. Since his return from King Kshyksi's court, he had hardly sat down or retired to his bed for very long. He constantly paced, wandering on the palace balconies, his hands clasped behind his back. When the servants or guards tried to speak to him, there was little, if any, response. Eating had become a task too. No matter what the palace's kitchens prepared, all meals were pushed around the plate with the same indifference.

What had happened with the three princesses was what was bothering him, of that much I was sure. I found it difficult to think about as well. How could this demigod, who had always thought so deeply about every thought and action, do something so rash and out of character as to insist on bringing the three princesses to Hastinapur? Yes, he had treated them with respect, but they were deeply upset. Perhaps I should at least find solace in Bhishma's anger towards himself. He seemed to know he'd made the wrong decision. Or was it his confrontation, and humiliation, of King Shalva that plagued his thoughts? Bhishma was a good man, good enough to spare a life, as he had with Shalva twice now. Yet, he had not been good enough to spare a man from humiliation. Humiliation is a political tool reserved for those who cannot do battle. Humiliation was a fate worse than death or defeat.

I had tried small talk. I was well aware that my gardening and medicine-making did not enthral him in the slightest, but in the past he'd at least feigned interest in conversations about these pastimes. He would always make me feel that my words, no matter on what topic, had as much of an impact as the arrows of his army. But no longer. He was now impatient and irritable.

I could not bear it any longer. He might have been the hero of Hastinapur, but equally important, he was my son, my found family. I didn't want to confront him about what had happened. I had said all I had to say on that. However, I needed to know what was devouring him from the inside out. If he opened up to me and it all poured out, then I could embrace him, as I had always yearned to do. I had always been a little jealous of Ganga, being there when he was a child, able to cradle and protect him from the world. It was hard to imagine the headstrong warrior that he had become being smothered in motherly affection.

My search for Bhishma took no time at all. I didn't even bother checking his quarters, the dining area, or the throne room. I found him exactly where I'd expected to, standing on a balcony overlooking the river—the same river where his brothers had perished and from where his true mother had emerged.

The sun had almost set and the sky was dark, barring the slithers of orange light that lingered, breaking up the encroaching cloak of night. The grass and trees had already begun to disappear, and the reassuring glint of the mighty river beyond had almost faded to nothing. It was quiet. In the near distance, a fisherman walked home towards the palace, his day's work slung over his shoulder. Bhishma was staring into the gloom of the far distance, but focused on nothing. I wished he could see the beauty of this kingdom. Something this striking deserved to be acknowledged every day. When was the last time he had noticed it?

For a short time, we stood side by side in complete silence. The atmosphere between us felt heavy, and my stomach churned. At last, I took a deep breath.

'Bhishma, I know that it is my duty to listen to you and to understand whatever it is you are going through, but I feel more compelled to give you advice than I have ever done.'

I saw my companion give a barely discernible movement of his head and took this as a cue to continue.

'You have not told me why you are so preoccupied, but I can take a pretty good guess. These three princesses, the confrontation with King Shalva, that is more than what happens to most men in a lifetime. I know that you are not an ordinary man. You are far beyond that, but your humanity is shining through. I can see how what has happened is destroying you.

'Those princesses should not be here, but we can put that right together.'

Bhishma remained silent. Was he thinking about what he wanted to say? Or had he not heard me? Finally, he spoke.

'You are right. I have made mistakes,' he said quietly. 'I may even have put this haven, this haven for all its people, our home, at risk. I may have …'

He turned to face me, and all the light and life that had once shone from his eyes was gone.

'… I may have put Hastinapur in danger.'

I wished that Bhishma was wrong, but he was not. Hastinapur was now trapped under a shroud of uncertainty. Discontent and anger skulked around the palace corridors and seeped through the walls. What danger had he brought into our home? There was nothing I could say, or do, to comfort him. He was right. All we could do now was try to fix it as best we could. I needed to make a plan. I would do this, since Bhishma was in no condition to resolve this crisis.

The next morning, while still mulling over what to do, I made my way to the throne room to meet Bhishma to begin the day's work. I got there before him, but as soon as he arrived, it was clear that his mood had improved little from last night. He walked the short distance to the dais with as little haste as I had seen anyone move. Prisoners walked to be flogged with a greater sense of urgency than this. As soon as he reached his golden throne, he slumped into the seat, a picture of despair. He looked more like one of the city's drunkards hunkered over a table rather than the powerful demigod that he was. Regardless of what he was going through, I felt the need to quietly upbraid him before the court sessions began. His demeanour would only worry everyone even more and cast an even greater pall on the court. I got to my feet and began to slowly make my way to him, greeting all those I passed respectfully.

The distance between me and Bhishma was just a few *aratni* when the golden doors at the back of the court were abruptly thrown open with a crash. The two guards stationed there stumbled forward in surprise, their armour and weapons clattering in a metallic arpeggio. There, standing in the doorway was Amba. Her expression was resolute, but the pain she felt was there for all to see.

The court was silent as Amba walked towards Bhishma. The only sound that could be heard was the clacking of her shoes on the tiled floor and the swish of her silk sari. While I hardly dared to take my eyes off her, I stole a glance at Bhishma.

He was sitting upright in his throne, curious about the sudden intrusion, yet seemingly unperturbed. At least he was able to keep his cool. Most kings and princes would have erupted at such a disrespectful entrance. Then, I realised. Amba's interruption was clearly not news to him. He had already foreseen it. Perhaps that explained his mood over the past days. He had known this encounter was overdue.

Recovering their composure, a few guards rushed forward to block Amba's path, but Bhishma called them away with a simple sweep of his arm as he got to his feet. The message was clear: Allow this princess to get as close as she wishes. I moved closer to Bhishma. Our court had done wrong, I knew that, but I had sworn to protect him as much as the kingdom. Even so, a part of me was wracked by guilt. As a woman, I knew how hard things could be. I knew that we should have protected the princesses.

Amba didn't check her progress. She came to a stop just a few inches from Bhishma.

'Everything has been taken from me,' she said calmly. Then, she swung around, and raising her voice, addressed the crowd. 'I do not understand how you can all sit here, in this court, and listen to this man. He is a criminal who has pulled three young women away from their home.'

Everyone exchanged stunned and shocked glances. They were not used to such outbursts from women, especially in such a symbolic place of male power. This room, where wars were strategized and fought, where people decided who would feast and who would starve, had never seen the likes of this. A chill seemed to have descended on the throne room.

I felt torn. Amba was right to feel aggrieved, but she could not be allowed to behave like this.

'You must go now,' I said. 'You cannot behave like this here. It is not right.'

Amba acknowledged me with the merest of respectful bows, but she did not take her eyes off Bhishma.

'I have just returned from speaking with King Shalva,' she said, her voice eerily calm now.

Bhishma's expression didn't alter at the mention of the king's name, but he did lean forward a little. Was he bracing himself for bad news? The fearful whisper that rose from the courtiers showed he would not be alone. Could this be a declaration of war? Hastinapur was surely not ready for such an announcement.

'Let us speak alone,' I urged Amba. 'You, me and Bhishma. We can put this right.'

She still did not take her gaze away from Bhishma.

'Your humiliation of the king, *twice*, has not only tarnished his reputation, but it has ruined my life too,' Amba said, her voice flat and filled with sadness. 'Because of what you have done, the king and I will no longer marry. I cannot be with him, ever, because of you, Bhishma.

'You have left me with nothing, no other choices in life. Therefore, I must ask, no, *demand*, that you marry me.'

So, that was why she had come. I already knew the answer to that plea. I didn't even need to look at Bhishma. The oath. That oath. It cursed this lineage over and over. She could not have what she had asked for.

To my surprise, when I looked at Bhishma, I saw, for the briefest second, a look of uncertainty flicker across his brow. Then, his bearing quickly settled to its usual impassive state. Knowing him as I did, though, I could see his cheeks were redder than usual. Was this a flush of anger? Or embarrassment?

'No,' he said.

Bhishma's voice was as powerful and unyielding as the day when he had made his terrible oath outside my father's house all those years ago. This was his final verdict. It invited no argument.

I had to intervene, for I could see this spiralling out of control.

Stepping between Amba and Bhishma, I faced the princess with a gentle smile.

'We can fix this,' I said. 'We will find you a match. You will be happy again and we will look after you.'

Tears appeared in Amba's eyes, but she wiped them angrily away. She had not come for platitudes or vague promises. She wanted this sorted out now.

'No?' she stormed, glaring at Bhishma. 'No? Do you have any honour? This is the *only* way you can preserve some integrity and restore your reputation and that of your kingdom.'

The words cut through me like a knife, but Bhishma was impassive. His mother Ganga had taught him well. He could keep a cool head in any situation.

'It would be the right and honourable thing to do,' he agreed, his tone quiet and steady, with no trace of anger. 'I owe you a great debt, and a union such as this would go a long way in repairing the rift between our kingdoms. But I cannot do as you ask. I am sworn to be celibate until the end of my days. This is an oath that I cannot break, even for you. Even if I would be a better man for doing so.'

Amba glowered back at Bhishma. Her calmness had given way to raw fury now. Her eyes were afire with rage, and her hands balled into fists at her side. She had heard enough. Once more I stepped into the place between them, my only thought to protect Bhishma who stood stock-still before her, a wide-open target.

Once more she barely acknowledged me, other than a short, impatient bow.

'Your choice has been made, and I won't waste time and energy trying to change it,' she said, stepping to one side of me, never once taking her eyes off Bhishma. Then, taking a pace backwards, she regarded her tormentor with a fearsome look, a look that sent a chill down my spine. 'Now, I must do something that I should have done sooner.'

Amba paused and then drew herself up, her right arm extended and the forefinger of her hand pointing at Bhishma's heart.

'Bhishma, son of Ganga, I put a curse on you.'

An audible gasp of shock rippled around the court, and my legs felt weak.

'I put a curse on you,' she repeated. 'I will be the cause of your death, whether I achieve it in this life or the next.'

Bhishma stared at Amba, showing no trace of emotion.

'That is your choice to make,' he said. 'I am sorry that this has happened between us. Now, please leave.'

I turned back to Amba, ready to plead with her to lift her curse. As soon as I saw her expression, though, I knew this would be a hopeless endeavour. She had been rejected by Shalva and then by Bhishma. Her lust for vengeance had now consumed her whole being. Despite all that had happened, there was no justification for this. I have never, ever hated anyone as much as I did Amba in that moment. This woman had just vowed to destroy Bhishma.

Amba did not even glance at me before she turned and began to walk towards the door. The courtiers shrank back, clearly unsure of how to react. A few of the braver guards looked at me questioningly. They wanted to know if they should prevent the princess from leaving. I motioned to them to let her go.

Imprisoning her was not the solution. She had sworn her oath and would carry it out whatever we tried to do to prevent it. Bhishma's fate was sealed. He was doomed to die at Amba's hand.

In the days following the altercation, it was impossible to dispel the shadow that loomed large over Hastinapur. We were in the weakest position we had ever been in. Not only did we face the prospect of war with our neighbours, but our most powerful protector had also been cursed and may not be able to help us.

As I walked around the court, I often heard Amba's name whispered by servants and dignitaries, usually accompanied by a furtive glance to check whether Bhishma or I had overheard them. They need not have feared my displeasure if I were to catch them celebrating their hatred of her. If I could, I would have joined them in condemning the princess, but that was not the behaviour of a queen. Besides, I could not show how worried I was.

After a few weeks of this tense waiting, whispering and planning, our agonising wait to discover the next move in this potential battle for Hastinapur was over, albeit we didn't know it yet. A servant came running to tell me that an emissary for the great Sage Parashuram had arrived and was asking for an audience with Bhishma and me. I granted this request right away and asked for him to be shown to the throne room. Sage Parashuram was not just a revered holy man, but he was also a very familiar name in this house. The great immortal sage, the founder of the mighty warrior caste, had been Bhishma's tutor when he was a young boy, and his name had only ever been spoken about in the same breath as the highest of praises. In better times, Bhishma had recounted many mighty stories of their time together and would repeat the sage's teachings often. When Bhishma fought, he fought in the way the sage had taught him, with so much power, precision and deliberation that it was little wonder that such a brilliant warrior as Bhishma thanked the sage every day for his teachings in the art of warfare.

I arrived in the throne room at the same time as Bhishma, who was smiling broadly. It was the first time I had seen him smile in weeks. He was visibly overjoyed to receive contact from his former tutor, whom he loved and respected. I could not help but notice, though, that the emissary seemed unduly serious.

'I am here on the behalf of Sage Parashuram', the emissary began. 'He asks that you meet him.'

'Now?' Bhishma said, perhaps caught a little off guard.

Despite his happiness at the opportunity to see the powerful sage, there was something in the emissary's tone that made him uneasy. Nevertheless, he remained his usual charming self.

'Please lead the way,' he said with a sweep of his arm indicating the direction of the door.

As I followed Bhishma through the court, I could see that the arrival of the sage's emissary had attracted a lot of attention. Like me, the courtiers seemed to sense something was afoot, and a large group fell in behind me to follow Bhishma and the emissary.

As always, Sarathee seemed to be one step ahead of me, and by the time I emerged from the palace, blinking in the sunlight, my chariot was ready for me. The charioteer helped me into my place and then took his, his face impassive as he took the reins. The timbers of the chariot creaked as he skilfully turned it and set off at a slow pace behind Bhishma's carriage. I did not look back, but behind me, I could hear the shuffle of the courtiers' feet in the dust. Whatever it was that we were waiting for was about to happen. I knew that now.

The sun had risen to its highest point of the day during the short time it had taken to reach the end of our journey. Our final destination was a simple field just outside the town's perimeter, and standing at its centre was Sage Parshuram. But it was not the sight of the mighty sage that made me reel with shock. It was that of Amba standing beside him, her face still etched with fury.

I watched in growing disbelief as Bhishma dismounted from his carriage and walked towards his tutor, bending low to touch his feet when he reached him. The sage allowed him to do so, but I was surprised at the cool reception given to Bhishma. I had always been told that Hastinapur's protector was the sage's finest pupil, the one of whom he was proudest. The feeling went both ways too. Aside from his mother, it was this sage who had taught Bhishma the skills he needed to be such a powerful warrior, who had educated him to a level far beyond that of anyone in the land.

The sage began to speak, his voice so low that I had to strain to hear each word.

'Recently, Princess Amba presented herself to the sages, many of whom you know,' he said. 'After she recounted the tale of being taken from her kingdom and they heard about the actions of the protector of Hastinapur, the sages came to see me.'

Sage Parshuram paused and looked deeply into Bhishma's eyes.

'My first reaction was to be angry and ashamed …'

I looked on in horror as Bhishma recoiled at the words. But the sage had not finished.

'… A teacher is only as good as their student. You have, therefore, degraded my good name by refusing to do what is right.'

I could hardly bear to look at Bhishma. I knew how harshly this would have hit him.

'I have decided to take up Amba's cause and fight for what is rightfully hers,' the sage continued. 'Will you marry this woman?'

Bhishma's head dropped low, and I could barely hear what he said next.

'No, Sir, I mean you no disrespect, but I cannot,' he said, his voice breaking with emotion. 'You taught me well and told me I must honour my word. Well, that is what I am doing now. I do regret the actions taken, and I do not want to fight you, but I will if you command me to do so.'

A flash of anger crossed the sage's brow. Drawing himself up to his full height and raising his voice so perhaps we could all witness what came next, he pronounced his verdict on his pupil's refusal to accede to his request.

'If you cannot do what I ask, you leave me with no choice,' he said. 'I challenge you to a duel.'

For a few seconds, I could hardly breathe. My heart raced. This could not be true. How could this happen? This teacher, Bhishma's idol, wanted to fight? A fight that neither could win. They were immortals. Neither of them could die.

Then, another terrible thought hit me. What if this duel was part of Amba's curse? Did her vow to be the cause of Bhishma's death mean by her blade? By her own hands? Or was it by an event that she set in motion? Sage Parshuram was a skilled fighter and just as much of a weapon as Bhishma's bow. Had I made this journey to watch Bhishma be slain before me?

I stepped down from the carriage and began to walk towards Bhishma. I would forbid him from fighting this duel. It was both a foolish and a worthless act. But I had barely taken a few steps in his direction before Bhishma raised his right arm, his palm facing me. His gaze was steady and the message clear. This was not my battle. I could not prevent what was about to happen.

'Bring a chariot for the sage,' Bhishma said, turning back to his esteemed tutor. 'This holy man seems to have decided that he is a match for me in my chariot, while he fights from the ground. Or does he expect me to match him in the dirt?'

A nervous murmur rippled through the crowd, and Amba glared at Bhishma. *How could she want this? How could anyone want this?*

My eyes drank in the scene before me as I tried my utmost to imagine the outcome of the forthcoming duel. Neither side could win. It was impossible. Yet, both were determined to fight. The sage was dressed in religious, rather than military, clothing. The white cotton of his ceremonial robes wouldn't protect a fly. Yet, he seemed confident of victory as he stood impassively, his bare feet dug deep into the orange soil. If he had not been a sage, then turning up on foot to engage in combat against a chariot would have been seen not only as suicidal, but also downright disrespectful. Yet, it was clear from the expression on the holy man's face that he was more ready for this fight than any warrior dressed head to toe in shining armour or perched atop a chariot of war.

'I am pleased that you would do me the courtesy of finding me a chariot to use,' the sage replied. 'I came to fight you here on the ground, however, with honour and respect. We don't need to try to mow each other down from our chariots like we are leading a desperate cavalry charge. I taught you better than that.'

Bhishma nodded slowly in agreement.

'You did, indeed, bring me up to fight on my feet. It does feel apt that we continue in this way, even though it saddens me greatly to stand against you.'

The two great warriors took several paces backwards, increasing the gap between them. I shivered as I watched them weigh each other up. Was it fear over the outcome or my response to the wind which seemed to be picking up around us? I caught my breath as the gusts caught at the sage's robes, revealing the golden bow beneath the folds. As if in response, the sage lifted the bow from its place on his shoulder and raised it into position. Within seconds, he had released an arrow. It soared into the air, but was met by one fired with pinpoint accuracy by Bhishma. The two projectiles exploded into a million fragments. Neither man paused, firing off a volley of further arrows, each one smashing into the next.

The crowd gasped as they saw the next arrow the sage had put in the string of the bow. It was the famed *Ashwapatra astra*, one of the arrows that had the power to destroy an entire army at once.

Glancing back at Bhishma, I could see he already had his bow drawn, an arrow in place. He had chosen the *Varunastra*, a weapon that once discharged could release torrential volumes of water. His leading arm was tense as he gripped the arrow rest, shaking slightly with the effort of keeping the string taut. His anger at the terrible situation he now faced seemed to flow from his heart into his bow. I watched as his eyes narrowed and he prepared to fire.

The atmosphere grew thick with tension, and the waiting crowd was silent. No one seemed to even dare breathe as we waited for the duel to begin. A part of me hoped it would never start, but it was too late to think that now. Then, with cat-like speed, Bhishma released the string, firing an arrow directly at the sage's head. It sped towards a position right between his eyes. Yet, the sage moved at a similar speed, firing his own arrow. Just as

Bhishma's arrow reached the halfway point in its trajectory, the sage's arrow pierced it from its tip to its feathers, splitting it into kindling and sending a torrent of water cascading into the dry soil. The sage's intact arrow sailed on, only to be deftly caught by Bhishma as he ducked out of its way. A look of raw anger flashed across his face as he snapped it into two pieces. Sparks flew as he threw the splinters of wood to the ground, stamping them into the dirt with his heel.

Without pausing for even a second, the sage grabbed another two arrows from his quiver. These were *Bhargavastras*, more *astras* of terrifying power. With deft movements, he placed them both on the string of his bow and fired them almost simultaneously. Both *Bhargavastras* met with the same fate as his first arrow, reduced to streaks of lightning across the sky, thanks to the accuracy of Bhishma's return fire. The sage rapidly released a further salvo, this time firing a volley of *Ashwapatra* arrows, two of which struck Bhishma's chest.

I gulped back tears as I watched Bhishma stumble back. Was Amba's curse coming true so soon? He snatched at the arrows embedded in his chest, snapping them in two, seemingly not caring that he had left the arrow heads behind. I winced as I saw the white and gold of his armour begin to turn red as the blood seeped through.

Bhishma was not the only one to have taken a hit. My attention was taken by the sage who was staggering backwards, spinning around before briefly turning his back on his opponent. When he turned back, I knew why. His holy white robes were soaked with blood and growing redder by the second. Despite the obvious wounds they were both inflicting upon one another, neither man seemed ready to step down.

The two warriors returned to their original positions, their expressions resolute. It was now obvious to all who were there that these two men were so powerful that this fight could continue for the rest of time. Neither would yield. It was difficult to truly comprehend that power. What everyone there also understood was the tragedy of the occasion, a teacher versus his best student. It was truly painful to see two individuals who had once loved and respected each other now struggling to find a way to destroy each other. Right then, everyone there was thinking the same thing: How would this end?

It was Bhishma who answered our question and who answered it in a way no one was prepared for.

Turning his back to the sage, he took a few steps forward, his right hand twitching slightly by his side. My eyes widened as I saw blood streaming from between two of his fingers, which had been ripped open by the effort of firing his bow with so much power. He raised his hand to the quiver strapped on his back, his blood leaving a faint trail across his armour. From that quiver, he produced *Brahmastra*.

A cry of shock rippled through the crowd. Everyone knew about *Brahmastra*, the arrow of the gods and the most powerful of all the *astras*. It was said to be capable of killing everything and everyone on Earth. Some people in the crowd turned in terror and began to run. No one knew how powerful this weapon could be, and they didn't want to hang around to find out. I was transfixed, though. I needed to see this. The outcome of this fight was now guaranteed if Bhishma fired that arrow. The arrow would destroy the sage, rendering his powers irrelevant as it cut through him.

I held my breath as I watched Bhishma raise the arrow and draw his bow. Time seemed to stand still as the sage stared first at the tip of the arrow and then deep into Bhishma's eyes. He was a proud master, about to be destroyed by a weapon of the highest power, wielded by his prize student. In a few moments, it would all be over.

The terrible end to the duel was not to be, though. It was not the plan the gods had in mind for either of these great warriors. Before Bhishma could fire his deadly salvo, the sky turned grey. A voice louder than a thousand shouts and more terrifying than anything I had ever heard boomed:

'Bhishma, stand down, now. We have seen enough. There are higher destinies at stake here.'

The gods had spoken. They knew this would have destroyed Earth.

I caught my breath as, with relief, I saw Bhishma lower his bow and close his eyes. He was pleased with the outcome, I knew. If the gods had not intervened, he would have killed the sage, and that was not something he'd ever be able to come to terms with. A pupil cannot kill his teacher; that would bring imbalance to the order of the world.

In the distance, I heard a shout and then a curse. I didn't need to look to know where it came from. It was Amba, making her displeasure known, defying the gods, cursing them for ruining her masterstroke. *Just go*, I thought. *Your time will come, damn you.*

The sage and Bhishma walked towards one another. The younger man's face bore a mixture of world-weariness, sadness and relief, a look that sharply contrasted with the pride on the face of his respected tutor. I strained my ears to hear the conversation between them. We had moved a long way past the angry proclamations of war, but their words were intended to be private.

'You fought well, my son, and I am very proud of you,' said the sage. 'You have heeded my teachings well, and I could ask for no better pupil. But now, you must retreat. I cannot be seen to leave the battlefield first.'

Bhishma bowed to the sage and thanked him. Taking a step back, he raised his voice to say what was meant to be heard by everyone there.

'Sage Parshuram, please allow me to yield. You have fought bravely, and I am honoured to have once been your pupil. I am glad that you believe I did your training justice and that I have conducted myself well. I ask that you let this be an end to this.'

The sage gave a nod of approval, indicating he accepted the terms, and they both turned to walk away. No one noticed Amba leave. As far as everyone was concerned, from the lowliest courtier to the gods above, the matter was closed. At least, for now.

Chapter Eleven

Bhishma returned largely to normal after the duel. He was more relaxed and jovial, and he seemed happy to spend time in the court, attending to business. I sensed he wanted to put the incident of Amba and King Kshyksi behind us, so I did not press him on why he had acted so out of character. If I were to guess, I'd say that he had finally allowed himself to process the grief at the death of his father and our perilous position since. The bond between the two had always been strong—so strong that Bhishma had given up everything to ensure his father's happiness. For a rare period, his human side had come to the fore, and he had acted purely out of raw emotion. No one could blame him for that. He had carried the hopes and dreams of everyone on his shoulders for so long.

My own focus was on rebuilding and strengthening Hastinapur. Too much had happened, and the courtiers were nervous and jittery, despite even the lavish festivities that surrounded the wedding of Vichitravirya and the two princesses, Ambika and Ambalika. The upbeat impact had not lasted for anything like as long as I had hoped. As for those outside the palace, I had no doubt they were even more concerned. I no longer went out to see for myself, though. Those daily chariot rides with Sarathee seemed self-indulgent now. My place was in the palace, alongside Bhishma, ensuring every part of our kingdom was running smoothly. I did not have Bhishma's godly powers, but I had to show that we were in a position of strength.

Bhishma was very much in charge of the affairs of the kingdom, as he had vowed he would be. That was a blessing because his skills in politics and diplomacy were unmatched. His mother and the good sage had taught him well, and there were no problems among his subjects that he was unable to resolve, often in an instant. It was satisfying to watch people from the kingdom when they came to seek his counsel. They'd arrive with worry etched on their faces and leave looking calm and happy. I learned much by listening and watching. My hope was that my young son did the same too. Each day, Bhishma would tutor Vichitravirya in all the skills he would need to become a just, fair and respected ruler. He had been joined in the palace by Sage Kripa, who was also an able and patient tutor and instructed him in politics, spirituality and ethics. The three of them would pore over books together, discussing what they found there for two hours every morning. Each afternoon, Bhishma could be found in the palace grounds, either practising with bows and arrows or walking through the moves my son needed to become a skilled swordsman. At least once a week, they would head off to the forest to hunt.

Bhishma and Kripa were always encouraging towards their pupil, never criticising if he did not succeed the first time. Whenever I asked Bhishma how Vichitravirya was getting along, he would say that he would be a fine king and that I must not worry. But I did. I loved Vichitravirya as a mother should, but I could see what others could also see but did not say out loud, namely that he was a weak child. Most children of his age were taller and had already begun to show signs of becoming men, but he had not. He was extremely, almost painfully, thin, and even a short period of exercise left him exhausted. He had little interest in the nourishment that might help him, pushing his food around his plate with a look of distaste. What troubled me even more was that he was permanently listless. He could not find an interest in anything. I was not surprised that he had little enthusiasm for his wives, Ambika and Ambalika, for he was still young. But I had watched him from the shadows when he went through his lessons with Bhishma and Kripa. He'd stare into space while his highly qualified tutors would talk expansively about the wonders of the stars, but he was not following the science. His mind was elsewhere. He would yawn his way through lessons in geography and history. Seeing Bhishma and Vichitravirya in close proximity was jarring too. Bhishma was so tall, handsome and muscular, the perfect, powerful ruler. My son was none of those things, and I was not sure he ever would be.

It is impossible to articulate how terrible I felt for having these thoughts when Vichitravirya became sick. I cursed myself over and over. Had I caused this? One morning, he had simply failed to appear for breakfast. I had run to his room in alarm and found him in bed, pale and drawn, his sheets soaked with sweat. He barely recognised me when I called out in alarm. Even as I raced to the guards to tell them to fetch Bhishma, I heard the sound I dreaded the most, coughing. It sounded like Vichitravirya was drowning, as his breath came in deep, watery rasps. Returning to the bed, I grabbed one of the silk gowns that had been slung over the end of a chair, purposefully rolling it into a tight ball as I walked. Vichitravirya was rolling from side to side, his face contorted in pain, his eyes unseeing. It was almost impossible to dab his face with the cloth, he was writhing so much, but somehow I managed it. When I drew back my hand, I saw what I had expected to see, but which no mother would ever want to see. The damp silk was covered with flecks of blood. Vichitravirya had tuberculosis.

Before I had come to the palace, I had known nothing about tuberculosis. No one in our village had ever had this dreadful disease. Yet, I learned about it quickly because it was rife in the towns around us. Many of our people had succumbed to it, and nothing could be done to help them. The disease did not discriminate and would quickly snuff out the life of all before it, old or young. Nothing could be done. There was no cure. Even though I knew this, I summoned our best physicians and healers to ask them, no, beg them, to help my son. One after another, they stood by his bedside, and each time, the expression on their faces told me more than I needed to know about the hopelessness of our situation. If I had all the gold and jewels in the world to pay for treatment, it would not have been enough. No matter how much I willed the gods to spare him, it would not be enough either.

Late one night, as Vichitravirya's cough worsened, I felt a cry of raw pain rise within my throat. For the first time in days, I had to leave his side and retreat to a dark corner, far away from his chamber. I knew I would be unable to stop myself from letting out a deep moan of pure misery. I didn't want him to hear this, even though in his now rare moments of lucidity, he knew what fate had in store for him.

It took a week for the tuberculosis to do its terrible work and claim my son. A long, agonising, terrible week. I did not leave his bedside the whole time, except to howl my grief alone in the shadows that night. As I stood by Vichitravirya's bedside, looking at his lifeless body, I could not cry. I was a hollowed-out husk, with no emotion or tears left. Or perhaps it was because I was too wracked with guilt to allow my despair to have full reign. Somehow, I felt I had caused this. I had dismissed my youngest son as weak and inconsequential, even if only in my thoughts, and he had been swept aside by this disease.

The moment that the light finally left Vichitravirya's eyes was the worst in my entire life. It was many times worse than losing Shantanu or Chitrangada. It was the time when I realised that Hastinapur was lost. For all the oaths I had taken to protect it, I had failed. Now my only son was gone, there could be no heirs, and thanks to Bhishma's oath, no chance of the bloodline continuing either. I was ashamed about it, but I selfishly prayed for the gods to take me too.

I had not been able to look at Bhishma during Vichitravirya's last few days. He had joined me at the bedside and done his best to comfort the young boy. Every time I saw him, it was a reminder of what we had sacrificed. After my son died, I barely heard Bhishma as he told me to take my time, that he would see to the kingdom. We both knew we'd need to have a conversation at some point, but I was not ready.

Once the funeral was over, I retired to my chamber. I could not bear to lie in my bed, the bed I used to share with Shantanu, so I curled up on the large pile of cushions arranged on the floor where I used to entertain guests in happier times. The cool silk of their covers became soaked in my tears, but I did not care. Each day, the servants would leave me platters of food to tempt me. But I did not want their ripe mangoes and berries, or mounds of warm rice and lentils. Everything tasted too rich, or too sweet, or too sour. Even nibbling at plain flatbread and yoghurt made me feel queasy.

How long did I lie there, every bone and muscle aching with sadness? A week? A month? I had no idea, no concept of time. I simply couldn't move. For a long while, I imagined that nothing would ever get me out of that room. That was until I heard a knock at my door and a servant came in with a message.

'Your father is here, my queen,' she said quietly, her eyes averted.

'My father?'

'Yes,' she said, her eyes still downcast.

I had barely seen my father since I left our home by the river. He hadn't come to my wedding and had been an infrequent visitor to the palace. We'd long since accepted that our lives had taken different paths. I'd been sure to send him an income so he did not have to rely on the fish anymore, and that seemed to have been enough. I imagined he enjoyed the trappings of wealth and the status that being the father of a queen brought with it, but had no wish to become emotionally involved. That was not the man he was or who he had ever been. That arrangement had suited us both. Then why had he come now?

'I don't wish to see him,' I said with certainty.

The servant nodded and looked up at me for a moment before glancing away quickly.

'He … he hasn't asked to speak to you,' she said nervously. 'He asked to speak to Bhishma. I thought you would like to know.'

'Bhishma?' I said, sitting up, suddenly alert.

Memories of the first time the two men had met flooded my mind—everything about my father's goading and demands and that terrible oath. What did the fisherman want now? I was already on my feet and rushing to the door. Catching sight of my reflection in the gilt-edged mirror on the wall, I momentarily stopped, shocked at my appearance. My hair was flecked with grey and my eyes framed by dark circles. My sari was crumpled and lined with deep creases. I paused just long enough to grab a cloak and quickly smooth down my unruly hair.

My legs felt weak as I rushed along the corridor. This was the furthest I had been for some time, and I had not eaten for a while. It was only when I was an arm's length from Bhishma's door that I stopped and began to wonder what I was going to say. My memory of that last encounter was being ordered away by my father and having to hide. Instinctively, I did the same again, slipping into a niche just outside the door. Luckily, it had been left ajar.

'... news has even reached us all the way down where we are,' said a familiar voice. 'Hastinapur is vulnerable. It is all anyone speaks about. The merchants tell me armies are amassing to the north and the south.'

I strained my ears to tune into my father's voice. He sounded different from before. During that last conversation, he had been playing a game, timing each move to manipulate Bhishma towards his ends. His tone had been wheedling, yet firm. Today, though, he sounded unsure and less confident, almost desperate.

'Do you think we are not aware of what goes on in Hastinapur and on its borders, Dasharaj?' Bhishma asked. 'I can assure you that we are, and I can tell you now that there is no danger.'

A deep sigh of frustration ensued. It was my father. Even after all these years, the sound was as familiar to me as if I had heard it yesterday. I could even picture him sucking in his cheeks and then blowing out air dramatically, his hands on his hips, a large frown creasing his forehead.

Bhishma had clearly chosen to ignore this posturing.

'If there is any danger, I will deal with it. I always have.'

'But you can't do this forever!' my father interrupted, his voice rising almost to a shout. 'That is my point.'

'I am not sure I understand your point,' Bhishma said calmly, 'or, whether there is any need for you to make one. Would you not be better off visiting your daughter while you are here? I am sure she has need of some kind words.'

Footsteps moved towards the door, and I instinctively shrank further back into the shadows.

'I can ask the servants to find you some food,' Bhishma said. His voice was closer. He'd clearly decided the conversation was over and was trying to show my father out. It was his footsteps that I had heard.

'No! No! We need to end this now.'

'End this?'

'End this, Bhishma. I have come here to do what I should have done a long, long time ago. I am here to release you from your oath. You must marry Ambika and Ambalika and secure heirs. There is no other option.'

Tears sprang to my eyes. I could not imagine what had driven my father to this. The cynical me would say he was looking out for his own ends. My father always had an eye on taking advantage. Perhaps things in the kingdom really were so bad that he feared the unrest could spread as far as our home. It didn't matter what his motivations were, though. I already knew the response.

'I appreciate what you are saying, and thank you for coming here,' Bhishma said, his voice polite, yet icily smooth and entirely unruffled. 'I have to tell you, though, that it is not in your gift to release me from my oath. It is not in anyone's gift. I did not make my oath to you. I did it for my father, and Hastinapur and the gods, not you …'

'This is madness ...' my father stormed. He hated to lose, but this conversation was more than that. He genuinely wanted Bhishma to do this. Perhaps I had underestimated him. 'There is no shame in changing course. Quite the opposite, in fact. Don't let your stubbornness put the kingdom in danger. You know I am right.'

'Dasharaj, I have given you my answer. Now, please, can I get you some refreshment ...'

'No!'

I heard a clatter of feet, and suddenly, my father appeared in the doorway and began to make his way angrily down the corridor, shaking his head as he walked. He didn't look back, so he didn't see me shrinking back into my hiding place. Moments later, Bhishma appeared at the door and turned to look in my direction.

'Mother,' he said quietly. He did not look at all shocked to see me. 'Please come in. It is so lovely to see you back on your feet. Can I get you anything, some water perhaps?'

I followed him into the chamber. Once inside, I turned to face him. There was no point pretending I had not overheard what had just happened. I had always been completely honest with Bhishma. Besides, he sensed my every thought.

'I ... I ... am sorry if my father upset you,' I began hesitantly. I had not spoken to Bhishma for so long that I felt almost shy in the presence of this charismatic man.

'He did not,' Bhishma interrupted. 'I understand why he asked me what he did.'

The silence grew between us as we looked at one another.

'Would you please reconsider his request?' I said, my words tumbling out in almost a whisper. I already knew the answer, but I hoped I was wrong. So much had changed since I first came to the palace and first asked Bhishma to reconsider his oath. Surely now? Now, when the alternative was inevitably going to weaken, possibly even destroy, Hastinapur.

'Will you please marry Ambika and Ambalika?'

Bhishma was silent, but he shook his head slowly from side to side. I knew he was never ever going to allow himself to relent on his oath. That was not who he was, and I had to respect him for it, however painful. Even so, his face was etched in concern, still searching mine for signs I was going to be alright.

'There is a solution,' I said.

Seeing Bhishma beginning to shake his head, I raised my palm to indicate he needn't worry. This did not concern his oath. In fact, it did not concern him at all. It concerned me and a secret I had harboured for very long. What I was about to do would be the hardest thing I had ever done, but the time had come. To fulfil the oath I had made to protect Hastinapur, I had to make this sacrifice.

'I need you to go and see Sage Vyasa,' I told Bhishma. 'That will solve our problem.'

Chapter Twelve

Watching from the balcony as Bhishma mounted his chariot, I felt a deep pang of guilt. It clawed at my insides, as extreme as the pain of giving birth. Should I have told him the full story before he left; should I have prepared him? Strangely, this was the only time that I had felt that he did not know the full extent of every thought of mine. I had buried this secret so deep and covered it in layer upon layer of denial. Now, though, it would be utterly exposed.

Bhishma did not look back as his chariot clattered away. He had a long journey ahead of him and would not be returning for some days. He would be eager to get on with it. In the meantime, I would be alone with my thoughts and this pain, wondering what this great man would think of me once he knew my truth.

I felt suddenly tired as I walked back to my chamber and sank onto my familiar silk cushions. Wrapping my sari closer around me, I closed my eyes, praying for sleep's respite. Just for a short while, I needed to distance myself from what lay ahead. Yet, as I drifted off, a vision of my previous life appeared to me as clear as if it was happening all over again.

I was back in my little teak boat, plying my trade on the Yamuna. This time, though, the familiarity of the scene gave me no comfort. I wanted to scream at my younger self, to warn her of her impending fate. Part of me was also jealous of this girl. Back then, she had no concerns other than the fact the people of the village used to tease her. They called her Matsyagandha, or 'she who smelled of fish'. Even so, she had not been hugely bothered. Each evening, when she returned to her father to hand him the day's takings, the fisherman would take the handful of coins she had earned and talk about the day when she would have riches beyond her dreams as the queen of all the land. Life was so much simpler back then.

The occasion on which I saw young Satyavati in my dream looked like any other day. Business had been a little slower that morning, and she was lying in the keel of her boat, her small bag scrunched up under her head like a pillow. The sun was almost at its highest point of the day, and most birds had retreated to the trees to get out of its glare. The gharials were not at all bothered, though, since they had the river to keep them cool. Every so often the air was pierced by the sound of thrashing and the river's surface was disturbed as a fish met an untimely end.

Unexpectedly, the girl's head was bathed in shade. I watched as, startled, her eyes flew open and there, standing on the water's edge was a sage. This was not just any sage, but the greatest of holy men. He was a vision of calm serenity in his orange robes, the aura around him seemingly battling with the sun itself to see which was more intense. His face was also lit up, a benign smile playing across his lips.

'My child, have I disturbed you?' he said softly as the girl leapt to her feet. 'Please excuse me.'

'No … no …' she stammered.

'May I trouble you to take me across the river?'

She nodded, smoothing down her sari as he stepped into the boat, his bare feet barely making a sound. It had been impossible for her not to feel self-conscious in such close proximity to this wise man.

The sage had settled on the narrow wooden bench, the fingers of each hand arranged in a small spire in front of him as he looked thoughtfully at the girl.

'What a vision you are!' he murmured.

She couldn't help but blush as she picked up her oar and began to row. There was no obvious response to this, so she'd decided it was best not to reply at all.

'I am surprised you do not have men queueing at the river's edge, just waiting for you to take them across the river. Who would not wish to be in the presence of such beauty? I am intoxicated by the vision before me.'

She'd averted her eyes and continued to row. Again, she was not sure if she should reply and, even if she should, what she should say. Strangely, despite the sage's persistence, she felt perfectly safe.

'You can speak to me,' he went on. 'I mean you no harm.'

'I know,' she said quietly.

'I'm sure you feel me foolish, but when I see something of great beauty, I feel compelled to remark upon it,' the sage went on, never once taking his eyes off the girl. 'There is much wrong in this world, so we must celebrate each beacon of light in the darkness.'

The young Satyavati remained silent and continued to row. Just then, a fish leapt out of the water, no doubt desperate not to become the gharials' next meal. The girl started, almost dropped her oar and then giggled self-consciously at her foolishness. At this, the sage laughed and clapped his hands together in delight.

'That is it,' he said. 'My heart is broken by your smile. You have enchanted me.'

She could not help but smile again at the sage's evident glee, despite her nervousness around her esteemed passenger.

'Please allow me to introduce myself. I am Sage Parashara and you, my vision of grace? What can I call you?'

After she told him her name, he clasped a hand on his heart as though it had been pierced by an arrow.

'Even your name is charming,' he had said.

The sage had himself gone quiet for a short while as the young girl continued to row. He looked lost in contemplation. They were not far from the opposite shore now, and Satyavati began to concentrate on hitting the familiar mark where she docked her small boat each time. It had always been a point of pride to her to land it just right so that the passenger barely noticed they'd arrived because the journey had been so smooth.

'I would like to make love to you,' the sage said.

The words had sounded so matter of fact that Satyavati initially thought she had misheard. She glanced at him and saw he was looking at her expectantly, waiting for an answer.

'Will you let me make love to you?' he repeated.

The girl's eyes widened. How should she respond? This was a great sage and she was a lowly fisherman's daughter. She must refuse, but how could she do so without causing offence? Her mind spun until she settled upon the decision that the only option was honesty. Thus, she couched her reply in the following terms.

'Sir, you are a Brahmin, the highest caste of them all, and I am a low-caste daughter of a fisherman. It cannot be so.'

The sage had not replied, still staring at the girl, apparently awaiting a better answer.

'If I am no longer a virgin, I will never be able to marry,' she stumbled on. Then, as an afterthought, she hurriedly added,

'Besides, I am not worthy of your attentions. The local people say I smell of fish. I am not good enough for someone as esteemed as you.'

At last, the sage appeared to be satisfied by the response. By this time, they had reached the shore and Satyavati skilfully steered her boat into the usual moorings, relieved this strange journey was at an end. She watched as the sage rose to his feet and rearranged the folds of his robe so they fell just so.

'If you make love with me, I will grant you two boons,' he said, looking at her steadily. 'The first is that whatever happens on this day, you will remain a virgin. The second that the fragrance of fish will forever more be changed into the finest perfume. Anyone who comes close to you will be as intoxicated as I at this sweet scent. It will overwhelm everyone.'

Even now, all these years later, I did not question how my younger self allowed herself to be seduced by Sage Parashara. There had been something so bewitching about him and the strength of his spirit. In my dreams, I watched as the sage sat back down in his seat and the young girl rowed him to the centre of the river. My thoughts did not intrude on what happened next. Not I, nor anyone else, could see the sage make sweet love to the young girl, because he had created a deep fog around the teak craft. All anyone would know of what passed was the ripples of water that rhythmically emerged from the thick cloud. That part of the story would remain a secret forever.

The sage had been true to his word. I had remained a virgin, and from then on, people would comment on my scent with admiration. Matsyagandha was forgotten, replaced by Gandhavati, or 'the fragrant one', as I became known. But that had not been the only souvenir of my experiences that day. No, there was physical proof of what had transpired between us. Nine months later, I gave birth to a son, whom I called Vyasa.

Looking back now, I wondered if this was always meant to be. The gods already knew my story and had put in place a way forward for me, a way to save Hastinapur. I had a son who could continue the bloodline, the son of a great sage. At the time, I hadn't known any of this, of course. I'd had to bear my son with great secrecy to avoid the shame of what had happened becoming common knowledge. I could hardly be a virgin with a child, after all. Once Vyasa had been born, I had personally taken him to Sage Parashara in the forest. I had beseeched him to bring Vyasa up as a sage, as was his birthright and he, of course, had agreed.

It had been agony to leave my child with Sage Parashara and his fellow sages, even though I had no choice. Even now, I could feel the pain of the loss as I had made my way back through the forest, alone, without my child. The pain was a heady mix of guilt and concern that I had done the right thing. Those emotions never truly left me. They became a part of me, inhabiting a small knot in the pit of my stomach that announced its presence every day when I awoke, questioning how I could walk away from my own son. In the months and years that followed, I sought out every piece of news I could about Sage Vyasa from those who often visited the forest to consult with the sages. To my immense pleasure, Sage Vyasa's name would often come up. His wisdom and power became legendary. Perhaps this was no surprise given his lineage. Sage Parashara would have been proud of him. To my immense sadness, I had never seen Vyasa since the day I had left him with the sages, even though I had often yearned to do so. Many times, I'd had to stop myself from running into the forest to seek him out among his adoptive family of wise men. This story had to remain a secret, even from my closest family. Now, though, that secret would be revealed.

The anxiety I felt awaiting Bhishma's return was overwhelming. I had no idea whether Vyasa would agree to come to court. Even if he did, would he agree to this *niyoga*? If he fathered children with Ambika and Ambalika, the widows of his deceased brother, Vichitravirya, it would ensure the Hastinapur bloodline, but it was impossible to know whether the sage would consent to my plan. It was a big thing to ask. Even with such momentous decisions at stake, there was one issue that bothered me more than any other. I could not bear it if Bhishma thought less of me once he discovered my secret. To be diminished in his eyes would be worse than death.

Each day, I would pace up and down the palace corridor, never far from the balcony that provided a perfect view of the entrance yard below and the road leading into the palace. The slightest noise would have me quickening my pace to look out over the ornate stone wall of the balcony, gripping its sides to steady myself. Even though Bhishma was not due for days, I still did it each time, my heart beating hard in my chest only to stop abruptly, a wave of disappointment threatening to suffocate me. I had not realised the palace yard played host to such a large amount of traffic each day. The wait was agonising.

Then, as quickly as it began, my ordeal was over. My dash to the balcony was rewarded with the sight of Bhishma standing proudly at the front of his chariot. The blood rushed to my face as I looked upon his great stature and assured stance. It took a few seconds to realise something was not right. Bhishma was alone. There was no sign of Vyasa or of a separate chariot following behind, ridden by the sage. This could surely mean only one of two things: Bhishma had either not found the sage or Vyasa had turned down his request.

My breath was already coming in short gasps as I began to run towards the stairs. My mind played out a series of terrible scenarios, each one more awful than the last. I had shared my secret, and yet, nothing had come of it. My son had not forgiven me for abandoning him.

By the time I reached the great hall, Bhishma was already there, standing tall, giving instructions to two courtiers on how to deal with his chariot. He smiled broadly at them before sharing a joke and patting one affectionately on the shoulder. It was impossible to read his mood as I hurried towards him, stopping directly in front of him.

'Tell me what has happened,' I said, still breathing hard.

I dreaded the reply but could not put it off. I had to know.

Bhishma gave a small bow. Searching his face, I could have gasped with happiness. His eyes shone with affection and kindness. He did not hate me.

'Everything is alright, Mother Satyavati,' he said in a low voice. 'Come, let us talk in private. You look like you need some refreshment.'

He indicated that I should follow him to the justices' room.

'It is you who has ridden a long way,' I protested. 'I should be calling for refreshment for you.'

We had reached the smaller room by now, and Bhishma shrugged to indicate it was not a problem. Before he closed the large, ornate doors behind us, he asked a servant to bring us drinks.

'As always, the most important thing to me is that you are happy and well,' he said.

Grateful for his words, I sank into a chair. Bhishma did the same, taking up a place directly beside me. I was struck by the distinctive scent of vanilla and sandalwood, mixed with the warm leather of his armour. He smelled fresh even after his long ride. I was desperate to voice a whole jumble of questions, but I let Bhishma tell the story in his own way.

'When I found Sage Vyasa in the forest, my first thought was that he did not look surprised to see me,' he said. 'I found that this was correct when his first words were that he knew what I was about to ask, even though at that time I was not fully sure of it myself.'

I caught my breath as the door behind us swung open. I turned around, hoping perhaps the sage had followed on a little behind and that was why Bhishma had arrived alone. But it was not my son. It was a servant carrying a jug of *bael* sherbet and two goblets. We stayed silent as she laid it down on the table beside us, poured out generous measures of the sweet, fruity drink and then quietly left. Neither of us reached for the refreshments.

'He then asked if I had come to ask of him something only a real mother could ask from a son.'

I did my utmost to keep my expression neutral, but tears were already pricking my eyes.

'So, you know,' I said quietly, my head dipped in shame that this great man would think less of me. I could not bear to look him in the eye.

Bhishma leant forward and spoke quietly.

'I didn't know, but I do now, but I do not think any less of you. Quite the opposite. Once again, you have been true to your vow to make every sacrifice to protect our kingdom. How could I not hold you in the very highest esteem for that alone?'

I let the words sink in for a few moments.

'Did he … did he tell you the full story?' I asked.

Bhishma nodded.

'I understand why you said nothing before. I can also see your plan. You are wise, Mother. Sage Vyasa can, with the help of Ambika and Ambalika, secure the bloodline with *niyoga*.'

I wanted to feel relieved. My worst fears had been unfounded, and Bhishma did not have a reduced opinion of me. But I could not relax yet. There was still an important question that I needed to hear the answer to.

'Will Vyasa come to the court and fulfil his mother's wish?'

Bhishma bowed his head to confirm that he would. I had barely let out a sigh of relief before he raised his hand to show he had not completed his response.

'He will come to the palace, yes. However, when I came upon him, he had already embarked upon a period of penance.'

I looked at Bhishma uncomprehendingly. I understood the concept of penance, where holy men would succumb to periods of great hardship, fasting, or lying on rocks heated by the sun. It was fundamental to attaining a higher form of mental awareness, rising above the daily cares harboured by those around them. These penances could go on for months and months, though, and we did not have the luxury of time. Our neighbouring kingdoms had already sensed our vulnerability and armies were being formed. My throat felt dry and I impulsively reached out and took the goblet of sherbet. Even as I drank large gulps, I barely noticed the sweetness of the *bael* fruit or the usually pleasing contrast with the tang of the lime water it was mixed with.

'How long?' I said, setting the goblet down beside me.

'He wants to be at full strength …'

'... how long?'

Bhishma sighed and brought his palms together in front of him, as if to counsel me to be patient.

'A year, Mother. One year.'

A year? Who knew what could happen in a year? Anything could happen. Hastinapur could fall to any one of its enemies and be destroyed for ever.

'No, no, no,' I said, shaking my head for emphasis. My concern had turned into raw anger. 'This cannot be. Did you not tell him it was urgent?'

Bhishma draw back slightly, letting his hands fall to his lap. I had gone too far. I was impatient and rude, but this was no time to lash out.

'I'm sorry,' I said quickly.

'I understand. I think we are all aware of the urgency. Vyasa certainly so. He, like I, is also eager not to let you down. He has been on his penance for a while now and is not in a good way. He is mentally stronger but physically much weakened. You know how these things can impact even a man as strong as the great Sage Vyasa. It is not easy to be patient, I know, but ...'

A large part of me wanted to shout with frustration, even lash out and say something I knew I didn't mean. Bhishma was right, though. In an ideal world, I would be patient. But our situation was not ideal. Far from it.

Making up my mind, I got to my feet.

'Where are you going?'

'I am going to call for Sarathee,' I said. 'I am so thankful for what you have done, but I need to go and speak with the sage. My son needs to understand our situation.'

Bhishma got to his feet too.

'Stop,' he said. 'There is no need to call Sarathee. I will go. I will speak again with Sage Vyasa and explain your position. I will leave right away.'

For the first time, perhaps ever, I caught a trace of sadness in Bhishma's expression. My story was not the reason for this sadness. He had reassured me of that. No, it was my impatience that had troubled him. Despite understanding the urgency as much as I did, he was concerned about the sage's warning. He sensed that breaking the penance and rushing to the palace might not result in the outcome we wanted. But what choice did we have?

Chapter Thirteen

With Bhishma gone for several days, I had taken his role in the day-to-day running of the kingdom. On the day that he returned, I had already spent some time talking with the justices in the morning, discussing a long-running land dispute between two wealthy Hastinapur families. After that, I took a meeting with two of our army generals. There was nothing I could tell them about the matters they wanted to discuss, which were to do with training their young troops. This was their area of expertise and Bhishma's. I was, however, able to provide the reassurance they needed that the necessary provisions to feed and nourish their new recruits would remain at their disposal. As soon as Bhishma was back, I told them, I would ensure he went through their questions in much more detail. Finally, I met with our talented chefs. After all the unrelenting tension of the past months, we needed a new, more positive focus, something to signal to our people that this kingdom was the vibrant capital it had always been. I hoped to have some good news to share soon, and that would require a celebration. How uplifting it would be for one and all if we could put on a feast like we used to do in better times, when the tables would run the length of the palace, groaning with fish, wild boar, *roti* and *khichdi*.

I knew Sage Vyasa had arrived at the palace long before a messenger ran in to announce it. The change in atmosphere was perceptible. The normally loud burble of day-to-day chatter was silenced, replaced by hushed whispers. *Was the arrival of my son really that shocking?*

Over the past few days, I had thought much about what it would be like to finally lay eyes on my son. The last time I had seen him, he was a tiny baby. Like all mothers, I was biased, but as I looked upon his smooth skin the colour of burnt sienna, I thought he was the most handsome child I had ever seen. Even at just a few hours old, his dark eyes had an other-worldly sense, as though he was all-seeing and all-knowing. Years had passed since then, and I had no idea what sort of man he had grown to be. People often talked in hushed, awe-stricken terms about the charismatic Sage Vyasa, who was renowned for his exceptional wisdom, but I was ashamed that I would not have recognised him if he passed me on the streets.

I raced to the entrance of the palace, my heart beating so hard in anticipation that I felt faint. Nothing though, nothing, could have prepared me for the sight that greeted me. As I arrived, Bhishma had just leapt down from the golden chariot with his usual jaguar-like agility. Still standing at the front of the chariot, his hands clasped around the rail, shoulders stooped, was a tall figure in the orange robes of a sage.

'Vyasa,' I breathed.

I don't know if he heard me, but at that very moment, the sage looked up. I couldn't help but take a step back in shock. His long, dark hair was unkempt and greasy, and the beard that trailed in a lengthy line down his chest was filthy and matted. His orange robe was dusty and worn, having clearly not been washed in weeks, and torn in places. Most noticeable of all were his eyes, which were almost charcoal-black and sunken deep in their sockets.

This man had seemingly not slept for a lifetime. Yet, those eyes exuded a spiritual calm and kindness. I felt as though I could see his soul reflected in them.

I swallowed hard as I desperately tried to collect my thoughts. I was glad that I had anticipated that the sage might not look his best after a lengthy period of penance followed by the journey through the forest to the palace. Mindful of the reaction of Ambika and Ambalika, I had directed their maid, Parishrami, to see that they stayed in their chambers on the pretext of helping them prepare to meet the sage. I had not forgotten the look on the faces of the two sisters when I had told them of my plan and the important role they were about to play in the future of Hastinapur. Their eyes had widened in alarm, and they had clasped one another in fear. It was a great deal to ask of them, I knew that, but we could not change course now. However, if they had seen the sage's crumpled form, it would have set them running in the opposite direction.

Whatever my concerns at seeing the state of the sage, I could not let them show. This was my greatest skill these days. I had been practising an air of confidence ever since Shantanu had succumbed to depression on hearing of his son's oath, and I was an expert now. I would never let anyone see how worried I was for the future of Hastinapur. My feelings, about everything and everyone, were my own, and would most likely be so for ever.

Bhishma had moved quickly to the other side of the chariot, his arms outstretched to help the sage down. It was heartbreaking to see how slowly my son manoeuvred himself around to accept this aid and to watch as he shuffled forward to the edge of the chariot's floor. From the way he braced himself, he could have been about to leap from the tallest mountain towards jagged rocks below, rather than be helped a short step down to the warm, welcoming sands of the palace courtyard.

Quite a crowd began to form as curious courtiers came to see the dishevelled guest. We all knew about penance and how only the greatest of holy men could withstand its rigours, but no one had yet seen a sage who had clearly been practising this ritual for such a punishing amount of time. For a moment, just like everyone else, I felt frozen to the spot, only able to stare at what was unfolding before me. I forced myself to step forward, arriving at the side of the carriage just as my son's feet connected with the ground. Bhishma stepped back, gave a small bow and passed the sage's hands into my own.

'My son,' I said, keeping my voice low. Then, raising my voice a little higher, I added, 'Sage Vyasa, you honour us.'

The warmth and energy pulsing through our connected hands was surprising. Despite his weakened state, Vyasa emanated a power that I had only ever felt from one other, Bhishma.

'Mother,' he said, his voice hoarse.

He began to stoop to kiss my feet, but I moved my hand to his shoulder to prevent him, fearful he would not be able to get up again.

'I am so happy you came, thank you,' I said. 'You need to rest now. Please let me show you to your chamber.'

I glanced at Bhishma, but his expression was neutral. He had done as I had asked, but he was clearly still unsure. Seeing Vyasa as he was now, I understood better why he had urged me to delay. But as far as I was concerned, nothing had changed. Our cause was as urgent as ever.

The walk to the chamber was slow and laborious, causing me to adjust my usual brisk pace. Bhishma followed close behind, and I couldn't help wondering if he was preparing himself to catch the sage should he faint with sheer exhaustion.

'There is so much I want to speak to you about,' I told Vyasa. 'I feel like I have waited several lifetimes to meet you. I want you to know …'

The sage, who had been walking beside me, stopped and turned to face me.

'I know, Mother, and there is nothing to be remorseful about,' he said. 'You gave me the gift of life, and I am here to fulfil the duty you have assigned to me. Do not be agitated.'

Once more, despite his exhaustion, a surge of energy seemed to pass from my son into my very soul.

'Thank you,' I said, and we resumed our walk.

When we reached the chamber, the guard outside opened the door, and Vyasa walked towards it. He motioned for us not to follow him and asked for a few moments to collect himself.

'You may then send me the girls,' he said, entering the darkened room before the door closed behind him.

My throat felt tight as I turned to face Bhishma, who had remained silent since his return. We would never question one another, but this was the nearest he had ever come to reproach. It was plain that Vyasa was in no condition for this task. As for the two queens, well, Bhishma knew better than anyone that our kingdom had put them through quite a lot already.

'It is duty,' I said firmly. 'We all need to do our duty.'

Even as I said the words, I barely recognised myself. Had I become so blinded by what I needed to do to protect Hastinapur that I had lost all humanity? Bhishma inclined his head. It was such a slight movement that it was barely noticeable, but it was a sign of agreement. It was not an admission that mistakes had been made, for he would never do that, but he was prepared to support me in this endeavour.

We walked together in silence to the queens' chambers, and one of the large double doors opened just as we reached the first one. Parishrami emerged and bowed.

'The princesses are ready, Queen Mother,' she said, 'as per your instructions.'

'Thank you,' I replied. 'The good sage is in his chamber. Please arrange for Ambika and Ambalika to be taken to him, one at a time.'

Parishrami acknowledged the instruction with another bow.

'And, when it is … done, … please come to find Bhishma and me.'

Turning to Bhishma, I added, 'I need you to attend to some matters that arose while you were gone.'

Leaving Parishrami to fulfil my instructions, Bhishma and I headed to the main hall and then on to our usual spot in the justices' room. I asked the servant who hovered close to the door to bring us some light refreshment and sat down at the table. Bhishma found a seat opposite and looked at me expectantly. It gave me great pleasure to see that his look of reproach was gone and his expression had returned to normal. He had accepted what I had already accepted. This was our only option.

'So, tell me, what has been going on while I have been in the forest?' he said, sitting back in his chair.

We both knew that neither of us was there to discuss matters of state, however pressing. It was merely a distraction to pass the time, but I played along.

'There have been some issues with getting proper supplies to the younger soldiers,' I began.

Strangely, the distraction technique seemed to work up to a point. Going through the day-to-day cares of the court was more diverting than I imagined it could be. We became relaxed enough to even laugh at some of the pettier goings-on we were expected to rule upon. It was a huge comfort to me to see Bhishma's face light up in a smile. I felt like I had not seen him this way for months. He likely felt the same about me. We'd had very little to smile about of late. Without us noticing it, a few hours flew by. Our discussion was drawn to an abrupt halt when the door to the justices' room opened and Parishrami entered.

It was clear right away that something was wrong. The maid looked anxious, her shoulders slumped and hands clasped together at her waist. Bhishma and I were on our feet before she'd even taken a few paces into the room. The relaxed atmosphere was instantly replaced with one of tension and apprehension.

'What, what is it?' I asked, trying and failing to sound calm. 'Are the queens alright?'

In a few brisk paces, Bhishma had walked around the table and was now at my side, staring intently at the maid whose eyes were wide.

'The queens … they are not harmed,' Parishrami began hesitantly.

She cast her eyes down, unable to speak further.

'You must tell us what happened,' I said, reaching forward to stroke her arm. 'We must know.'

Parishrami looked up and took a deep gulp of air.

'I took Queen Ambika to Sage Vyasa's quarters,' she said. 'She rushed out, not long afterwards. She said she was terrified. She was so scared by the sight of the sage that she covered her eyes.'

I stole a glance at Bhishma, who did not return it. He was staring intently at Parishrami.

'And Ambalika?' he said.

Parishrami looked at Bhishma. She was finding it hard to speak.

'She ... she was also terrified. When she came out, she was deathly pale.'

Looking from Parishrami to Bhishma, I struggled to understand. From the look on Bhishma's face, though, I could see he fully understood the implications.

'What? What does this mean?'

Bhishma seemed to be struggling with an inner demon, unable to answer my urgent question. Parishrami returned her gaze to the floor.

'I can't be sure,' he said quietly.

'Can't? Or don't you want to tell me?'

My tone was combative once again, so I checked myself. I felt so close to Bhishma that at times I could not help speaking my mind. But this was not the relationship we were supposed to have. We were only partners in the sense that we had both sworn to protect the kingdom.

Softening my voice, I spoke again.

'If you know anything, please, I beseech you to tell me. Have I made things worse with my rashness?'

Bhishma sighed as he turned to me.

'We must speak with Vyasa,' he said. 'Your motivations were sound, and I supported you. I still support you.'

'But?'

'There is a possibility that ... that whatever baby ensues from this union may be damaged by the circumstances of their conception.'

Damaged? I let the thought sink in. Would this nightmare never end? Whatever I did to put right the wrongs of that original oath only seemed to make the situation worse.

'Damaged? How?' I almost sobbed.

Bhishma shook his head.

'I need to know,' I pushed.

'There is a possibility that since Ambika averted her eyes, the child will be born blind.'

Each word he said hit me like a rock.

'And Ambalika?'

'Her child might be pale and unhealthy.'

I let each painful word sink in. My plan had collapsed. Bhishma had been right all along. It had been too soon. We should have waited for Vyasa to finish his penance and regain his full strength. My rash impatience had destroyed our final chance.

'No!' I shouted. 'This is not going to be so.'

Parishrami's head shot up, alarmed by my loss of composure. Even Bhishma looked taken aback.

'I am not going to accept this.'

My fists were balled at my sides as I began to pace the room, my breath coming fast.

'I've had enough. I have been fighting and fighting since I came to this palace, and everything has conspired against me. But this is going to change. It *has* to change.'

I swung around to face Parishrami.

'You. You need to go back to the queens.'

Ignoring the look of shock and surprise on her face, as well as any possibility of eye contact with Bhishma, I ploughed on.

'Tell them ... tell them they are to try again.'

Parishrami looked alarmed but did her best to mask her fear. It was Bhishma who stepped between us.

'Are you sure? How are you so certain that you can undo what has been done? I say that you cannot.'

Bringing my hands up, palms outwards, I signalled that any thought of defeat was not going to deter me. Nor was I going to change my mind. I'd had enough of people telling me what I could and couldn't achieve, or that I had to leave it to others to discuss. I was not going to be a passive bystander anymore. Let the history books call me impatient and impulsive. Sometimes, that is what those in charge need to be. That is how tough decisions are made.

'Now, go!' I said to Parishrami, my finger pointing to the door.

The maid hurried to the door and her footsteps could be heard, running along the hall towards the stairs to the queens' chamber.

Even as she left, I began to regret my outburst. For all my regrets that day about not listening to Bhishma's wise counsel, I had done it again. There were no excuses, but I just couldn't see a way out of the relentless downward spiral that was sucking Hastinapur and me to certain catastrophe. The pressure inside me to do something, combined with pain, sadness, hurt and grief, never stopped.

'I don't know if I can do this anymore,' I said, walking to the door.

My hand was on the door, but before I could push it open, Bhishma was by my side. He leaned in to speak in a low voice. His face was so close to mine that I could feel the warmth of his breath.

'It will be fine,' he said. 'You have done more than any mortal woman could do and been through more than any mortal woman too. I am proud of you. Be patient. Things are difficult, but they will get better soon.'

He was right, of course. He always was. Patience was what I needed now, more than ever. I had to learn to be calm. I felt ashamed at my outburst, yet torn as to whether I had done the right thing. Only time would tell.

In the months that followed, I watched anxiously as the queens progressed through their pregnancies. To my relief, everything seemed to be proceeding just as it should. The pair even seemed quite relaxed, more relaxed than they had been since they'd first arrived at the court. They also seemed to enjoy the attentions they were receiving as they edged towards their confinement. Word had got around of the *niyoga* and the impending royal births. To my relief, no one said anything about my relationship with Sage Vyasa, at least not in my hearing. If I dared to say it out loud, which I did not, I would have said there was an air of optimism in the palace and on the streets. For the first time in ages, the future of the kingdom rested on a steady foundation. On my walks around the palace corridors, I certainly came across fewer groups huddled together, gossiping nervously about the future.

Pleasingly, Bhishma and I had resumed our previous relationship, supporting one another as before in dealing with the issues of the palace. He consulted me with the same seriousness as ever, always complimenting me on my decisions. He too had a lightness about him that I had not seen for some time.

For my own part, I tried to push the tensions of that day behind me and believe that we would, as Bhishma had said, see better times. Among my biggest regrets was how difficult it had been saying goodbye to Sage Vyasa. There was so much I wanted to speak with him about, but he was eager to return to his penance. I made him promise that he would, in the future, return and spend some time with me, and he gave me his word. Even so, I did wonder how many years it would be before I would see him again. Instinct told me it would not be for a very long time.

It was a few months before I noticed how little I'd seen of Parishrami since that day. I liked this maid and felt saddened that she might be avoiding me. I had always seen a little of my younger self in her. We even looked a little alike: We were around the same height, with a delicate frame and long, glossy hair. Her eyes were the colour of warm hazel interspersed with chestnut flecks and always shone with confidence. She was perhaps a little headstrong at times, but empathetic and perceptive too. I concluded that she had been embarrassed at my outburst in the justices' room. I had not been myself at the time.

Despite resolving to rectify this immediately, it was much later that I managed to find the time to seek her out. As soon as I found her, though, I knew exactly why she had been keeping away from me. She too had the same swollen belly as the queens she served. By the way she shied away from making eye contact, I immediately suspected something was amiss.

'Is there something that you wish to tell me, my child?' I said.

Once more Parishrami averted her gaze, but one hand soothed the obvious bump which could not be hidden in the folds of her sari. I had found her in one of the smaller dressing chambers adjoining the queens' chambers. By the tidiness of the rows of neatly folded saris and throws, I suspected the maid had been spending a great deal of time in this room. The queens were both impeccable in their manners, but even they were not this meticulous.

'Why do you not wish to be seen?' I pressed.

I was sure to speak gently. The last time we had spoken, I had been harsh, and I'd seen the fear in her eyes as she scuttled away to tell her mistresses that they must return to what they dreaded most. Slowly, gently, I coaxed the story out of her.

Parishrami had returned to the queens, and they had screamed in alarm at the idea of returning to Sage Vyasa.

'They begged me to take their place,' she said. 'Forgive me for saying it, but they could not bear to be in the same room again.'

I did not interrupt. It was clear this maid wished to tell her tale in her own way.

'I went to the sage myself,' she said, before pausing and raising her head to return my gaze. 'I kept my composure. I am sure my baby will be strong and healthy.'

The pride with which she told me this tale left me in no doubt that this was true. There was no way I could chide her for not doing as I had asked. Now, with the benefit of hindsight, I could see that what I demanded and the way I had demanded it was unreasonable. Parishrami had done what she believed to be the right thing, and I could not punish her for that.

'Thank you,' I said, stepping forward to embrace her. 'Rest assured, we will look after you, and your child will be given everything he needs.'

As I left the chamber to seek out Bhishma, I tried to work through what this meant to my plan. Reaching the stairs, I stopped and changed direction, continuing my journey along the adjacent corridor. I would share the news shortly, but there was no hurry. Nothing could be done at this moment. For now, I just wanted to spend some time outside in the palace garden, feeling the heat of the sun on my face. Our fate, the fate of Hastinapur, would be decided, but not until a few months from now.

Chapter Fourteen

Eighteen years passed since the visit of Sage Vyasa to the palace. It was remarkable how much, yet how little changed. I was overjoyed at the birth of my grandchildren. Ambika had been the first to go into labour. Even when the maids confirmed to me what I had already known, that her son, whom she named Dhritarashtra, had been born blind, I did not mind. He was the most adorable baby. My heart filled with love the moment I saw him. I didn't think I had any more love left to give until Ambalika too presented me with a grandson, Pandu. There were those that whispered that he was disappointingly pale and unhealthy, but in my eyes, he was a bundle of loveliness. And then Parishrami presented me with a third grandchild, Vidur. Vidur was in rude health, the most robust and bright-eyed of the three.

For the first time, I understood why it is often said that being a grandparent is so much better than being a parent. In those first few years, I spent so many carefree moments with the three boys. Against all convention, the main hall of the palace turned into a giant nursery, their toys scattered about the stone floor. At first, the courtiers, especially the warrior chiefs, would tut a little as they navigated through the miniature carved wooden animals and silken bean bags. But even these fighting men could not help being moved by the antics of the three. Before long, they were on their hands and knees too, pushing toys back and forth to the little ones, laughing with pleasure.

Right from the start, even before they could properly walk, Pandu and Vidur looked out for their brother. They were the first to press toys into his hands or guide him to the best spot. The three seemed to have their own private language. If Dhritarashtra cried out in frustration, the other two would rush to his side, their hands clutching whatever it was that he needed, then guiding their blind brother to take it. They always seemed to know what he wanted. Perhaps they already sensed his nobility and that they would always be serving their brother. Dhritarashtra was, after all, the eldest, and therefore destined to take the throne.

Each of them had very distinct personalities despite sharing the same age and upbringing. Out of the trio, Dhritarashtra liked his own company the most and could often be impatient. He was definitely the most likely to lash out if his needs were not accommodated promptly. This could, of course, be put down to his blindness. Pandu was the most playful of the three, the joker amongst the boys. He had an almost permanent smile on his face and loved to spend time with others. By far, the most serious was Vidur, who learned to read and write well before the other two and loved nothing better than an afternoon curled up with his books. I could not resist teaching him to play *pachisi*, a game he took to with great joy. The strategies of moving around the cowrie shells fascinated him.

The day when Bhishma told me that it was time for the young boys to go to the ashram was one of the most difficult days of my life. It was the same for Ambika and Ambalika too. They were such doting mothers. We all knew that that this time would come, but even so, we could not bear to let them go.

'We must make sure to train them in all the arts they will need, to be the strong rulers we want them to become,' Bhishma reminded me.

It was the right thing to do, but the thought of the years I would spend without seeing them had been heartbreaking. I would miss so much about not being with them, and how unfair it seemed not to be able to witness each stage of their growth into young men. I had accepted it, though. This was the plan, and if it was to be realised, I had to give way to Bhishma. There was no better teacher in the whole world and, once again, he would be joined by Sage Kripa, who had proved to be such an able tutor with Vichitravirya. If I had any role now, it was to look after the two queens. They shared the loss of the children as keenly as I did.

If I had imagined it would be difficult as I waved the young boys away in Bhishma's carriage, the reality was many, many times worse. After they had left, the halls of the palace seemed empty, and the silence was unbearable. Courtiers crossed the floor of the great hall unencumbered, as though the boys had never been there at all. Yet, I was not the only one to feel the pain of their loss. Now, the conversations I overheard were all about what the boys used to do.

'Do you remember that time Pandu ...'

'That Vidur, I cannot believe he beat me at *pachisi*. I'm four times his age ...'

'Dhritarashtra, that boy has the stoicism of a warrior ...'

Each day had seemed to drag into the next. Of course, I had a huge amount to occupy me. My time was spent attending to the needs of Hastinapur. Without Bhishma there, I had indeed taken the full role of ruling the kingdom single-handedly rather than remaining the figurehead that my Queen Mother title would indicate. I feared, though, that I was not the greatest ruler as was prophesised. I missed the guiding hand and wise counsel of Bhishma. My only comfort, when difficult decisions needed to be made, was to ask myself what Bhishma would do. For just a moment, it would feel like he was sitting there beside me. To imagine the warm glow of his powerful presence, even for a second, gave me pleasure. But this welcome feeling was always quickly snatched away from me when I realised I was alone. It was not just his wise counsel I missed. I missed my friend. There was a perpetual large void in the court without his company.

Despite my responsibilities, I returned to taking daily tours on the chariot with Sarathee. I did not leave the palace for long, but I needed this small respite. My favourite spot was the public garden, situated just outside the city, with its pleasing combination of orchard and flower gardens. I especially enjoyed sitting in the shade on one of the small stone benches within the leafy bowers. The prime spot was one which overlooked the pool of water that had been excavated who knew how many years earlier to keep the gardens fully quenched. Whoever had done this had seen to it that the pool was planted with lilies, lotus flowers and an abundance of other water-loving plants. Together, at the right time of the year, these now-mature plants produced a cacophony of colour which never failed to lift the spirits. If that did not do the job, there was a small group of tame peacocks who were always curious to see any visitors.

Sarathee would always remain with the chariot, waiting patiently for my return. He'd wait a little longer when I was done, making sure it was I who broke the silence between us after climbing back onto the chariot. My faithful friend instinctively knew I needed to prolong my meditations for just a few moments longer. It was one of the few periods of peace I had. When I was ready to speak, I would ask him about his family and what he did when he was not driving this chariot. I particularly enjoyed the stories about his grandchildren. Somehow, hearing of their antics made the pain of not being with mine a little easier. Every few days, I would ask him about what he was hearing in the city. I could not do it too often, because the thoughts of the people of Hastinapur echoed my own. They were impatient for the return of the boys and the coronation of the next king. I was grateful that the news of the birth of the boys had kept our enemies away, but the threat of invasion never seemed far away from Hastinapur. Everyone fully expected one of our neighbouring kingdoms to test the waters. It was only the fear of Bhishma's wrath which kept them away. We needed a more permanent solution for the future of Hastinapur.

When word came through that Bhishma was about to return with my grandchildren, I could barely contain my excitement. The lengthy period without them suddenly seemed a distant memory, as if it had passed in a flash, even though at the time, each day had seemed to last 48 hours. As I walked about the palace making preparations, my step was as light as that of a young girl. Everything had to be perfect for their return. Ambika and Ambalika were just as cheerful and enthusiastically joined in, instructing the maids to clean and air the boys' chambers and decorate them with the best silk drapes in the palace. When my grandchildren had left, they had all been young boys, but they would be returning as men, and their chambers must reflect their new status. The two queens were also sure to speak with the palace chefs. We needed a grand feast, the grandest feast the palace had ever seen. We had not been the only ones keenly awaiting their return. This was the moment everyone had been looking forward to. Of course, we would be arranging another celebration for the coronation of Dhritarashtra, which I anticipated would be a little later. But there was no harm in bringing some more lightness and optimism to the palace. We had waited so long for this.

On the day itself, I awoke at dawn. There was no need, for I had already supervised all the arrangements and had had their chambers rearranged at least three times apiece. But I just couldn't sleep any longer. I took up my usual position at the balcony overlooking the palace courtyard. The sunrise that day was more beautiful than I had ever seen it. I was sure it was the gods telling me that this was the dawn of a new era. All my efforts to protect Hastinapur were to be rewarded. My grandsons were returning, educated and trained by a demigod. What enemy would risk taking them on?

It was not until midday that I spied the chariot approaching. I could hardly believe what I saw. Bhishma's proud stance was unmistakable as he guided the chariot through the palace gate. But beside him were three men. Three tall, well-built figures, who stood in the same confident manner as their tutor. Even as I turned to run down the stairs to greet them, I heard a cheer go up outside. Quite a crowd had gathered to see the new king and his brothers. The people were clearly as moved as I. Hope had, at last, returned to Hastinapur.

Almost blinded by tears of joy, I ran into the courtyard. Bhishma had already alighted from the chariot and was smiling broadly as he bowed deeply to me. His eyes shone with the same happiness that I felt. Then, with a sweep of his arm, he indicated that the young men should alight too and greet their queen. I watched in awe as Pandu jumped down first, sure-footed and confident.

All traces of his youthful pallor seemed to have vanished. He was every inch a self-assured, healthy prince. Vidur followed him. His frame was a little slighter, but his scholarly air did not disguise the fact that this was a handsome and confident young man. Finally, both brothers turned, their hands outstretched, and Dhritarashtra caught hold of each one. As he stepped down from the chariot, he looked every inch the king he would inevitably become. He stood tall, his square chin raised, breathing in the air of his kingdom with approval. Bhishma had done us proud.

Dhritarashtra, trained to be a leader from the start, turned in the direction of the sound coming from the small yet growing crowd and waved. He smiled as the courtiers cheered and cheered.

'We have returned,' Bhishma said, his palms pressed together in front of him. 'The boys are men, and they are ready.'

I had to stop from flinging myself into Bhishma's arms. That would not be the behaviour expected from the queen mother. But I was so grateful to this man for what he had achieved. I had also missed him so very much.

'Thank you,' I said instead, keeping my voice as steady as I could.

I was interrupted by Pandu, ever the joker, who swept me up in his arms and spun me around. Despite my vow to always behave with dignity, I could not help giggling like a young girl.

'Tell them you missed me the most,' he urged, nodding over his shoulder at his brothers. 'We can send them back to the forest if you just say the word ...'

'Enough,' I laughed. 'I have missed you all equally. Come, I want to hear everything.'

As I led the small group into the palace, I noticed the brothers had fallen into what seemed like a well-practised routine.

Pandu and Vidur walked on either side of Dhritarashtra, not touching, but close enough that he could follow their step. They instinctively knew that since their brother had not been to the palace for so long, the entrance with its small flight of steps would be unfamiliar. Without sight, Dhritarashtra would need to relearn how to navigate by himself. Until that time, though, his brothers were his guides.

With a start, I realised Bhishma had noticed me watching my grandchildren and noting the reason for their actions. I couldn't help but smile as I saw him. '*Yes, they are there for one another. This is their training,*' his look seemed to say. Once more, he had read my thoughts. Oh, how I had missed this man!

The celebrations for the return of the group went on for three whole days. One feast led to another, and the walls of the palace echoed with the sounds of music and laughter. All business was suspended and the main hall decked out with row upon row of tables groaning with food. A table had been set on the dais at the top end of the hall, the place reserved for kings and queens, but Pandu in particular could not stay there for long. He was forever running onto the floor of the hall, grabbing a young female courtier by the waist and dancing around the tables with her.

'I've been in the forest learning and learning,' he called over his shoulder, when I stepped forward to semi-reproach him for his un-prince-like behaviour. 'You have no idea how dull life was!'

I glanced at Bhishma, who was shaking his head and laughing at the same time.

'You see what I have had to put up with?' he asked.

It was refreshing to see Bhishma so relaxed and at ease. Yet, despite our close bond and continued honesty with one another, I would never admit to him that Pandu was my favourite. But I knew that Bhishma, like me, saw the young prince as a breath of fresh air. After all the angst that we had been through over the years, this was what we needed. We'd have a serious king in Dhritarashtra, and his younger brother would win the hearts of those around him. As for Vidur, he had the intellect that would win the respect of all whom he encountered.

Inevitably, it all had to end. There was serious business to be done. Now that Bhishma and my grandchildren had returned, the formalities needed to be dealt with ahead of Dhritarashtra's coronation.

The servants had managed to get the main hall back into shape in a remarkably short space of time. Working through the night, they had cleared away the plates of leftover food and half-drunk goblets of wine and sticky jugs of sherbet, and swept the stone floor clean. The wax in the wall lamps was replenished and the golden ornaments atop each surface were polished until they shone, as were the grand double doors at the entrance. The dais had been returned to its usual arrangement, with a large throne at the centre ready for Dhritarashtra, and another just beside it for Bhishma, who would remain as an important advisor. A little way away from it was a smaller throne for me, and two more, one for Pandu and another for Vidur. The rest of the ministers were seated in carved wooden chairs fanning out on either side at ground level immediately below the dais.

I had taken my place on my throne early, as had Bhishma. The ministers had been similarly prompt, eager to get the business of the day concluded. I was quite sure that many of them had their eye on the next feast, the one that would accompany the coronation, and were therefore eager to get this formal part out of the way as quickly as possible. I was in no hurry to rob my grandchild of the due ceremony his status deserved, but there was also a small part of me that agreed with the sentiment. I far preferred it when the court was united in happiness and merriment.

The doors at the end of the hall opened and Dhritarashtra walked through first, his brothers close behind in the now-familiar formation. The oldest brother looked quite sure of himself as he walked across the main hall. This was a man who welcomed his destiny. Despite the challenges his blindness had brought, he was ready to do his duty as king. He had been prepared by Bhishma for the role and was proud to finally perform it.

When they reached the foot of the dais, they stopped. Bhishma was on his feet and began to speak, welcoming everyone.

'I am not alone in saying that we have all long looked forward to this day,' he said, looking at each of the assembled ministers. 'We are very proud of our new king Dhrit…'

He never finished the word. Vidur had leapt to the dais to stand in front of his mentor.

'Sir, if you will forgive me,' he said, bowing low to Bhishma.

A frown played across the older man's face. He had not expected this from his most studious charge. Of all the boys, Vidur was the least likely to act impulsively. That was more Pandu's style.

'If you will permit me, I would like to address the room,' Vidur said, looking first at Bhishma, and then at me.

Bhishma turned to look at me, and I stared at him in confusion. This was so unusual. These confirmation ceremonies in the run-up to a coronation had been unchanged for centuries. The traditions were set in stone. I felt sure Bhishma would have schooled the three brothers in what was supposed to happen. We had little choice now, since Vidur had already changed the flow of events through his interruption. I nodded to Bhishma to indicate

I would allow it, and Bhishma raised his hand to Vidur to show that he too agreed.

'Thank you,' Vidur said, before turning to face his brothers and the ministers seated either side of them. 'I know this is highly unusual, and for that, I must apologise. However, I would be remiss if I did not speak up now, before it is too late.'

A heavy anticipation fell like a dark shadow, cloaking the main hall, as everyone waited to hear what Vidur had to say. Even Pandu looked deathly serious as he stared at his brother.

'There might be those who believe me to be disloyal when I say what I have to say,' he went on. 'But trust me, this is quite the opposite. I say what I will say out of complete loyalty and devotion to the kingdom of Hastinapur.'

I watched as Vidur paused, seemingly building up strength. *What could possibly be so momentous at a time like this?*

'I believe that Pandu, not Dhritarashtra, should become king.'

A gasp of shock rippled across the room. Dhritarashtra looked shaken and Pandu profoundly taken aback. Even then, his first thought was for his older brother and he stepped forward to protectively hold his arm, perhaps believing he may collapse with surprise. Dhritarashtra angrily shook him away, his face still inclined in Vidur's direction, waiting to hear what he had to say to explain this terrible betrayal. The only person who had not moved, nor made any show of surprise was Bhishma, who remained in his seat, looking attentively upon the younger brother.

'As I say, I voice this opinion with the best interests of Hastinapur at heart,' Vidur went on. 'Yes, I know that Dhritarashtra is the eldest and by all convention should take the throne. I am equally certain that he would be a just and fair king.

'Yet, after a prolonged period of weakness, Hastinapur needs an exceptional king, a *strong* king, not a blind one. One who can fully take care of its subjects and who can deal with any threats.'

When Vidur had stopped speaking, the hall remained in silence. No one, not even Bhishma, had anticipated this. It was Pandu who found his voice first.

'This is not my preference,' he said, sounding unusually unsure of himself. 'We have always known that Dhritarashtra would rule. We have sworn to protect him and guide him whenever he needs us.'

Dhritarashtra, though, was silent. I could see the pain in my oldest grandson's face through the anger. Despite the challenges of his sightlessness, he had always had one goal in his life, the goal he had built everything around: the knowledge that one day he would fulfil his destiny and rule. Now, his brother, part of the tight-knit group whom he trusted more than any other, had changed everything.

Pandu looked increasingly stricken too. It was obvious that Vidur had not shared his thoughts with him beforehand. Now that what had been said was sinking in, I was certain that Pandu would be in inner turmoil, torn between his intense loyalty to each brother and his duty towards Hastinapur. Bhishma's training had focused on helping Pandu become a formidable warrior to protect his older brother's kingdom. Now, though, he was being told that he should take a completely different place in its future.

I became aware that all eyes were upon the dais, looking between Bhishma and me. The ministers were unable to take such a momentous decision. That fell to the protector of Hastinapur, the wise, all-seeing demigod, and the queen mother. We would, together, make this choice.

My heart was beating hard in my chest as Bhishma turned in his throne to look at me. I could read nothing in his expression, nothing that would guide me. Yet, he was giving me the final say. I could see that.

I closed my eyes for a moment, and in that split second, all became clear. Bhishma and I had always shared an oath. Our conviction had been that we would do all we could for the kingdom, giving everything we had to secure the strongest future available to it. That was the only way we could both make up for what had happened in the past. My final check was to ask my oft-asked question: *What would Bhishma do?* Opening my eyes, I looked out over the court.

'I agree with Vidur,' I said. 'Pandu is the strongest candidate to become king, and this is in the best interest of all of us. Pandu will rule.'

I avoided looking at my eldest grandchild, even when I heard a loud sob of fury from his direction.

Chapter Fifteen

The coronation celebrations were barely over before Hastinapur came under attack. We'd been going through the day's business when a messenger ran into the main hall. Breathless and speaking fast, he informed Bhishma that a large army had broken through our northern-most border and was, even now, making steady progress towards the palace.

'Then we will meet them,' Pandu said, jumping to his feet. 'We will show them that we are not weak.'

Bhishma was also on his feet, motioning to a minister to come forward and issuing rapid instructions to him. I waited patiently until he had finished, doing my best to quell my growing sense of alarm. I could not let anyone, least of all Pandu, see how much I feared what lay ahead.

'Mother,' Bhishma said, turning to take his leave, 'If you will excuse us.'

'Of course,' I said. 'I just don't understand …'

'… understand?'

I marvelled at how calm Bhishma was, even though he was just hours away from going into battle. There was not a trace of impatience in his voice. I felt a little foolish. Now was not the time.

'I just thought that we looked stronger now,' I said quickly. 'We have crowned a new king. There were years and years when you were away, training Pandu and his brothers. Why didn't they attack then?'

Bhishma shrugged.

'Fairness? Or perhaps they were not up to full strength either. Now, though, they want to test us, to see how strong we are.'

I pretended I understood, although I really did not. I didn't press the point, nor express concern about Pandu, even though this was his first campaign and he had barely been king for a few days.

'He will be fine,' Bhishma called over his shoulder as he made to leave. 'I trained him well.'

After so many years of pretending everything was fine, I should have been a master at the art. Even so, I struggled to contain my emotions over the next few days. It was impossible to stop my mind wandering to what was happening in the battlefield. My imagination kept feeding me the most awful pictures of Pandu lying blood-soaked and injured on the battlefield, or worse. I had no fears about Bhishma. I knew he would be fine whatever happened. He had proved himself to be the mightiest of mighty warriors a hundred times or more. But Pandu? He was a mortal man. What would happen if he were badly hurt?

It was a whole week before they returned although it felt a lot longer. Then, just as I was beginning to truly despair, Pandu flung open the doors to the court and almost bounced in. He looked in rude health, and a huge grin played across his face.

'Grandmother,' he said, giving a low bow. 'You are looking at the victorious King Pandu who has slain all before him. Well, perhaps not all. I let Bhishma and the rest of the men take a few.'

He jabbed a finger over his shoulder in the direction of Bhishma, who had just entered the hall, and said in a stage whisper, 'I have to let the old man have a go. These demigods can be quite temperamental, you know …'

Bhishma was standing directly behind my grandson by then, shaking his head slowly from side to side. He too was smiling.

'It is a wonder this young man managed to fight anyone,' he said, reaching forward to ruffle Pandu's long, dark hair. 'He never stops talking.'

'But everything is all right?' I said, still not quite ready to be as relaxed as the two standing in front of me. 'The enemy is … defeated?'

'Defeated, vanquished and cast down into the dirt,' Pandu said with another bow. 'Those we spared have gone back where they came from. They won't be troubling us again.'

I found myself laughing, not out of amusement but relief. That feeling of pure relief was one of the most overwhelming emotions I had ever experienced. My legs felt so weak that they threatened to give way. I needed to sit down.

'I am so glad you are back home safe and sound,' I managed before heading back to my place on the dais.

'Which is more than can be said for many of the enemy,' Pandu said, his face radiant with success. 'Let me clean up after our journey, and I will return to tell you everything.'

I watched as he and Bhishma left to freshen up after the rigours of battle. Pandu was talking non stop, his arms waving as he emphasised each gesture, with Bhishma only managing to chime in now and again. The peals of laughter from the young king were audible even as the two neared the outer reaches of the grand hall. It was a pleasure to see that the two got on so well. They were relaxed in one another's company, even more so now after the intensity of their shared experience. For just a moment,

I allowed myself to feel a glow of pride that my plan with Sage Vyasa had worked. It had been a truly painful episode, but we had achieved what I had hoped for. We had made Hastinapur safe.

Something else occurred to me as I watched the figures disappearing through the large double doors. Pandu's swaggering step, so full of vigour and confidence, was not that of a weak man. Despite the prediction that he would be at a disadvantage following the reaction of his mother to Sage Vyasa, the paleness of skin that had characterised his childhood had all but disappeared. He had grown up into a strong, vibrant man. I saw no weakness. Perhaps Bhishma had, for once, been wrong about something.

My greatest hope now was that this would be the last of the battles to demonstrate Hastinapur's strength. I was no master military tactician—that was Bhishma's forte—but surely our other enemies would hear about the crushing defeat of the invaders from the north and would decide not to risk it? That would seem to be sensible.

As I quickly discovered, however, when it came to men and war, they are rarely sensible. Barely a month passed before another messenger appeared with urgent news. This time, an army had breached the southern border. The force was small, he said, but heavily armed and well prepared. Pandu was on his feet and shouting for his chariot to be prepared even before the messenger had completed his briefing. My headstrong grandchild was eager to go into battle again. Bhishma, the more experienced warrior, listened intently to the messenger, but then he too headed to the door to begin the process of instructing his generals.

Would this ever get easier? It crushed my very soul to watch two of the people I loved most in the world heading off to face our enemies. The same uncertainties flooded my brain, the same images of my grandchild lying wounded in the dirt. As before, my only option was to carry on, manage the kingdom and pretend I was not in the least bit concerned.

Fortunately, I was no longer alone in administering to the day-to-day needs of Hastinapur. Vidur now joined me as Hastinapur's Prime Minister and quickly proved to be invaluable. His skills were very similar to those of Bhishma when it came to wise counsel, which was no surprise since the older man had trained him in the arts of diplomacy. At times, it was almost as though Bhishma was at my side once more as we worked together through the business of the court. While more serious than his brother Pandu, Vidur was well liked, and the ministers listened keenly to what he had to say. They knew they had a learned man in their midst and were quick to consult him. I had never anticipated that Vidur would play such an important role at the palace, but once he was there, I wondered how I had ever managed without him.

Vanquishing the enemies from the south took less time than those from the north. Although Bhishma warned Pandu not to boast, my grandson could not resist describing the victory, almost blow by blow, when they returned to the court. In what was quickly becoming a familiar routine, Pandu would describe the battle while Bhishma stood beside him, smiling softly with an expression not unlike what one might expect from a doting father.

'They had elephants, Grandmother,' Pandu said, stretching his arms out wide to indicate the size of the beasts. 'Elephants! But we drove them into the river along with their cavalry.'

Pandu leaned in conspiratorially. 'Here is a question for you. Do you think elephants can swim?'

I shook my head and raised my hands to indicate that I had no idea. I had only ever seen a handful of elephants, but none near water.

'Yes, they can!' Pandu exclaimed with a flourish. 'But it turns out that our enemies cannot. Never mind. Next time, they should plan their campaign a bit better and not try to flank us around the river.'

Looking around the court, I could tell the ministers were lapping up Pandu's bravado. They knew, as I did, that battle is a vile, bloody affair, but the king's stories made them relax. Hastinapur was in good hands. Bhishma had trained the king well.

'Well, I hope that is the last of it,' I said when Pandu had finished his story. 'We have shown our enemies that we will not be cowed. Hastinapur is safe.'

How I wished that was so! But it was not to be. The stronger we became, the more our enemies attacked us. It became almost a point of pride for our neighbouring kingdoms. A belief appeared to have developed that if any army could defeat Hastinapur, then it would be on a fast track to claim the title of the strongest of them all. The victorious kingdom would not need to waste any more blood on other battlefields, or so the thinking seemed to go. Month after month, one messenger after another appeared, breathlessly announcing a new force heading towards us. Pandu never seemed to tire of it. It was quite the opposite. To him, it was almost a sport. And each time, riding out at his side was Bhishma. I was quite certain Pandu loved riding out to battle a thousand times more than dealing with the mundanities of court life. He'd almost said as much.

'We should all do what we are best at,' he grinned before yet another conflict. 'I am the bravest warrior and Vidur is the learned fellow. He loves his dusty books and his torturously complicated diplomatic arguments that no one but he understands. When it comes to your grandchildren, you, my dear Queen Mother, have the best of all worlds.'

Did it get easier? No, it did not. Each time Pandu and Bhishma returned victorious, my grandchild would tell his stories of war, laughing and joking as he did so. I knew his humour was an effort to keep me calm, and I did not fear for him as much as I once did, but the worry never completely left me. If we lost Pandu, I didn't think I would ever recover from it. It was not just that; once more, Hastinapur would be plunged into danger. Pandu was such a ray of sunshine and hope that it would be like the world had ended for me.

For the first time ever, I found myself looking forward to the monsoon season, which lasted from July to September. Months earlier, when I had spoken to Vidur about my misgivings around Pandu and Bhishma and the constant battles, he had sought to appease my nerves by telling me that any general would take the prevailing weather conditions into account before planning an attack. No one would want to go to war when there was a danger that their armies would nearly drown in the annual rains, he had told me with his usual certainty. Not only that, it would be impossible to resupply an army if the ground was sodden, he had explained, reiterating that getting around during this season was always a challenge.

I really thought we'd make it through. But, in mid-June, when the sun was still high in the sky and the daytimes long, warm and inviting, a messenger arrived.

'Ah, one more try before the weather closes in,' Pandu said, rubbing his hands together in glee. 'You see, Bhishma, we get all the luck!'

Bhishma shook his head with mock incredulity. 'You, my young King, enjoy battles far too much,' he laughed.

Looking at Bhishma, I could tell he was getting as much pleasure out of it as his young protégé. He rightly took great pride in how well he had trained Pandu. After all the anguish he'd been through when I first came to the palace, this was most likely a welcome relief too. He had never feared battle, and he was actively doing what we had both sworn to do.

As always, as I listened to the chariots rumbling away, I sent up a silent prayer that would protect the two men and their army. Perhaps this would be the last time I would need to do so for a while. One more victory, surely that was all we needed. Then, we would be left alone.

I must have managed to convince myself that this was the last time because it was a little easier. I threw myself into palace affairs, and the days passed relatively quickly. Even my dreadful visions of death and injury came to me less frequently. I began to contemplate calling for Sarathee. I had hardly been away from the palace for weeks and would never have previously imagined doing so while Pandu was on a campaign. Perhaps I would do so the next day.

Vidur and I were just finishing the day's business when the large doors of the main hall flew open. Swinging around at the sound, I was greeted by a terrible sight. Bhishma was standing there, holding up Pandu, one arm tightly around his waist. My grandchild was on his feet, but barely, with his head down and shoulders slumped.

Clamping my hand across my mouth to prevent myself from screaming, I began to run towards the two figures. *No, no, no, this was what I feared most!*

'It is all right,' Bhishma said quietly as soon as I was close. 'He has been wounded, but it is not serious.'

'Not serious?' I said, my eyes wide.

My grandson had an ugly gash across his chest. The front of his leather armour was no longer gleaming white. It was brown with blood and more livid red liquid was soaking into it all the time.

Pandu lifted his head and gave me a weak smile.

'It took four of them all at once to get this close,' he murmured. 'You should see what I did to them.'

Pandu began to straighten up, but the effort was too much. The muscles in Bhishma's arm tensed as he took all of Pandu's weight. He'd tried to make it look casual, like he had an arm around a good friend, but I could see the worry in his eyes.

'Can you help him to his chamber, please?' I said. 'I will send the healer to you. He will know what to do.'

Bhishma inclined his head and began to manoeuvre Pandu towards the stairs. With all my heart, I did not want to let my grandson out of my sight, but I had a job to do. I hurried back the way I had come and began issuing instructions. While one messenger was sent to urgently locate the healer, I asked the maids to prepare refreshments to be taken up to Pandu's chamber. Bhishma, always so strong and charismatic, looked like he had not slept, eaten or drunk anything for days. His only focus had been to get his young charge back to the palace. I entrusted a further group with gathering all the necessary equipment I thought the healer would need, especially plenty of water and cloth to clean the wound. It was only once everything was in place that I too hastily made my way upstairs.

The sight of Pandu lying on top of his bed made my heart sink. He looked so exhausted and pale. Bhishma was holding a cloth over the wound, pressing down hard, but it was already soaked in blood.

'How did this happen?' I whispered, reaching out to touch Pandu's forehead. It was hot and clammy.

'It was how he said,' Bhishma said in a low voice. 'A group of infantrymen attacked him together.'

He paused and added with a rueful grin, 'I am quite certain that when he is better, he will tell you the story properly. He will no doubt conclude that the enemy has decided that he is the most ruthless foe and mighty warrior and thus must be eliminated on priority in order to secure victory.'

With a groan, Pandu raised his hand a little.

'It is true,' he said in a rasping voice.

'Shh, don't speak,' I said.

At that moment, the door opened, and to my relief, the healer hurried in.

'Come,' Bhishma said. 'Let us let him get on with his work. We are in the way.'

We both stepped back and watched as the healer and his assistant began to attend to Pandu. They started by carefully peeling back the outer layer of armour, Pandu wincing as the dried blood came away from his skin. Then, slowly and gently, the healer began to dab at the wound, using a cloth soaked in the water we'd provided, to which he had added a mix of herbs and wood ash. I could only marvel at how brave my grandchild was being. The open wound must have smarted so much.

'Will it be all right?' I said. 'Will he ...'

Without once taking his eyes away from his patient, the healer nodded.

'It looks bad, but it is not life-threatening,' he said.

Bhishma and I exchanged glances. The look of relief on his face no doubt matched my own.

'Come,' he said. 'Let us leave him to do his work.'

Then, turning to the healer, he added, 'We will wait outside.'

Once out in the corridor, I found myself drinking in great gulps of cool air. I realised that I had been holding my breath for much of the time in Pandu's room.

'Thank you,' I said to Bhishma.

'Thank you? I didn't do anything. I should have kept a better eye on him.'

'We both know that is impossible. There is no controlling that man,' I said, smiling for the first time since they had returned. 'No, I was thanking you for bringing him home.'

We were both silent for a moment, and I am sure we were contemplating the same thing: What if Pandu had not made it?

'You'll be pleased to know we won,' Bhishma said. 'I think our enemies have got the message. I don't see any more attacks, not for a good while.'

Before today, this would have been music to my ears, but I was not yet ready to change the subject and pretend everything was going to be alright. We had been foolish, thinking we had achieved all we set out to do. The challenge of protecting Hastinapur was not over simply because we had a strong king who could vanquish all enemies. Today had proved that. If that sword stroke had been a little deeper or in a different place, we would have been having a very different conversation.

'We can't let this happen again,' I said. 'We can't allow it.'

Bhishma looked confused.

'I just said that I don't think there will be any more battles ...'

'... no, not that. We've been complacent.'

Bhishma remained silent. He would never contradict me, but I sensed he did not agree. Perhaps he didn't see where I was going with this.

'We were all so relieved when Pandu became king. Vidur was right. He was the person for the job, and he has proved that again and again. But our job is not over. It will not be over until we secure Hastinapur for the next generation.

'We must find Pandu a wife. The king must have a queen, and we must secure the bloodline.'

I'd been pacing up and down as I spoke and when I finished, I turned around to scrutinise Bhishma's reaction. It was not what I expected. He was frowning.

'Forgive me, but I feel you have forgotten something quite important,' he said. 'By tradition, the eldest child should marry first. You appear to have given no consideration to Dhritarashtra.'

His tone cut me to the core. For the first time since I had known him, Bhishma sounded reproachful. What made it most hurtful was that he was right. I had barely given my eldest grandchild a second thought. I had rushed to his side and comforted him after the decision was taken to crown Pandu, but we'd hardly spoken since that time. Dhritarashtra had taken himself off to his chamber and rarely appeared in the main rooms of the palace. I had been so swept away by my concerns over Pandu during the campaigns that I had not once checked to see if Dhritarashtra was alright.

Looking back over the past few months, I winced with shame and embarrassment. The only time Dhritarashtra had been in court, he would have heard his brother talking vividly about all his successes on the battlefield, successes which his older brother would never enjoy. He'd have heard us laughing at Pandu's wild stories. How it must have hurt to not only have his life's ambition snatched away, but to also be constantly confronted by how much he had lost. How could I have been so thoughtless? Vidur had taken a central role in running the kingdom, but no thought had been given to doing the same for his brother, who was struggling to come to terms with what had happened. How had I not thought of this?

'You are right,' I said, gulping back the tears that threatened to overwhelm me. 'I feel awful. I will make amends, I will. And please, can I ask for your help in finding brides for *both* Dhritarashtra and Pandu?'

I had barely finished speaking when the door behind us opened and the healer's assistant beckoned us inside. He was smiling broadly, which seemed to indicate that Pandu was going to make a full recovery.

'Bhishma, can you go to him?' I said. 'There is someone I need to speak with.'

Without waiting for an answer, I turned and headed in the direction of Dhritarashtra's chamber. I hoped I was not too late to right the wrong.

Chapter Sixteen

Bhishma's suggestion of a match for Dhritarashtra was perfect. In fact, it was more than perfect. Few people have impressed me as much as Gandhari. Her quiet grace and stoicism masked a strong wit. Almost from the moment we met, I felt drawn to her. This was a woman who knew her own mind and who would not be swayed by others.

I admit that I had been a little taken aback when Bhishma first brought her to the palace. She was wearing a yellow silk blindfold as he guided her into the main hall. I hardly knew what to make of it as she was led to the dais for the introductions. I hurried forward to greet her, taking both her hands in mine so she knew that I was there.

'My child,' I said. 'What is the meaning of this?'

Gandhari had smiled and gently squeezed my hands to acknowledge me.

'If I am to marry Dhritarashtra, I wish to share his experiences. All of his experiences. I will remain blindfolded forever.'

What an extraordinary woman! While Gandhari was taken to her chamber to freshen up after her long journey, Bhishma and I had retired to our usual meeting place in the justices' room so he could tell me what had happened. The story he told convinced me more than ever that this was a perfect match.

Gandhari was the daughter of King Subula. When Bhishma had arrived in the court of Gandhar to ask if Dhritarashtra could marry Gandhari, he had received a warm welcome from the king, but his son and Gandhari's brother, Shakuni, had been openly rude and contemptuous.

'Why do we get the blind brother?' he had sneered at Bhishma. 'The real prize here is Pandu, is it not?'

Bhishma had been calm and respectful and spoken up for Dhritarashtra. Yet, it was Gandhari who swayed the argument. She had told her father and brother that this was the match that she wanted. It was then that she had produced the silken cloth and applied her blindfold, tying it on herself. The king and Shakuni had been aghast and done all they could to talk her out of it, but Gandhari would not change her mind. She had not removed the scarf since and clearly never would.

Dhritarashtra was instantly entranced by Gandhari. Though he could not see her delicate beauty as we could, he was overcome by her selflessness when she gently lifted his hands to let him feel the scarf before promising to wear it forever. It pleased me greatly to see my eldest grandson smile once more. After the reprimand from Bhishma, I had been careful to pay attention to Dhritarashtra and had spent much more time with him. He had been a little wary of my intentions at first and it had grieved me how little he trusted me, but over time and with my persistence, we formed a closer bond. But it wasn't until Gandhari came to the palace that he fully relaxed. In fact, he became a different man. The anger and resentment evaporated to be replaced by a lightness of spirit. He and Gandhari were a constant presence in the main hall and in the palace gardens, where they would sit close to one another, talking quietly for hours.

Dhritarashtra and Gandhari's wedding was a lavish four-day celebration. Despite his opposition to the event, Shakuni came to Hastinapur and brought many gifts. Many of our neighbouring kingdoms sent royal emissaries too, which made me believe that perhaps Bhishma had been right and the long period of unrest was over. We had finally turned the corner and hope could return to Hastinapur. It was so pleasing to see every one of our courtiers so relaxed and happy too. All the uncertainties in the aftermath of Bhishma's oath seemed to be long forgotten.

Once the feasts were over and the tables cleared away, we were free to turn our attentions to finding a match for Pandu. I had charged Bhishma with the task of finding the best match, but it was my grandson himself who made his choice. True to form, the headstrong young man announced one day that Shurasena, the King of Yadava, was allowing his daughter Kunti to choose her own husband. He would, he declared, go to Mathura to collect his bride. In his mind, there was no possibility that the princess could choose anyone else. He was assured of victory here as much as he had been every time he had ridden his chariot into battle.

Sure enough, Pandu arrived back at the palace just a week later, a young woman standing at his side in his chariot. It was, of course, Kunti. She was mesmerising, almost ethereal in her beauty. Her figure was slim yet shapely, and her skin seemed to shimmer like amber. Perhaps most noticeable were her dark, almond-shaped eyes that crinkled at the sides when she laughed. And she did laugh a lot as Pandu told the story of how she had been unable to resist his charms and that it had been no contest once she had set eyes upon him among all the suitors who had travelled to Mathura.

Everyone had crowded around as Pandu led his future bride into the court. They knew they were in for a treat. Whenever the king returned from one of his battles, he would always regale them with elaborate stories about what had gone on. This, however, was the most important conquest of his life, or so he announced as he introduced Kunti.

'Fortunately, though,' he added with a comical bow to Kunti, 'I did not need to fight for one moment to subdue my enemy, the other suitors. They instantly recognised a superior foe.'

Watching Kunti as Pandu held court, the assembled crowd roaring with laughter at his antics, I had a sudden feeling that something was not quite right. That she was as smitten with Pandu as he was with her was unmistakable, but instinctively, I saw sadness in her eyes too. Was it sadness? No, perhaps it was something else. Try as I might, I couldn't put my finger on it.

As Kunti settled into the palace, I found it more difficult to get to know her than Gandhari. She was always charming and ready to talk, but whatever it was I had seen that first day was an ever-present shadow. It was like she was holding something back, something she didn't want to share.

And then, I knew it. I knew what that look meant. I had seen it a thousand times before, reflected back at me whenever I looked in the mirror. This princess had a secret.

When I understood this, everything made sense. She was happy, but something haunted her. For several days, I battled with my conscience, wondering if I should ask her about her secret. Would she think me nosey or interfering? I was neither. I simply knew what a weight off my shoulders it had been when I had finally revealed my own secret. And if I had not revealed it, well, I didn't want to think about that anymore. That was in the past. Even as

I ran it through in my mind, I already knew it was nonsense to imagine that asking Kunti a direct question would elicit a direct answer. If someone had done the same with me all those years ago, I would not have said a word. The only reason I did, finally, reveal my secret was because I had to. The time had been right.

I resolved to say nothing for now. One day, when we knew each other a little better, I would give her the opportunity to share, but I would not force it.

Pandu and Kunti's wedding was quite the celebration. I was mindful to keep the scale of it on par with the festivities we'd held for Dhritarashtra and Gandhari's wedding. I had learned my lesson. But even so, it was a much more raucous event. While Dhritarashtra and Gandhari were happy to sit and talk with their guests, Pandu wanted everyone to dance and sing. Simply eating and talking was anathema to the king. I lost count of the number of times during the celebration that he would suddenly appear, clasp his hands around my waist and demand that I dance with him.

'It is your turn, Grandmother,' he said, spinning me around.

No amount of telling him that I was getting too old for this and it was not dignified would stop him.

'You have more life and energy than any woman half your age!' he said.

That young man was irrepressible. After twirling me around the floor, he did the same to Ambika and Ambalika, who both giggled like young children. He even managed to get Bhishma dancing. Bhishma, the demigod, who was always more comfortable conversing with his generals or ministers!

When I was finally allowed to return to my seat, panting with exhaustion at my exertions, Bhishma joined me.

'That Pandu!' he said.

'But look,' I said, 'What do you see?'

'Your grandson behaving like a crazy person?'

'No. Well, yes. But what I see is a hall full of very happy people. Did you ever imagine this could happen?'

We were silent for a moment as we drank in the scene before us. There was once a time when both of us could never even dare to hope for such a moment. Pandu, no, *all* my grandchildren, had brought such happiness to Hastinapur.

It took a great deal of time for the palace to settle down to normal routine following the festivities. Everyone had enjoyed themselves so much that they yearned for another wedding and then another. The atmosphere was light, though. It was impossible not to be buoyed by the atmosphere of hope and joy.

Pandu, despite no longer being on perpetual campaigns because Hastinapur was at peace, chose not to take over the day-to-day business of the kingdom. His brother Vidur and Bhishma were far better for this, he declared, and better qualified for the task.

'It is for the good of the kingdom,' he declared, hand on heart.

It was the smile that played across his lips that showed he was teasing. He had heard that phrase so many times as he grew up, as Bhishma and I did all we could to strengthen Hastinapur. Instead, Pandu would pass most days hunting or training his army, or sometimes walking in the forest with Kunti.

I was pleased to see that Dhritarashtra had begun to spend a lot more time within the main court, Gandhari always at his side. He had a particular interest in the judicial system. He was meticulous in his work too. In any dispute, he was never too quick to judge, but would seek out the full picture from both sides before spending time on his deliberations.

Day by day, there was less and less for me to do. All the tasks that I had shouldered while Bhishma had been elsewhere were now taken by my grandsons. Gandhari and Kunti had also taken over much of the running of the palace, directing the maids and chefs to make sure the ebb and flow of palace life ran smoothly. Meanwhile, Bhishma, Vidur and Dhritarashtra were on top of the administration in Hastinapur. It was a strange feeling. I had been racing through life at full pelt for so long that it was difficult at first to slow down and let go. For a while, I felt listless, even a little irritable. Then, I would remind myself that this was what we had wanted and I should take solace in that.

I returned to my daily chariot rides with Sarathee. How pleasing it was to see my favourite gardens just outside the city once more! They were as well kept as ever, and breathing in the scent of the abundant flowers never failed to lift the spirits. My other most treasured destination was the river. There was something so calming about sitting on the bank, staring out over the water. I was suddenly my 20-year-old self once more, on my breaks between ferrying customers. I'd smile at the antics of the birds which swooped low to pick the insects off the water's surface, and then quickly dart away to avoid whatever lurked beneath the surface. My most cherished sight was the brightly coloured great hornbill. I kidded myself it had returned to pay me a visit. Yet, this could not possibly be the same one I had seen with Shantanu more than four decades ago. That hornbill, like my dear husband, would be long gone. A part of me wondered if I should ask for a small boat to be built for me. I could row myself to the middle of the river to look at that hornbill more closely when he paid another visit. Perhaps, though, I was getting too old to be rowing myself across the river.

On some days, Kunti would accompany me on my journeys away from the palace. We had gradually grown closer, not least because we discovered that we shared a passion for nature. To begin with, when we visited the gardens, we would sit mostly in silence beside the pools or would take long circuits on foot, laughing as we weaved our way around the tame peacocks. Over time, she spoke more, though. She was much more serious than her husband, but then everyone seemed serious as compared to Pandu. It was clear she thought deeply about things and liked to work things through in her mind before she gave an opinion.

After we'd been to the garden several times, I asked Kunti if she would like to accompany me to the river and she happily agreed. We set off early in the morning so we could have some time there before needing to retreat to the shade to get away from the midday sun. The day was just beginning to break as we headed through the city, and the people were starting to emerge from their houses, ready to begin their day's work.

'This reminds me so much of where I came from,' I said. 'Not the city. I came from a tiny village, where there was barely a handful of houses. I mean heading to the river at daybreak.'

'Do you miss it?' Kunti asked.

Did I? What a question! I was not really sure, even though I had spent so much time of late reflecting on my early life. Perhaps I did, a little. Things had been a lot simpler then.

We reached the outskirts of the city, and Sarathee deftly executed the sharp right turn to pick up the track that would lead us to the river. In the far distance, I could already see the rays of early sunlight reflecting off the surface of the water.

'Bits, yes,' I said at last. 'So much about that time changed my life.'

Kunti looked thoughtful, but didn't reply. For a short time, the only noise was the clack of the horses' hooves and the rumble of chariot wheels against the sand and rocks of the track. When we were a short distance from the river, Sarathee stopped the chariot and helped us both down. As was our custom, he would steer the chariot into the copious shade shared by the banyan tree and wait there until we were ready to return.

'What do you know of Pandu's father?' I asked as Kunti and I fell into step with one another, walking towards the river's edge.

I had often wondered about this. Twenty years or more ago, everyone in the court knew of the *niyoga* and of my relationship with Sage Vyasa. It had been accepted, even celebrated, because it had changed everything. But stories like these get forgotten. Life moves on. I didn't mind. I would even have preferred it. I also couldn't assume that Pandu had spoken to his wife about it.

'I … I know a little,' Kunti said cautiously. 'Sage Vyasa is your son.'

We had reached the water's edge now and settled down in the soft grass. I kicked off my slippers and Kunti did the same. It was refreshing to dangle our feet in the cool water.

'Let me tell you my story,' I said, staring out over the water.

Strangely, I no longer found it difficult to talk about what had happened that day. I spoke about my little boat, the appearance of Saga Parashara, the mystical fog and his two boons. The hardest part of the story was describing how I took my infant son to the forest and left him with the sages.

'I kept it secret for so many years,' I said. 'It was too painful to even say it out loud. But then, I had to share it. Sometimes, things happen and you are left with no choice.'

Turning to face Kunti, I saw that she was crying. Her whole face was wet with tears.

'I'm so sorry, I didn't mean to upset you. Forgive me. I thought …'

'No, no,' Kunti said, wiping her tears and returning my gaze. 'You did not upset me. I am so grateful that you shared your story.'

My young companion looked in turmoil. Then, she swallowed hard.

'I … I have a secret,' she said.

I had not spoken about my secret to encourage her to tell me hers, but now that I thought about it, I realised that we were always going to reach this moment. The gods had brought us together. Two women who had both borne the weight of a huge secret alone for so long. Who better to help one another?

'You don't have to talk about it.'

'I do. I want to. If it was to be anyone, I am glad it is you.'

I didn't speak as I waited for Kunti to gather her thoughts. I knew how difficult this could be. I remembered the feeling of sheer terror when I realised I would need to reveal everything to Bhishma. I had not even managed to do it myself, instead leaving it to my son, the good sage. What courage and strength of mind this young woman had!

'I too was visited by a sage,' she began. 'The legendary Sage Durvasa.'

She blushed a little, adding quickly that she would spare me the details.

'He said that he was so delighted by me, by my patience and devotion, that he would give me a divine mantra. This mantra would enable me to invoke any god of my choosing and he would bless me with a child.'

She shook her head and closed her eyes.

'I was a silly, foolish young girl,' she said, laughing softly at herself. 'I decided to test the mantra. Even now I don't know why.'

'Curiosity?'

'Yes, possibly. Naivety too, I suppose. Whatever it was, I chanted the mantra, and it worked straight away. I invoked the sun god, Surya. I had no reason to doubt the sage, nor the power of his mantra, but how could I have summoned up one of the greatest deities to my room? I was mortified.'

Kunti put her head into her hands.

'And he blessed you with a child?'

'Yes, a son.'

My poor Kunti! She didn't need to voice the pain and embarrassment of her predicament. I knew it so well. Yet, even worse than those first thoughts of the shame of bearing a child as an unmarried mother was what came next. I could still vividly remember that trip into the forest where I had given up my small baby and, even worse, that walk home alone. That feeling of complete emptiness was overwhelming. Tears came to my eyes at the memory.

'Where is he now?'

Kunti leaned forward, her palms together in prayer, and stared at the river before her.

'I don't know,' she said quietly. 'I put him in a basket and brought him to the Ganges. I set him afloat.'

She had barely said the last word before she let out a sob of anguish. I could picture her as a young girl, walking away from the river feeling like her heart would break. All because of a foolish, impetuous mistake.

I put an arm around her shoulders and squeezed her tightly.

'You must not blame yourself. I am quite certain that the gods will have looked after him. He is, after all, a demigod. Perhaps you will even meet one day?'

Kunti tried to smile. 'I hope so.'

Both of us were silent once again, lost in our own thoughts about a single event that can change everything.

'Come, it is growing too warm to sit here in the sun,' I said at last. 'Let us return to Sarathee.'

I helped Kunti to her feet and tenderly brushed away the last of her tears.

'I hope you didn't feel obliged to tell me your secret because I had shared mine. No one should feel they have to give up their secrets. They should only ever have to be revealed if the situation is absolutely desperate.'

Kunti managed another weak smile to show she understood.

'I am grateful to you for sharing it, though. Perhaps, in some small way, it has helped you to voice it. I know that it made a big difference to me.'

We were almost back at the chariot by now, and I waved at Sarathee who had already spotted us and was preparing the horses.

'You have my word that I will not share it with anyone, ever,' I said while we were still out of the charioteer's hearing.

Chapter Seventeen

Kunti was radiant. As we travelled back to the palace, the smile upon her face was infectious. Even Sarathee, who tended to look quite serious when he was driving the chariot, was grinning. Sharing her secret had lifted a weight from her shoulders. Just telling one person was all she had needed. I understood exactly how she felt. I had been in her position for years and years. Each time I had smiled, or laughed at a joke, I had checked myself. I'd silently chide myself: *How could I be happy when I had left my child in the forest without a second thought?* The pain had not lessened with the passing of the years. The only time it had finally been vanquished was when my son had come to court. The circumstances had been less than ideal, but at least I finally saw for myself that the sage was happy and was living the life he wanted to lead.

Perhaps I should have confided in someone sooner. But who would that have been? There had been no one I trusted enough. Then, once I had formed a close bond with Bhishma, I hadn't wanted to say anything because I didn't want him to think any less of me. Eventually, I had had no choice but to tell him.

There was no point holding on to regrets or asking 'what if'. I needed to live in the here and now. My oath to protect Hastinapur had not changed, and this meant supporting Pandu and Kunti was my priority.

We pulled into the courtyard just after lunchtime. It was clear right away that something was up. There were never this many people around at this time of day. It was just too hot. Littered around the yard were little piles of wrapped-up goods and boxes stacked one upon another. They told a familiar story: A campaign had begun and no doubt Pandu had left in a hurry, instructing his generals to gather their men and follow.

'Bhishma said this was all over,' I said quietly to myself as I dismounted.

I glanced at Kunti and saw that she too had read the meaning of the chaotic scene. Her smile had vanished entirely.

Pausing only to exchange a reassuring glance, I made my way into the palace. I had barely reached the top of the steps when I saw Bhishma. By the look of it, he had been on his way to intercept me.

The impulsive part of me wanted to shout that he had said this was all over and things would be peaceful now. I hadn't dared to believe it was true, and I was right. But I stopped myself. I had been too harsh on my good friend in the past. We both still had the best interests of the kingdom at heart.

'Mother,' he said. 'How was your ride out this fine day?'

'Fine, fine,' I said, a little too quickly.

'Things look quite busy here …' I added.

Bhishma looked past me at the activity in the yard.

'Indeed, Pandu is on the move.'

'But', I paused while I chose my words, 'Who is the new threat?'

Bhishma laughed softly.

'Pandu,' he said.

'Pandu?'

Bhishma swept his arm towards the main hall of the palace, indicating we should go there, even though the vast area seemed just as busy as the yard with people scurrying back and forth.

'Come, let us get out of the way,' he said, 'so we can talk.'

We walked across the main hall, weaving our way around sacks and boxes and servants rushing back and forth, with armfuls of kit in their hands. It was difficult not to cry out with impatience. I was desperate to know what was going on.

When we reached the justices' room, I did not sit down. Turning to face Bhishma, I looked at him expectantly.

'He has gone to meet King Madra,' he said.

'King Madra is attacking us?'

This surprised me. We had been at peace with Madras for many years, certainly before I had even come to the palace. The king had even attended the weddings of both Pandu and Dhritarashtra.

'No. There are rumours that the king is already in Hastinapur, but we don't know why. However, Pandu is intent on mounting a campaign against Madras.'

I shook my head. This did not make any sense to me. We were at peace.

'Why? Why now? Perhaps he is coming to pay his respects. Pandu is putting himself and the kingdom in danger.'

If I lived a thousand years, I would never understand men and their passion for war.

'It is not about fighting,' Bhishma said, once more knowing exactly where my thoughts were. 'A kingdom does not remain strong by standing still. Sometimes, changing the contours of the map is the best way to secure the future. It is a demonstration of … of strength.'

benefit. Even more so, it could be dangerous for future diplomatic relations with the respective kingdoms. No one wanted to hear that their husbands, brothers, sons and nephews were needlessly sacrificed to save face. Even if they did somehow manage to emerge victorious, it would leave their army so depleted that it might struggle against subsequent attackers.

Pandu had always fallen firmly into the camp of never yielding. To be fair, with Bhishma on his side, both as a trainer and an accomplished fighter, there had never been much cause to even consider it. In almost every battle they fought, they had rapidly received submissions from the enemy to negotiate surrender. There would be a pitched battle for a few days, certainly no more than a week, and an approach would be made. I prayed that this would be the case this time too, that there would be the bare minimum of fighting and Pandu and Bhishma would be home within weeks, with the king happily recounting a fresh story from the battlefield.

Even I was surprised when I heard the unmistakable noise of a large number of chariots thundering towards the palace. Hardly two weeks had passed since Pandu had left. That was barely time to get to Madras and back, let alone engage with the enemy. It was still early, and the sun had just appeared above the far horizon. As was increasingly happening these days, I had awoken early and was taking a turn around the corridors, collecting my thoughts before the day ahead.

Looking out from my usual balcony perch, I first saw the dust kicked up by the distant chariots. Then, the unmistakable image of Bhishma appeared. He was out front, standing proud, his chariot and golden armour glinting in the first rays of the sun. Pandu was just behind, but his carriage was slightly obscured by the larger figure of his mentor. I could just about make out the top of Pandu's head and breathed a sigh of relief. They were safe.

I took the split-second decision not to wake up Kunti and ran down the stairs, unable to stop smiling. Once Pandu settled back into the palace, she would have him all to herself. Now, though, I could spend some time alone with two of my favourite people. It would be like old times. I was already picturing myself laughing uproariously at Pandu's stories while Bhishma shook his head pretending to disapprove. The closeness between the two after a campaign was always wonderful to see.

I reached the courtyard just as Bhishma's chariot swung through the palace gates. He spotted me straight away and waved. I was just about to return the gesture, when my hand froze in mid-air. Pandu's carriage had swept in just behind Bhishma's, and he was not alone. Standing beside him was a statuesque beauty, clad in a simple white silk sari. Her slender arms were covered in dozens of delicate gold bangles, which travelled in a row from her wrists to the midpoint of her forearm, leaving the rest of her arms exposed up to her shoulders. Her long, glossy hair was looped in a simple style atop her head, held in place by a golden tiara. Not a single hair looked out of place despite the long journey. The woman's youth and beauty were almost breathtaking.

When I looked back at Bhishma, I saw he had been following my gaze. Yet, when we exchanged glances, his expression gave nothing away. He simply leapt off his chariot in his usual athletic manner and walked to my side.

'Mother,' he said in a low voice. 'We are home safe, as I promised.'

'I am so glad,' I said. 'And curious.'

Bhishma resumed his blank expression. This was something for Pandu to explain.

I watched with growing impatience as Pandu jumped from his chariot and then walked around to the other side to help the tall beauty down. She took his hand and stepped down with the well-practised and unmistakable grace of a princess. What was most noticeable about the scene was the warm smile the two exchanged. No words were said, but it was as though the pair had known each other for a hundred years. What was going on? Just weeks earlier, he had been exchanging the same looks with Kunti.

The two began to walk towards me. Pandu had his usual swagger, a confident grin upon his face, but I knew him well enough to see that all was not as it seemed. He was unsure, but as was his way, he was determined to brazen his way through it with a joke and a smile. Tucking herself in a few steps behind him, the woman looked much less sure of herself. It wasn't until Pandu was just a few steps away that he broke his silence. Breaking into a wide smile, he bowed low, sweeping his hand skywards with a flourish before bending low to touch my feet.

'Grandmother,' he said.

'My King Pandu.'

I stayed silent as he straightened up and then glanced nervously over his shoulder at the woman.

'May I present Madri to you?'

Madri stepped forward, and now that she was close to me, I could see that she was trembling. There were goosebumps on her bare arms, and her dark eyes were wide with fear. I worried she may pass out at any moment and put a hand out to stop her bending down to kiss my feet.

'Please, my child, do not fear me,' I said.

Madri's head remained low. She did not wish to meet my gaze.

'Pandu?' I said, turning to the king.

I needed an explanation.

'I would like to say it was the greatest battle ever seen,' Pandu began.

I put up my hand. This was not the time for his epic stories, and the king immediately understood.

'We marched to Madras, but the king didn't have any appetite for battle,' he said, his tone now serious. 'Not a single arrow was dispatched. Not one.'

Unable to resist, Pandu chuckled. 'King Madra heard about the great warrior Pandu and surrendered immediately rather than face my wrath.'

I did not return his smile and his own quickly evaporated.

'We had not long arrived in Madras and picked out the spot for the battle. The king arrived with a handful of guards and came to speak to me. Standing beside him on his chariot was Madri.'

The woman was still looking at the ground, but dipped her head a little to show this was true.

'The king said he wanted to prove his peaceful intentions by offering his sister Madri as a gift of good faith.'

I was still not sure I completely understood. This was not an unusual act, or so I had been told. But I sensed that Pandu was holding something back.

'I would like to make Madri my second wife,' he said quickly.

A confusing mixture of emotions threatened to engulf me. I was surprised that Pandu had fallen for this woman so quickly, yet he was clearly smitten by Madri. I was also profoundly saddened for Kunti. She had always been so loyal to Pandu; her every action was weighed in consideration of what would be best for her husband. How would she feel about sharing him with another woman? As always, I thought of the wider implications too. What would the courtiers think? Everything had settled down, and the kingdom was stable for the first time in years. This could very well upend everything we had achieved.

I looked at Bhishma and knew he was having the same thoughts, only he'd had longer to go through the implications.

'In all cases, the answers to your questions are in how we present this,' he said. 'Both to the individuals concerned and the wider court ...'

'I will not accept this gift unless Kunti sanctions it,' Pandu said, interrupting Bhishma's flow.

Suddenly, the king's expression changed and the blood seemed to drain from his face. He was not looking at me, though; he was staring at the palace steps. Without turning around, I knew that Kunti had arrived.

It was Bhishma who moved first. He darted up the steps and took Kunti's hand before leading her down them towards us. As he did so, he leaned in and spoke to her quietly.

'We are very sorry to awake you so early with all of this commotion. It is lovely to be home, though, and to see you again.'

There was no way to read what Kunti was thinking. Her face was completely blank as she looked first at Pandu and then at Madri.

'My Queen,' Pandu said. 'How long ... how long had you been there?'

'Long enough to hear everything.'

Kunti's voice was icy calm. No one said a word as we collectively held our breaths, and I had to stop myself from rushing forward to put a protective arm around Kunti.

Pandu swallowed hard.

'I meant it. I will not marry Madri if you do not agree to it.'

All eyes were on Kunti, and my heart went out to her. No one should have to make a choice like that about the one they love, especially not in such a public forum. I sent up a silent prayer of thanks that this woman had such inner strength, as I now knew so well.

I watched with a mixture of pain and pride as Kunti tilted her head to indicate her consent. Then, without a word, she stepped forward and embraced Madri.

'Welcome, sister,' she said.

Then, she took the younger woman's hand and led her towards the palace steps. In that one moment, I knew, more than ever, that Kunti had been the perfect match for Pandu. Even as I watched the pair talking in low voices as they walked inside, I still felt uneasy. It had taken years, but Hastinapur had finally felt at peace with itself. Would this sudden change in circumstances create an imbalance?

In the weeks that followed, I found that my fears over the reaction of the kingdom to this match had been unfounded. Everyone had quickly taken the new queen into their hearts. Madri, though, who was by nature shy and reserved, had taken a little longer to settle in, despite the attention paid to her by her new sister, Kunti. I could not really blame her. It must have been a challenge to adapt to her new life under the glare of the ever-curious courtiers, who watched her every move.

It was Vidur who suggested the solution. We were meeting to discuss some palace business when, completely unprompted, he wondered out loud if Pandu might need to take a break with his two wives.

'Ever since he was crowned, he has been out fighting on one campaign or another,' he said. 'He must be exhausted. Hastinapur needs a king at the peak of his powers. Why not give him some recovery time? He can spend some time in that beloved forest of his and simply relax with Kunti and Madri.'

What a wise man Vidur was! This was exactly what this small family needed to adapt to their new dynamic. It had been a wise choice to appoint him Prime Minister.

'But what of the kingdom in his absence? Do we just carry on as we do when Pandu and Bhishma are on campaign?'

Vidur looked thoughtful.

'I have considered this,' he said. 'And I have a suggestion which may please a number of parties. What about asking Dhritarashtra to stand in?'

It was the perfect idea. Dhritarashtra had never got over being passed over for the throne, so this would be his dream. The kingdom had been in a completely different state when that decision had been taken and was now in a far stronger position. Vidur had also reorganised everything so the kingdom ran smoother than ever before. The threat of war had largely subsided and, of course, Bhishma was still there, a reassuring presence that underpinned it all.

'Yes,' I breathed. 'Yes, let's go and speak with all of them right away.'

Chapter Eighteen

It was rare for me to actively dislike anyone. Right from the time I was a small child, if I found myself unable to agree with someone's point of view, I would try to find something about them that I could get on board with. I found this impossible with Shakuni.

Gandhari's brother had arrived in the palace on almost the exact day that Dhritarashtra had taken over the throne, and he never left. Before this time, he had been a rare visitor to Hastinapur. On the odd occasion he had visited the palace, he had kept his distance from his brother-in-law, preferring to lobby ministers or trying to curry favour with Vidur. He'd made no effort to speak to me either, which I was fine about. In particular, he kept his distance from Bhishma. It was rumoured that he had never forgiven Bhishma for suggesting his sister marry 'the blind prince', as he would sneeringly put it when he thought he was out of earshot. By the malevolent looks that Shakuni sent in Bhishma's direction whenever they were in the same room, I could well believe it.

There was something about this man that instinctively made me uneasy. He was nothing remarkable to look at, shorter than most of the men at the palace, with a large, round belly, which he seemed to enjoy showing off. He had the annoying habit of stroking it tenderly like a cat when he spoke with people. The most noticeable thing about him was his dark, almost black hair, which was rarely brushed, and his full beard and moustache. It was almost impossible to see his mouth under all that facial hair or to tell if he was smiling or scowling. One glance at his raven-like eyes, though, seemed to confirm it was mostly the latter. Despite his apparent lack of attention to his personal grooming, he was a vain man. He invariably wore a large, brightly coloured silk turban adorned with multiple chains of pearls and gold, with many more elaborate chains slung around his bulging neck.

My greatest concern was that Shakuni had a disconcerting air of cunning and deviousness and always appeared to be plotting something. Not long after he arrived, a new chair appeared on the royal dais. No one could tell me where it had come from. It had simply been placed just to the right and a little behind the ornate golden royal throne. Each day, when Dhritarashtra took up his position on the king's throne to receive applications from the various people who would seek royal counsel, Shakuni could be found sitting in this new seat. He would lean forward as each new supplicant made his plea, listening intently. Then, he would whisper something to Dhritarashtra, who would incline his head to take it all in. It was only after Shakuni had made his feelings known that Dhritarashtra would speak to the person before him.

I had no idea what Shakuni was saying, nor indeed why he felt the need to appoint himself the king's unofficial advisor. Everything had been working smoothly before he arrived. Worse still, the long pause that ensued while Shakuni whispered to Dhritarashtra gave the palace an air of detached menace. The people in front of the dais would shuffle their feet nervously, most likely wondering if they were right to bother such important people with their troubles, even though that was exactly what we were there for.

I had tried to speak with Dhritarashtra, but he brushed away my concerns.

'I am the king now,' he said. 'I hardly need to remind you that this is the foremost position in the kingdom. You, and my people, must trust my judgement.'

Gandhari said nothing. The fact that she continued to wear her blindfold day after day was an indication of the depth of her loyalty to her husband. She would have stood by him whatever he said or did. She did not appear to be cross or unsettled by her brother either.

Over time, fewer people came to the palace to seek advice. Word was getting around. The court was not the same light-hearted place it was under Pandu, nor did it offer the wise and considered counsel that was available under Vidur. The advice that Dhritarashtra gave was often mean-spirited or offered no leeway for discussion or diplomacy.

It struck me that an individual leader could make such a difference, but that had been the point all along. My vow to protect the kingdom had been born out of guilt at its loss of Bhishma as its figurehead. He was head and shoulders above everyone as the right choice for king. We had, I believed, managed to recover from that blow, at least as far as we were able. Yet, we now seemed at risk of lurching into another crisis.

As I racked my brains trying to come up with a solution that did not, yet again, put Dhritarashtra at a disadvantage, I turned to my oft-used fallback position: What would the mighty Bhishma do? I realised with a start that I barely saw my good friend these days. Where once we were so close, spending hour upon hour to make sure that the kingdom was safe, he barely came to the main hall these days. He left it to Dhritarashtra, perhaps safe in the knowledge that Vidur was working hard in the background, ensuring that the wheels of power continued to roll smoothly despite the deficiencies of his older brother and Shakuni.

It took me a while to track Bhishma down. I searched the corridors, then the chambers in the main part of the palace, and eventually found him outside in the area near the stables, where all the chariots were kept. The unused chariots, in a neat row, appeared to tell the story of a kingdom at peace. In reality, though, it felt anything but.

'My mother Satyavati,' Bhishma said when he saw me approaching.

It was his usual greeting, but was I imagining it, or did it not sound as warm as before?

'Are you looking for me? Or is it Sarathee you need? I think he has only been back for a few days ...'

He let the comment hang in the air. I had been sending Sarathee into the forest quite regularly with supplies for Pandu, Kunti and Madri. When I first began doing it, Bhishma had teased me, telling me that the forest was already plentiful in natural food and there was no need to send anything from the palace. We both knew why I did it, though. I missed Pandu so much and felt starved of his company, which brought light to even the darkest of rooms. Sarathee never had much to report from his trips to the forest. The routine there seemed quite simple. The three spent much of their time enjoying one another's company, going for walks or riding horses. The only recent change of note had been news that Pandu and his wives were becoming frequent callers on Sage Kindama, who had a small dwelling near theirs. Sarathee reported back to me that the sage had been encouraging Pandu to get on with starting a family, since he must fulfil Lord

Brahma's debt and procreate. Pandu didn't seem to be in any rush, observed the charioteer.

The moment he had said it, my first thought was that there *was* a rush. Pandu, like me, must look to the future, and that meant ensuring a strong bloodline.

'No, no, it was you I was looking for. I just wanted to speak to you,' I said, suddenly unsure of what I wanted to say.

Bhishma looked at me expectantly. I hated how we were no longer a significant part of one another's lives.

'I'm worried about Shakuni. I don't even know why he is here. He just seems to make Dhritarashtra tense with all that whispering.'

Bhishma laughed softly.

'Ah, I would agree that there are many things you could criticise Shakuni for, but I wouldn't lay that one at his door. That young man has been wound more tightly than any bowstring since his birth. Don't you remember how quick he was to lash out even as a boy?'

Bhishma was right, but Shakuni wasn't helping.

'Besides, Vidur is there for any significant decisions,' he went on. 'There is no real chance of things going awry, whatever Shakuni is trying to do.'

I admired Bhishma's optimism, but I was not as convinced. Something didn't *feel* right.

'I think it is time for Pandu to return. He's been away too long.'

Bhishma's expression changed to one of bemusement.

'It's been six months …'

'… but it is time. Things just felt better when he was here. Everything ran as it should, and that was what we have both worked so hard for.'

My good friend shrugged. He knew I could not be dissuaded from this course of action.

'Very well. Would you like me to speak with Sarathee? You had also better start thinking about how you can tell Dhritarashtra. It is not something he will welcome, nor will Shakuni, if your instincts are correct.'

Bhishma was right, but now that I had made up my mind, I knew it was the right decision. Pandu was the king that Hastinapur wanted and respected. Far from being the weak king that his childhood appeared to indicate, he was a popular figurehead. We needed to get the balance of the court back in order.

I felt full of hope as I watched Sarathee depart the following day, although that hope mixed with a slight feeling of dread that I would need to break the news to Dhritarashtra. He would not be happy to step aside once more. Perhaps he would be even less amenable than before, now that he had had a taste of the power he craved. I tried to comfort myself with the thought that my eldest grandson always knew the arrangement was temporary and that Pandu would return. Another positive would be that Shakuni would almost certainly vanish once it became clear that his place behind the throne was no longer available. I was sure that peace and calm would be restored to the palace in a matter of days. Just the thought of Pandu's laughter pealing out across the main hall and seeping down the endless corridors made me smile. This was the right thing to do.

As I took my usual early morning turn around the corridors, I calculated the number of days until Pandu's return. Based on Sarathee's usual visits, I reckoned it would be less than a week. On this basis, I would endeavour to speak with Dhritarashtra the day before his brother returned. All being well, we'd smooth things over and then Pandu's presence would do the rest. Shakuni might even skulk away before the royal party returned. The plan sounded perfect.

Each morning, I awoke with mixed emotions. My first thought each day was that my beloved Pandu was on his way home and the palace would be restored to happiness. Then, almost immediately, I was consumed by a deep feeling of dread. I needed to speak with Dhritarashtra.

I rehearsed and re-rehearsed what I might say. Nothing seemed to be quite right. I was almost certain he would retort that the throne was his rightful place and he had proved that now. How could I tell him that he was not suited to the role? And I had to contend with the knowledge that all the while we would be having this conversation, Shakuni would be glowering at me.

It took me a while to work out that this was not a burden I should be carrying alone. This was something I needed Bhishma for, perhaps Vidur too. Both had been instrumental in the original decision, so it made sense that they helped me this time. The relief was immense when I realised I had been so foolish for not thinking of this earlier. While Bhishma felt it was too soon to bring Pandu back, I had no doubt that he agreed that Pandu was the best king for Hastinapur.

I turned around and headed towards the staircase. If my calculations were correct, Sarathee was due back the day after tomorrow. We could get all of this ironed out and then prepare for the festivities.

I couldn't help giggling to myself as I jumped down the stone staircase, taking two steps at a time. I was behaving like a little girl, not the respected older stateswoman I was supposed to be. I was the queen mother.

The main hall of the palace was deserted. It was still quite early. I decided to see Vidur first. He always awoke early too and could invariably be found in one of the small anterooms off the hall, getting ahead of the business of the day. No doubt Bhishma would be out with the horses or practising his archery skills outside. I had barely reached the anteroom when the doors of the main hall burst open with an alarming crash. Nothing could have prepared me for the shock of seeing Pandu, not Sarathee, stagger through them, his eyes wide with fear.

'What is it?' I said, running towards him, just as he slumped to his knees.

Pandu looked crushed, his body heaving as he tried to catch his breath. He must have been driving that chariot at speed for hours. People began appearing through countless doorways, staring in wonder at the commotion. Vidur was already at my side, followed shortly by Bhishma.

'Fetch him some water,' Vidur said to a maid.

His voice was icy calm, but I knew him well enough to know he was deeply concerned.

Still Pandu did not speak. He simply couldn't find the words. The maid returned with a pitcher of cool water and poured a goblet for him. His hand shook alarmingly as he took it and gulped the liquid. Huge drops escaped and splashed upon his tunic. At last his thirst was sated, and he wiped a large hand across his mouth. His first four words shocked me to the core.

'I have been cursed,' he said.

My legs felt weak as I looked first at Pandu, whose head was once again slumped low in abject despair, and then at Bhishma and Vidur. No words could be worse.

It was Vidur who reacted first. He ordered two guards to help Pandu to his feet and lead him to one of the soft couches that ran the length of the main hall's walls. He spoke to his brother in hushed tones, telling him to take his time.

'Tell us the whole story.'

Bhishma stood at my side as I strained to hear each word as Pandu began his story in a shaky voice.

'Sarathee came to the forest, as instructed, to deliver his message. You know I would never refuse a request from the queen, so we all began to pack straight away.'

Pandu closed his eyes. I knew he was picturing the scene before him.

'We were happy,' he said, his voice barely a whisper now. 'Relaxed. The same for Kunti and Madri. The two are like sisters now.'

Once more, Pandu wiped his hand across his mouth. He was still breathing hard, but it was not because of his exertions now. It was because of what he was about to say.

'We were ready to go, all ready, when we heard a tiger. It must have been nearby because its roar was so distinctive. You know me—I can never resist a challenge. I was already weighing up my chances before Madri announced she would like its skin as a gift.'

Pandu shook his head.

'I should have … I should …'

'We all know you once you get something into your head,' Vidur said gently. 'Please continue.'

Pandu sighed.

'I had everything at the ready, all my hunting equipment. It was all to hand. Of course it was. It was packed and ready to go. I picked up the trail very quickly. In a matter of minutes, I heard the noise of what sounded like a deer in distress.

'I was sure the tiger had made its move and brought down its quarry.'

Pandu lapsed into silence. It was becoming too much. He could not bear the thought that we were judging him harshly.

'I mean, you would assume that, wouldn't you?' he said, his palms outstretched.

A few people in the small crowd nodded in assent, but no one interrupted.

'I crouched low and loaded my arrow. Just like I had done a thousand times before. Like you taught me, Bhishma. Then, I let it fly.'

Pandu looked stricken.

'I heard a loud scream. A human scream. I had shot Sage Kindama and his wife ...'

I caught my breath. Pandu had shot a sage? It could not be possible.

'... They'd been locked in an embrace, sitting in the shade of the banyan tree, and a single arrow pierced them both. It went right through, from the sage's back, into his wife ...'

For a few seconds, the room was completely silent as the gravity of the news sank in.

'Were they ... did they ... live?' I managed to say. My mouth felt dry.

For a few seconds, Pandu did not respond, simply turning his head from side to side. Then, in a hoarse whisper, he gave us a few more terrible details.

'The sage's wife died immediately, and by the time I reached them, the sage was taking his final breaths.'

My eyes were filled with tears, and I could no longer see the scene in front of me, all of us gathered around my grandson. My mind was too occupied imagining the scene he had described: the sage and his wife, slumped against a tree, blood oozing from their lifeless bodies.

A holy man. Pandu had shot a holy man. I wanted to leap ahead in the story to the curse, but I knew I needed to hear it as it happened.

'I did everything I could, I really did. I knelt by the sage and tried to stem the bleeding. Sage Kindama would not have any of it, even though the wound was deep. He batted away my hand.

'It was then, with his dying breaths, that he uttered his curse.'

Collectively, we held our breaths as we waited to hear of Pandu's fate. If Bhishma had not been standing so close, I felt sure I would have collapsed on the floor any moment.

'Sage Kindama declared that I would die the moment I embraced a woman.'

In a single moment, everything I had hoped for and dreamt about was shattered. Pandu would never ever be able to produce heirs, as we all hoped. His lineage was over. Forever. If he ever went anywhere near his two wives, he would die instantly.

The trial was brief. Too brief. Even so, it felt like it was spread over a thousand years. Each word lasted a week, each sentence a month. Why? Because any one of those words or sentences could have condemned Pandu, my perfect, wonderful, vibrant grandchild. They could have been the one that sealed his fate.

Justice is black and white, or at least that is how it tries to portray itself. I could have kicked myself looking back at all those years where I had overseen the judicial system of Hastinapur in the absence of Bhishma or Pandu. Supplicants would come to the court seeking redress for events that had upended their lives. Had I ever truly understood what that meant? Had I known how important each decision we made was to these individuals standing before us, trembling with anticipation? I did now.

The case before the highest court of Hastinapur was outwardly simple. Was the death of Sage Kindama murder or a terrible accident? Yet, the outcome of that either/or decision was devastating. If it were decreed to be murder, Pandu would be put to death for this most heinous of crimes. Even if it was agreed to be an accident, the punishment would be severe. No one, not even a king, can kill a holy man and simply move on with their lives.

That Pandu would never return to being king was a given. Pandu had declared that himself, even before the trial. Even if Pandu was convicted on the lesser charge, his life in Hastinapur, as we knew it, was over. He could not rule. Not after this. He asked his older brother Dhritarashtra to take his place as a proxy, thus helping him to achieve his lifelong wish and take the throne on a permanent basis. Pandu had said that Dhritarashtra would rule until his son was ready to do so, but we all knew this was impossible now. I loved my eldest grandchild, of course I did, but even I knew he was not the best man for the job. I had seen that already. We all had.

As I might have anticipated, Shakuni was beside himself with glee at the news. He did not have the good grace to even hide his excitement at the turn of events. Despite disparaging the 'blind brother' as he still sneeringly called Dhritarashtra when out of earshot, he'd long since understood the infinite possibilities of being the king's self-styled personal advisor. In the run-up to the trial, I realised that Bhishma, Vidur and I would need to find a solution to this or Hastinapur would almost certainly be made vulnerable by Shakuni's greed and ambition. For now, though, all I could do was to insist that Shakuni would not attend the trial.

The sight of him gloating would be too much, and he was bound to try to sway Dhritarashtra towards making a decision in his own best interests.

As long as I lived, I would never forget the sight of Pandu on the first morning of the trial. He was slumped in an ordinary chair in front of the ministers of the court, flanked by Kunti and Madri on smaller chairs either side of him. It looked so different from his normal stance, leaning back casually on his golden throne, a wide grin on his face, a loud laugh never far from his lips. His entire stature was diminished. Whatever punishment he received could not be worse than the one he had inflicted upon himself. Pandu was a broken man. Kunti and Madri were ashen-faced, their hands laid on their laps, gaze averted from the court.

Even though Shakuni was not in court, his presence was there. The text and tone of Dhritarashtra's opening statement betrayed the poison that had been dripped into his ear.

'The death of a sage—in whatever form—must be punished …' he began stridently.

I closed my eyes. My heart was thumping so hard in anger and frustration that the blood in my ears stopped me hearing the entire statement. I heard only snippets. Yet, each statement piled on the agony.

'No one, however noble their blood, is above the law of the kingdom …

'I may be Pandu's brother, and love and admire him deeply, but I am also the king …'

Glancing at Bhishma, I saw he was looking as calm and composed as ever. He'd anticipated this. His head was cocked slightly to one side as he absorbed what was being said, but he gave away nothing of what he was thinking. Vidur, who sat beside

Bhishma, was equally unruffled, listening intently and scribbling notes into a large ledger in front of him. I had put my entire fate into the hands of these people and knew I was right to do so, but it was still impossible to let myself relax.

When Dhritarashtra had finished, Bhishma got to his feet from his position to the right of the dais holding the royal thrones. There was a murmur of voices among the ministers. Everyone wanted to know what was to become of Pandu. He had been (*had been!*) a popular and much-liked king.

Pandu, who had mostly stared at the floor during his brother's speech, looked up to see Bhishma. His eyes were great pools of pain and sadness. This was a man who had accepted his fate. When their eyes met, master and pupil, Bhishma's head dipped in a sign of reassurance. I don't think many people would have even noticed it. I did, though. I had been on the receiving end of this look from the demigod a number of times through my life. It had the power of penetrating one's soul. I hoped it gave Pandu the comfort it had always given me in my darkest hours.

'Gentlemen and nobles of the esteemed court, and respected judges, I stand before you today not merely as an advocate for the accused, but as a seeker of justice in a matter that transcends the bounds of time and culture,' Bhishma began, his voice loud, yet steady. 'In the hallowed halls of this palace, we are here to review a tragic event set against the backdrop of wisdom and enlightenment.'

The main hall was silent, the atmosphere thick with anticipation. Everyone's attention was fixed on Bhishma and what he had to say. His presence was so commanding that it was almost intimidating.

'Our good king Pandu finds himself on trial for a deed most grave—the accidental death of a revered sage in the heartland of our ancient forests. We stand here at the crossroads of destiny, where the scales of justice must be delicately balanced against the inexorable weight of circumstance.'

I watched, transfixed, as Bhishma slowly walked to the centre of the dais and bowed to Dhritarashtra, reaching out to touch his face as a gesture of respect to the blind man, before turning to the people who crowded the main hall. As always, his physical presence and authority were impossible to ignore. His hair was white now, flowing gracefully around his broad shoulders, which were as muscular and toned as when we had first met at my father's house, what seemed like a hundred years ago. His eyes too were as deep and piercing as ever, reflecting the profound insight and knowledge he had amassed year after year. Despite his age, his vigour and mental abilities were undiminished, a testament to his divine lineage.

'It is crucial to recognize the inherent complexity of the human experience and the profound uncertainties that shroud it,' he said, his arms drawn wide, as if to embrace each person in the hall. 'In the annals of time, our actions are often the outcome of a delicate interplay between choice and fate. What happened on this particular occasion stands as a testament to the fragility of life and the unforeseen consequences that may arise from our endless dance with destiny.'

Bhishma paused to let the words sink in. He needn't have done so. Everyone there was hanging on to his every syllable.

'I do not need to tell you all how sages are held in the highest regard, thanks to their spirituality and single-minded pursuit of knowledge. The loss of one such revered figure is without any doubt a tragedy of monumental proportions. However, it is incumbent upon us to delve into the depths of intent and circumstance that led to this lamentable event.'

I stole a glance at Dhritarashtra. He'd done his best to set his face in a neutral manner, as though listening carefully to the evidence. He had not, however, managed to smooth out the deep frown that played across his brow. His opening statement played on the drama and emotions of the event, no doubt fed to him by his brother-in-law, whereas Bhishma spoke with reason. It was impossible that he had not realised this.

'We cannot lose sight of the fact that King Pandu did not set out with malice aforethought, nor did he harbour any ill-will towards the sage in question. Quite the opposite, in fact. He and Sage Kindama had spent much time with each other in the past, not least because their forest dwellings were close by. Their wives enjoyed each other's company too. No, the unfolding of events was propelled by the capricious currents of chance, a sequence of happenings that drew together the king and the sage in a fateful encounter.'

I listened with sadness as Bhishma described the details of the accident. However much I wanted to block my ears, I made myself listen once more. As he came to the sage's dying words, I prayed that they would have a different outcome. A new, happier ending, but of course, they did not. I felt a warm tear running down my cheek and brushed it away. It would not do for the court to see their queen in such distress. Kunti and Madri could not help it, though. The faces of both of Pandu's wives were soaked in tears.

Looking around the court as Bhishma began his closing address, I saw that they were not the only ones in distress. Many of the nobles looked stricken, their faces pale. Even some of the experienced justices could not hide their expressions of sympathy.

Bhishma was now pacing slowly back and forth across the dais, seemingly making eye contact with each and every person in the room as he spoke.

'As we navigate the corridors of time in our pursuit of justice, let us not be blind to the nuances that define the human condition,' he said. 'King Pandu is an unwitting actor in this cosmic drama, a mere mortal at the mercy of the consequences of an inadvertent collision between two lives.

'King Pandu has been a just, fair and capable ruler. He is not seeking exoneration, only your understanding. I implore this venerable court to temper its judgment with wisdom, to weigh the evidence with discernment, and to recognise the shades of grey that colour the canvas of human existence.

'May the scales of justice find equilibrium in the face of the enigmatic dance of life and death.'

After this powerful speech, there was no question that the court would agree that this was an accident. A terrible, terrible accident. Even so, the punishment was severe. The justices ruled that Pandu was to be banished to the forest to do penance for the rest of his life.

My grandson accepted his fate without complaint. He wanted to go. He knew he had done something awful and accepted the verdict without question. He was distressed about leaving the palace, but it could be no other way. Most of all, though, he felt he had let Bhishma down. He loved and admired the man, as we all did, but the pair had an especially close bond. It had been forged as they fought side by side on the battlefields.

It broke my heart to see the interaction between them immediately after the verdict. The terms of the sentence still hung in the air, and Pandu was on his feet, but looking at the floor. Bhishma had immediately crossed to him and placed both hands on his shoulders, leaning in close to speak to him. No one could hear what was said, but Pandu bowed his head to his mentor, his face pale. How different this scene was to the many times I had seen them together in the past! Pandu with a wide grin on his face, laughing loudly, while Bhishma chuckled and shook his head in mock exasperation. What I would give to relive that just one more time!

I was shaken out of my trance by the approaching figures of Madri and Kunti. Both women looked shattered, but they clung together for comfort. I was glad that they had become like sisters. They would need each other more than ever now that their husband was being sent from them. I resolved to make it my mission to make sure they were looked after and did not become like ghosts, haunting the palace corridors, ignored and alone.

'Queen Mother,' Kunti said, bowing low to kiss my feet, 'I have, no, we have, a request that only you can grant.'

Taking the hand of each of Pandu's wives in mine, I formed the best smile I could in the circumstances by way of encouragement.

'You know I would always do anything I can for you,' I said. 'You have made such a difference here, to Pandu, to everyone, and I want to repay that …'

'… Then, let us go with Pandu,' Kunti said, unable to stop herself from interrupting. Today was not the day for protocol. 'We want to stay together.'

I caught the barely discernible sound of Madri taking a deep breath. Whatever I said next would determine the course of their lives. But how was I to respond? The curse said that Pandu would die the moment he embraced a woman. If I let them all go together, that would be putting him in danger. Temptation would be before him every day.

'Don't worry,' Kunti said, 'We understand what we are asking. But we will be able to keep him safe. You have my word.'

I looked at Madri, who mouthed 'we will', her eyes wide with concern, before glancing at Bhishma. This felt like too big a decision to take on my own. But Bhishma was still speaking intently with Pandu. In a split second, I made up my mind.

'I agree. I trust you to do what is right. You have earned that trust, both of you. Now, please go and prepare all you need.'

Both women embraced me before they left. Again, this was not the protocol, but this felt like a day when nothing was as expected. Their hugs were out of warmth and relief.

The small party were given two days to prepare themselves for their lifelong exile. While Pandu and his wives busied themselves in their arrangements, the preparations for Dhritarashtra's coronation started in full swing. I, like so many others, would have preferred to wait, but the king was not prepared to do so. It was not hard to see why. The trial had barely ended before Shakuni was back in court, by Dhritarashtra's side, whispering in his ear with a cunning smile and honeyed words, planting seeds of doubt and ambition. By the sour look on Shakuni's face, he was not impressed with the verdict. He no doubt believed it was another disappointment from the 'blind king' he seemed to have such a hold over, but he was not about to pass up his moment of glory. As far as Shakuni was concerned, he wanted to be elevated to what he believed to be his rightful position as the king's top advisor as soon as possible.

Everywhere I walked among the opulent chambers of the palace, preparations for the coronation were unfolding with grandeur. The air was thick with the heady scent of exotic flowers, their vibrant hues adorning every corner of the majestic hall. Lengths of silken fabrics, dyed in the rich colours of Hastinapur's standards, cascaded from the walls, billowing in the light breeze.

Jewelled chandeliers hung from the ceiling, casting a soft, golden glow upon rows of wooden tables, which awaited the throngs of dignitaries and esteemed guests. Even the palace grounds had been adorned with tapestries and canopies of gold-threaded silk, which made them glitter like a celestial garden. Everywhere resounded to the rhythmic beats of ceremonial drums as the musicians rehearsed their roles in heralding the regal investiture.

The royal kitchens were a hive of activity, with servants running in and out to the noise of pans clashing and chefs shouting volleys of orders. The feast would inevitably be a culinary extravaganza, unfolding across a series of days, each more extravagant than the last. The scent of exotic spices was already perfuming the air, mingling with the smell of slow-cooked meats and fragrant rice. I knew that if I strayed into the kitchens, I would be presented with a kaleidoscopic vision of colourful desserts which would dazzle the eyes.

My status dictated that I should be at the epicentre of this grand spectacle, orchestrating the myriad details that would weave the tapestry of Dhritarashtra's ascension to the throne. My heart, however, was not in it. It was not only that I was consumed by grief at having to say goodbye to Pandu in the next few hours. A shadow was also cast by my deep-seated reservations about the worthiness of Dhritarashtra to assume the mantle of kingship.

I had never had any doubts that Pandu possessed the qualities that should rightfully adorn a monarch. He was brave, fair and unwaveringly committed to the welfare of our kingdom. What he lacked in patience when it came to statecraft had been balanced by the skills of Vidur, his younger brother, and, of course, Bhishma. They were the perfect complement to one another. This would not be the case now. Dhritarashtra did not have the skills of his younger brother, nor any interest in listening to Vidur or Bhishma. His blindness was not his fault, but he could never accept that it did, at times, put him at a disadvantage. It had also made him vulnerable to the whims of fate and the subtle machinations of Shakuni, who had been able to easily sway him towards ill-fated paths, leading him astray from the principles that should guide a ruler.

As I moved through the bustling corridors, my heart was heavy with the knowledge that beneath this veneer of splendour lay a kingdom teetering on the edge of uncertainty once again. Dhritarashtra seemed blissfully oblivious of the gravity of his responsibilities. His affections were ensnared by the counsel of an advisor whose motives remained shrouded in secrecy, a man whose influence I instinctively feared. I had no idea what was behind the subtle manipulation delivered in low whispers by Shakuni, but I was quite certain it was intended to lead my grandson down a treacherous path.

In the silence of my chamber, I found solace in the flickering candlelight, contemplating the choices that had led us to this precipice. The tapestries of gold and silk, the jewelled chandeliers and the sumptuous feasts seemed like distractions from the harsh reality that awaited our kingdom. My eldest grandson might have been about to wear the physical crown, but the weight of true kingship rested on the intangible virtues of wisdom, integrity and devotion to the welfare of the realm. These were qualities that Dhritarashtra didn't have but that Pandu possessed in abundance.

There was nothing that could be changed. In a matter of hours, Pandu and his wives would be gone. Then, with barely a backward glance, Dhritarashtra's ceremony would begin that very evening. He would stand up before the crowds who would, with hushed anticipation, hear his proclamation echo through the hall, pledging to uphold the legacy of our kingdom and safeguard its prosperity.

I had resolved not to show any signs of sadness when I said my goodbyes. The situation was hopeless enough without my adding a burden for Pandu. I failed in my endeavour, however. Just seeing Pandu, Kunti and Madri standing beside their chariot and their modest array of luggage brought tears to my eyes. Very soon, they were flowing down my cheeks. That small array of belongings did not seem enough to sustain them forever. *Forever!*

Pandu was the first to step forward to say his goodbyes. Neither of us gave a thought to protocol as we clasped each other close.

'We will be fine,' he whispered. 'We have found happiness in each other.'

When we broke apart, I saw a brief glimpse of the old Pandu for the first time after he was cursed.

'If anything happens and we are attacked, you still have Bhishma,' Pandu said, and then added with a small grin, 'He's getting on a bit, but he was pretty handy once upon a time, at least when I was there to guide him.'

Bhishma too was smiling and cuffed Pandu's cheek, just as they used to do in the old days. Then, as if remembering the gravity of the situation, Pandu checked himself.

'And, of course, Dhritarashtra has already proved himself to be a just and worthy ruler. Hastinapur is in good hands.'

Bhishma gave Pandu a look of almost fatherly approval, and I felt the tears rising once more. Now, it was time for Madri and Kunti to say their farewells. Madri went first, and I pressed into her hand a small gift, a necklace. It was one of my favourites, which she had often admired. I had so much to say to her, but this seemed the simplest way to express my affection.

When Madri stepped away, Kunti came forward. We embraced like mother and daughter.

'I will keep my promise,' she said. 'You can rely on me.'

I knew this was true. She and I had shared so much in the short time we knew one another. This woman could be trusted. Impulsively, I made up my mind. Perhaps there was a way out of this, after all. A way that would preserve the future of Hastinapur, but protect Pandu.

'Remember your secret,' I said, leaning forward to speak quietly into her ear. 'This is the right time to use it.'

Kunti did not look surprised. From her expression, I knew that she had been considering the same thing. She and I were even more alike than I had thought. She did not voice her reply, though, simply placing a hand over her heart to show she understood.

Then, all too quickly, the small group climbed aboard the chariot and Pandu flicked the reins to begin their journey. As I watched them disappear, drums behind me started up. The coronation ceremony had begun. As I turned towards the palace, ready to play my part and do my duty, my thoughts were with the future, wondering about the fate of a kingdom that now rested upon the shoulders of a king whose qualifications were overshadowed by the allure of misguided counsel. Once more, I pledged silently to navigate the treacherous waters that lay ahead, standing alongside Bhishma in our seemingly endless posts as silent guardians of a kingdom in peril.

Chapter Nineteen

The monsoon season had been less severe than usual this year. Some years, the rains were so heavy that each drop felt like a pebble, hitting one over and over whenever one was outside. My feet would sink deep into the sodden ground, and sticky grey mud would splash up onto my sari. This year, for some reason, the rains had been kinder, gentler. I liked to think the gods recognised my advancing years and were being merciful. Or perhaps they saw that Hastinapur has been through enough.

There were certainly enough breaks in the rain for me to frequent my now favourite spot by the lake behind the palace, as I was doing today. Barely anyone ever seemed to come here, and I often wondered why. The sweet fragrance of plumeria was so soothing. It had the power to transport one away from everything and everyone, for a few moments at least.

I stared out across the lake, dotted with the exotic shades of white, pink and purple of the hundreds of sacred lotus blooms that covered its surface. Each day I looked, there seemed to be more lotus flowers, happily proliferating, spreading their message of calm beauty far and wide. How long had I been at this palace now? Twenty-five years? Thirty? I could not remember the exact count. So much had happened in this time.

When Pandu had gone away to his exile, I had told myself that I would not mourn. He was safe, and he was with Kunti and Madri. I fully intended to keep myself busy. I told myself I'd pick some of those beautiful lotus flowers and start to make medicines once again. I used to do that when I first came here. Shantanu, ah my precious Shantanu, would laugh at me and say that I didn't need to do this. But I felt I had a gift. My lotus-flower medicine helped many people in the court, and Bhishma would always carry a vial of it whenever he went into battle. Not that he needed it. He so rarely received a scratch, let alone a real wound. I had not picked, nor crushed, a single lotus flower for years, though. All I seemed to do was to pace around the edge of the lake, awaiting news.

My faithful Sarathee travelled into the forest once a month to bring back news of Pandu, just as he was doing right now. To begin with, Bhishma reminded me that exile meant exile and they should be left undisturbed. But we need to send them supplies and make sure they are cared for, I begged.

'The forest is abundant with supplies,' Bhishma had laughed gently. 'Pandu and his wives can feast on *shelva*, *karvanda*, mango and *jambul* whenever they wish. They don't need us to send fruits and vegetables from the palace.'

But I had wheedled and wheedled, and eventually he relented a little, but only so far that I could send Sarathee to receive news twelve times a year. He understood that I had to know Pandu was safe and keeping his distance from his wives. Sage Kindama's curse was never far from my mind. My grandson had told me he would be strong, and I trusted Kunti and Madri, but I could never be sure. If they gave into temptation just one time, that would be enough.

There was another reason why it was so important Pandu stayed resolute. Kunti had done as we had discussed. She had used her boon. I had often wondered, sitting in my place by the lake, how she had told Pandu about her gift. When one has been in possession of such a secret for so long, is not easy to say it out loud. I knew how difficult it had been to reveal to Bhishma my true connection to Sage Vyasa. But I hadn't really revealed it, had I? I had instructed Bhishma to go to see my son, and the good sage had told him the truth himself. Even now, I could relive the twisting knot of agony in the pit of my stomach as I'd imagined what Bhishma would think of me. If I had been reduced in his estimation by just one tiny bit, it would have destroyed me.

I couldn't ask Sarathee for the story of what had happened when Kunti told Pandu of the boon. We had known each other for so many years now, but there were some things we never spoke about. I sensed he knew so much when I looked deep into his kind eyes, but wouldn't dream of pushing the point. Instead, I left it to my imagination. I pictured Kunti shyly revealing her secret, as she and her husband stood alone in a light-dappled forest clearing, and Pandu's sweet face breaking into a broad smile. He would have been overjoyed, of course he would. Despite all that had happened, his bloodline would continue.

Kunti had sent me a note via Sarathee. Written on a palm leaf in small, neat handwriting, it told of how she had used her boon five times. She had first evoked the god of justice, Dharmaraja, and bore their son, Yudhishthir. Even when he was just a baby, it was clear he would be as righteous as Dharmaraja himself, she wrote. Then, she and Pandu had prayed to the wind god, Vayu, and bore Bhim, who was very powerful. 'Bhim never seems to stop eating; I assume it is to keep his strength up,' Kunti had added. 'His constant hunger means he eats more food than all his brothers put together.' Their third child, Arjun, was a gift from Lord Indra, the thunder god. Dear Kunti, she was always so generous. She shared her boon with Madri, who evoked the celestial twin brothers, Ashwini Kumars, and bore Pandu two sons, Nakul and Sahadev. Kunti's note had been short, but it had been a comfort. I had read it over and over. After a while, the palm leaf had begun to fade and crumble. By then, though, I knew every word by heart.

I was always hungry for more news, and it was all I could do to stop myself from sending Sarathee back into the forest every single week. Each time Sarathee left, I would sneak little gifts for the boys. Then, I would count the moments until the charioteer's return. In my mind, I would conjure up a vivid picture of every stage of Sarathee's journey as he headed towards my kin. By now, he would have reached the edge of the forest, the place where the *mahua* trees begin, I would think. This is the time of year when their green fruits begin to appear and the villagers rush to gather them to make jaggery and liquor. Then, he would reach the waterfall, where he'd told me that he always stopped to gather fresh water, dipping his gourd deep below the milky surface of foaming water to fill it. He would pass the sacred grove, taking a wide path to avoid disturbing the sages who meditated there in the shade of the sacred banyan tree. Then, after two days of travel, he would arrive at the clearing where Pandu had made his dwelling.

Sarathee told me that Kunti and Madri were always there to greet him. They would immediately fetch water so he could wash the dust of the forest path from his hands and feet and then lay out a simple meal of *saag*, *roti* and *dahl* on fresh palm leaves. He'd smile as he described how the calm of the occasion was always shattered by the noisy arrival of the five boys. They'd have been at their studies with the sage all morning and were always keen to let off steam.

'They are wonderful boys,' he'd say every time when he returned. 'The sage who tutors them says they are exceptionally bright.'

I would never upbraid Sarathee and tell him he had told me the same thing dozens of times before. I loved to hear about them and could have heard the same things one hundred times more. My great-grandchildren were exceptionally bright. How I yearned to meet them!

Staring out across the lake and dreaming of the family in the forest, I checked myself. *I was doing it again.* My mind was far away among the trees with Pandu, Kunti, Madri and their boys. I barely gave any thought to my other grandson, Dhritarashtra. The winds around me began to pick up, and the leaves of the trees that were dotted around the lake shook as if in quiet reproach.

'Yes, I know,' I said to the peepal tree closest to me. 'You are not the first to notice. Vidur is too polite to say it, but I can see it in the way he looks at me sometimes. He thinks Pandu is my favourite.'

For so long, I had pushed my dark thoughts aside. Whenever I felt the truth lifting its head, I would push it away. Maybe, though, I should confront this truth.

The light was beginning to fade a little as the sun dipped behind the tallest trees on the far side of the lake. I closed my eyes and inhaled deeply. *When had these feelings begun? Why did Dhritarashtra make me feel so uneasy?* Whenever I thought of him, a dark shadow would envelope me. I sensed something terrible might happen and that it involved my eldest grandson, yet I couldn't understand what it could be.

I knew I should have been overjoyed that Dhritarashtra and Gandhari had borne my great-grandchildren, and so many of them. One hundred infants. Their entry into the world had not been easy, though. When Gandhari had been pregnant, I had been so fearful. She had been so distressed every day that I feared the jealousy and resentment that for so long plagued my eldest grandchild would consume her too. Gandhari, the faithful wife who had donned a blindfold so she could better understand her husband, had always been so upbeat in the past. What had finally brought her down was the news that Kunti and Pandu had borne a son, Yudhishthir. I heard her raging at Dhritarashtra.

'Our child won't be the eldest,' she sobbed. 'Our family will miss out on the throne *again.* I know we must respect what fate has in store for us, but it is just so upsetting.'

Perhaps the pregnancy had exhausted her so much that her brother Shakuni's constant stirring had finally had an impact. Whatever it was, the poor woman had been pregnant for two whole years. I will never forget the day when she finally went into labour. Her screams and cries of pain and then grief could be heard across the whole kingdom. As I thought back to my first sight of her baby, the sadness climbed in my throat, threatening to swallow me. It hadn't been a baby at all. Just a lump of vivid pink flesh. The maid told me that Gandhari had beaten her stomach until she miscarried, but I did not question Gandhari about this claim. Her misery was too great.

I had done the only thing I could do and went to speak with my son, Sage Vyasa. We had not seen each other since my grandchildren were conceived, but I knew he would know what to do. I tell myself now that what I did, I did for Dhritarashtra and Gandhari, out of guilt for all they had lost, the blindness, the throne, everything. But in truth, I was also doing it Hastinapur and for me, for the terrible oath Bhishma had taken outside my father's house all those years ago. It was I who had made the kingdom vulnerable. It was my fault that there were no strong heirs to carry us forward.

The good sage had listened without saying anything when I begged him to intervene. His expression gave nothing away of what he was thinking. Bhishma, who had travelled with me to speak with him, always my good friend and protector, had given me no counsel either. When I reproached him, he would only say he would always obey the wishes of his mother. The sage gave nothing away of what he was thinking either. After I made my request, he had reached out and put his hand on my cheek. I had no idea if he was prepared to help.

It was only much later that I learned what had happened. Sage Vyasa had visited Gandhari and taken her stillborn child. He had used his knife to cut the flesh into one hundred pieces. Each piece had then been carefully placed in a clay pot and covered with ghee, before he hung them up on a tree deep in a cave, one by one. We had waited a whole year for the outcome. The atmosphere in the court had been terrible. The hallways had been dark and silent save for the low drumming of bare feet hurrying along the smooth floors. Each mealtime had been a muted affair as everyone all but swallowed their food whole so they could quickly scamper away from the misery that swamped the main chamber.

Then, one day, it all changed. The grief that had covered the palace like a shadow lifted, like the sun appearing from behind dark clouds after the last of the monsoon rains. Gandhari came hurrying into my chamber to tell me a miracle had occurred. The first pot had opened and their son Duryodhana had emerged. He was, she said, the most beautiful baby who had ever lived. But then, each day after that, more beautiful babies had emerged from their pots. In all, a total of ninety-nine boys and one girl emerged from those pots before the tree that bore their weight for so long withered and died. My own son, Sage Vyasa, had indeed worked wonders. I had never seen anyone as happy as Dhritarashtra and Gandhari. Their wishes had been fulfilled.

The court had changed completely after that. For a time, people danced and laughed and lingered over meals. Their faces, once grey, fearful and weary, looked younger, almost new in their relief. The very air around us felt lined with gold. Of course, the greatest noise of all was created by the tribe of great-grandchildren, who constantly rushed around, clattering into walls and laughing uproariously at their antics. A team of nannies would follow in their wake, concern etched on their faces as they dived to pick up precious pots and ornaments that were carelessly dislodged from their resting places by the unruly mob. The most boisterous of them all was the eldest, Duryodhana, the most headstrong and determined baby I had ever seen. His siblings were all drawn to him, fascinated by his swagger as, even as a young boy, he strode about the court like he owned the place. They constantly circled him like bees in a hive. The only person ever to take their attention away from their leader Duryodhana, was the next brother in line, Dushasana, who was a complete hothead. Dushasana was utterly devoted to his eldest brother and anyone who dared stand in his brother's way needed to answer to Dushasana. He would sometimes be quite rough in the justice meted out to both his brothers and the various servants who attended them, never caring to investigate whether the misdemeanour was just an accident.

I adored my great-grandchildren, of course I did. Watching them grow was a privilege. I was as diligent as any doting great-grandparent too, as I pushed podgy fingers away from sharp objects or swatted wasps who flew too close to the flailing arms and legs of the children, who always seemed so oblivious to danger. I would usher them away from the open fires to make sure the sparks did not touch their soft golden flesh and forbid them from pulling the precious lotus flowers from the lake, lest they toppled in and sunk into its depths. I couldn't have done more. But so often, standing in my quiet corner of the lake as I did now, I dreamt of what my other great-grandchildren would be like in court. My five exceptionally bright great-grandchildren would continue their studies, I was sure. They wouldn't be distracted by play or show off to one another. They would be too self-assured for all of that.

The leaves rustled overhead. *You're right, I am doing it again,* I smiled, looking up into the branches. But things were not as they should have been. Things had gradually gone back to how they were before. Dhritarashtra's demeanour had not improved with time. Despite the joy brought to him by his large family, everything about him betrayed a soul hardened by bitterness, presenting a stern and unyielding façade. His eyes, though unseeing, glinted with a cold detachment. Shakuni had done his work, ensuring that the ruler was more concerned with the preservation of his power than the prosperity of his people. Sadly, Dhritarashtra had not made his brother-in-law's work that difficult.

As I had always feared, the king had not mellowed with age but had instead become an embodiment of imperious self-importance. The weight of Shakuni's constant whispers had encouraged him to rule with an iron fist that crushed the once-vibrant spirit of his court. What had once been a centre of energy and joy under Pandu, and even when my one hundred great-grandchildren had been born, now more often echoed with hushed whispers and wary glances. The corridors, adorned with tapestries depicting tales of valour and prosperity, seemed to recoil under the oppressive air that accompanied the king's presence. His every decree bore the sting of arbitrary rule, and the once-jubilant gatherings of courtiers had transformed into sombre assemblies.

The only person the king appeared to soften around was his queen. Gandhari had weathered the storms of his reign with the same quiet fortitude with which she had initially put on her blindfold. Even then, though, behind closed doors, the tension between the king and his queen was palpable. I swear the portraits adorning their chamber walls had somehow absorbed the endless silent reproach that hung in the air. Certainly, their once-rich colours had dulled. Dhritarashtra and Gandhari's whispered conversations, at one time filled with shared dreams, now carried the weight of unspoken grievances.

This was not, as Dhritarashtra would occasionally remind me, my concern. He was king. I had had my time. However uncomfortable I was, I had to accept things as they were. Bhishma too. All we could do was watch and wait and hope the next generation would put things right.

It was, I realised, much later than I had thought. It was now difficult to make out the shape of individual branches in the half-light of dusk. Smoothing down the silk of my sari, which was cool to the touch, I turned to begin my short walk back to the palace. How long had I been standing there? I had no clue, but my legs felt stiff and a little sore. The weight of my years was such a burden to me now. I hated my weakness.

A shout in the distance snapped me out of my moment of self-pity. A cry of agony, the likes of which I had never heard before, and I'd had my fair share of tragedy. My heart began to pound as I hurried towards the source of the sound. Fear made my legs feel even weaker, and my temples pounded. I cursed myself for moving so slowly. I needed to be there. That cry called to me.

Rounding the corner of the large wall that divided the palace from the lake, I abruptly stopped. I could not believe what I saw in front of me. It was Sarathee's golden chariot and standing in front of it, shoulders slumped and head held low, Sarathee himself. Drawing upon what little strength I had left, I rushed to him. Placing my hands on his trembling shoulders, I gently shook him.

'Sarathee, Sarathee, what has happened? You have only been gone two days. Usually, you stay in the forest for at least …'

My words dried on my lips as Sarathee at last raised his head. His whole body was rigid, and the skin of his shoulders was cold beneath my fingers. But his eyes, those eyes that used to twinkle with pleasure as he spoke of the family in the forest, were utterly blank. His expression told me all I needed to know. Something had happened to Pandu. I felt my knees begin to buckle.

I opened my eyes to see Bhishma looking down at me, his face etched with concern. I was lying on the damp ground, my head was cradled in his lap as he gently stroked my forehead.

'Pandu?' I said, my voice barely a whisper.

Bhishma shook his head slowly.

'He is gone,' he said.

I wanted to cry out, but no sound came. My grief was so deep it might never emerge, and if it did, it might destroy me. I would need to wall it up inside me, keeping it in a dungeon beside my sadness at losing Shantanu, and my two boys, Chitrangada and Vichitravirya, and most of all, my shame for all I had put Bhishma through, the greatest man I had ever met.

'How?' was the only word I could manage.

Bhishma stared ahead as he talked. I realised that he too was doing his best to hold back the tidal wave of grief that threatened to overwhelm him.

'Pandu was always destined to be weak,' he began and then shook his head. 'Except we all thought he had escaped that curse, because he was such a bold warrior. Everyone admired his skills in battle, and he single-handedly helped restore the good standing of Hastinapur.'

Bhishma was silent for a moment, thoughtful. I did not interrupt.

'But he did have one weakness. Well, if you could call it that. He loved his wives too much. He knew the cost to him if he touched them. You warned him. I warned him. Kunti and Madri must have told him a thousand times. But …'

His voice trailed off. I heard a sob and looked up. There, standing behind Bhishma, was Kunti. Getting to my feet as quickly as I could, I raced to embrace her. As she sank into my arms, I heard a soft moan of abject despair.

'He held you?' I asked.

I felt her head shake from side to side to indicate it hadn't been her.

'Madri,' she said softly. 'But even before their lips touched, he fell to the floor. Dead.'

That last word was an arrow to my heart. I knew it was true, but hearing it spoken out loud made it all the more final.

Looking beyond Kunti, whose whole body heaved with sobs now, I searched for Madri among the small crowd standing beside the chariot.

'Where is she?' I asked Bhishma, who was now once again at my side. 'I can't see Madri.'

Bhishma shook his head slowly.

'She is gone too. She felt responsible and asked to join her beloved Pandu on the funeral pyre.'

My eyes blurred with tears. Pandu *and* Madri? It hardly seemed possible. My arms fell to my side, and Kunti shrank away. Poor girl, she should know I didn't blame her. I didn't blame anyone. It was just the most terrible tragedy.

'We need to be strong,' Bhishma said, tenderly wiping away the tears that now fell freely down my cheeks. 'We have a job to do.'

For a moment, I didn't understand. A job to do? What job? How would I possibly ever be able to function normally ever again? Then, I looked in the direction where Bhishma motioned. Standing there, in a forlorn huddle under the protective gaze of Sarathee, were five boys. My great-grandchildren. Home at last.

Chapter Twenty

To my relief, Shakuni was not around when I went to speak with Dhritarashtra. It was late in the afternoon, and I found the king in his chamber, seated on a low couch with Gandhari. The maid told me the two were preparing for supper, but one look at their faces and I knew immediately that they had retired to discuss what had just happened.

'You have heard the news,' I said.

My grandson raised his hand, sweeping it towards the sky. I was not sure I understood the gesture. Was he saying Pandu was with the gods now? That it was of no consequence in the grand scheme? What did he mean? Somehow, though, I didn't want to ask.

Gandhari, sweet, faithful Gandhari, stepped in to fill the silence. 'We are so sorry,' she said simply. 'We were all so fond of Pandu.'

Were.

My heart beat harder in my chest, but I forced myself to collect my thoughts. I had sought out the king for a reason. I must fulfil this purpose.

'That is true,' I said. I could not bring myself to say we *were* fond of Pandu. Not yet. Perhaps not ever. 'Are you aware that your nephews are here? Sarathee brought them to the court. There is no need for this family to stay in the forest, not anymore. Not now …'

Dhritarashtra made no reaction, but I knew he was listening intently. My beloved eldest grandson, who always put on such a show of defiance, yet I knew he was in as much pain as all of us. He had adored his younger brother.

'I have sent them to refresh themselves after the journey, but I would like to present them to you as soon as possible. Not as their uncle, but as the king of Hastinapur.'

Silence, but I noted that Dhritarashtra raised his head a little, as though sniffing at the night air. I had little choice but to press on. My mind spun with how to address what I had to say. As my eldest great-grandchild, it was inevitable that Yudhishthir would inherit the throne now they were back from exile. The king needed to take his role in paving the way for this to happen. A smooth succession when the time came. A succession which would keep Hastinapur safe.

'I came here to ask you to give the princes a proper welcome, to treat them well and to give them their rights.'

Without warning, Dhritarashtra leapt to his feet, his face darkened with a flash of anger. My instinctive response was to step back, but before I had done so, Gandhari had swiftly stood up and gently placed a hand on her husband's arm.

'Of course, we will do that,' she said. 'We are both very curious to meet them at long last.'

At his wife's cue, the king's stance softened a little and at last he spoke.

'You can rest easy. I always do everything I can to extend all courtesy in my court.'

Was I imagining it, but had he deliberately stressed the word 'my'? I could not reproach him for this. Now was not the time. He was king and had been so for many years. His role was not under threat, but he did have a duty to prepare the next king for his duties. The time to discuss that would come, though. Right now, it was all too raw, too soon.

'Thank you. May we present you the five Pandavs this evening, before supper?'

Dhritarashtra inclined his head to indicate this was acceptable, and I left the chamber as quickly as I could.

I made my way down to the main hall well ahead of the appointed hour and was surprised to see how many people were there already. Suppers in the halls had become increasingly quiet of late as the noblemen found various excuses to stay away. Now, though, word had got around about the five princes, and curiosity had got the better of them. Even Dhritarashtra was early and was sitting in his usual place on the dais, flanked by Shakuni on one side and Gandhari on the other. Further to one side sat Bhishma and Vidur. Was I mistaking it, or did Bhishma look as weary as I felt? I had seen less and less of him in recent times too. It was as though he was there if needed but preferred to keep the intrigues of Dhritarashtra's rule at arm's length. I did not blame him.

A hush of anticipation descended upon the court as the large doors opened to reveal the five young princes. They had changed their garments since their arrival, but someone, I didn't know who, had provided them with sombre clothes, no doubt to mark their recent bereavement. My heart went out to them as they made their steady way towards the dais with a poise and solemnity that belied their tender years. The eldest Pandav, Yudhishthir, a boy on the cusp of adolescence, bore the weight of responsibility on shoulders that seemed too fragile for the burden life had thrust upon him. His eyes, however, reflected a resilience that spoke of an inner strength and a lightness of being. I had seen that look before, in the eyes of his father Pandu. Behind him, walking with sure steps, his four brothers did not once take their eyes from their uncle.

It took huge presence of mind to tear my eyes away from my approaching great-grandchildren, but I wanted to read Dhritarashtra's reaction. As usual, Shakuni was whispering in his ear. His body language spoke of a helpful advisor describing the scene before him, yet the glint in his dark eyes seemed to say something different.

By the time I turned back, the Pandavs had almost reached the dais. They stopped a short distance away and, one, bowed low to the king. This was tradition. Dhritarashtra wouldn't see it, but he'd know immediately if it had not happened. Shakuni would be quick to tell him. Then, the boys turned to their right and did the same to Bhishma. A feeling of pride swelled within me. Pandu, Bhishma's most loyal pupil, had passed on his teachings to his sons and taught them to love and respect the demigod as much as he did. Bhishma got to his feet and returned the gesture. His eyes betrayed how much this meant to him.

It was Yudhishthir who spoke first, with a measured voice that carried the weight of newfound responsibility with surprising confidence.

'My King, it is an honour to be presented to you. May I please commend to you my brothers, Bhim, Arjun, Nakul and Sahadev. The circumstances of these introductions are not ideal, but we are, nevertheless, very pleased to come before you.'

Silence descended upon the main hall. Many of the nobles leaned forward in anticipation of the response, their gaze alternating between the small group of boys and the king. Even now, I had no idea which way this would go. I doubted

Dhritarashtra would warmly embrace his nephews. He had never been like that. His expression already indicated that he was suspicious of them. But I hoped he would be true to his word and would at least make them welcome.

To my surprise, he did not address the boys directly, but instead spoke to the court as a whole.

'It is with a sense of duty and compassion that we open our hearts and arms to these young princes, embracing them into the folds of our great family,' the king began. 'In doing so, we not only honour the memory of their father but also reaffirm our collective commitment to the values that define our great kingdom.'

It was not the most comforting, nor compassionate, of speeches, but at least it was not openly hostile and did acknowledge that the Pandavs were a part of the family. Now, though, Dhritarashtra began to address the boys directly.

'My nephews, I extend the welcome of the court, and we hope you will enjoy being here. You will live a life that is very different from what you have known, but this is the rightful place for you now. I am hopeful that my children, your cousins, will help you settle in and explain to you how we live here.

'I call upon my eldest son Duryodhana to make the introductions ...' he paused and gave a low chuckle. 'You will have many names to learn.'

I was just reflecting on how many times I had heard this joke from the king about his many children, when my thoughts were interrupted by the arrival of Duryodhana at the front of the dais. I had not noticed it before, but this evening, Dhritarashtra's son had chosen to dress in his most lavish robes. The golden silk fabric they were made from was inlaid with dozens of colourful precious stones. The multiple chains looped around the boy's slim neck were also dotted with jewels. By far, the most remarkable part of the ensemble, though, was the expression on his face. Duryodhana was a handsome boy, with strong cheekbones which ran parallel to his jawline, giving the impression he had been carefully chiselled from stone by the most exacting craftsperson. His eyes were large, dark pools, and his lips were full, which added to the effect. Yet, he had a habit of narrowing his eyes and pursing his lips into thin lines when he was displeased, which entirely altered the impact of his beauty, making him look cruel and vindictive. And this was what he was doing. To add to it, he had placed himself exactly in front of his father, his legs planted wide and arms behind his back.

Things happened very quickly. Out of the corner of my eye, I saw Bhishma leap to his feet and begin rushing forward. He always anticipated things much before us mere mortals. He was too slow, though. Even before he reached standing position, Duryodhana had leapt off the dais and was standing just in front of his cousin Yudhishthir, so close their noses almost touched. Then, he drew back his arms and roughly shoved Yudhishthir backwards, sending him sprawling to the floor. As Yudhishthir's brothers raced to help him to his feet, Duryodhana stalked the length of the main hall and went through the large doors without a backward glance.

I could barely believe what I had just seen, nor could anyone else. The court was not exactly in uproar, for no one would dare criticise the king's eldest son, but the low whispers between one noble and the next combined to create a wall of sound. One look at Dhritarashtra told me that Shakuni had already filled him in on what had happened, but the king did not look overly concerned. He was simply having an intense conversation with his advisor. I could swear I saw him smile and shake his head.

Was that it? Was he not going to admonish his son for such a grave act of rudeness?

If I did not act immediately, this would pave the way for the future. Dhritarashtra may have agreed to give all courtesy to the future king, but his son had not. Duryodhana had to be disciplined and made to understand that he should respect his cousin.

I began to make my way down the hall in the footsteps of Duryodhana, which was not easy as the nobles too were dispersing and the way was thronged with slow moving bodies. They'd come to see drama and had not been disappointed. They were in no hurry to leave as they swapped their reactions. No one was even trying to lower their voices to hide their conversations as they discussed what this new development might mean. *This is how it starts*, I thought, quickening my step.

I was close to the door when I felt a familiar presence by my side. *Bhishma*.

'This is not your battle,' he said in a low voice.

I swung around to face him, not comprehending. Of course it was my battle. It was *our* battle, the same one we had been fighting together ever since that day at my father's house. How could he not see that?

I glanced at the large doors in front of me and then back at Bhishma. I needed to address this now.

'No, we need to talk now,' he said.

I allowed myself to be turned around and walked beside Bhishma, both of us dodging between the tide of nobles leaving the hall. I knew without asking where we were going. To our usual spot, the justices' room. The dais had already cleared as we went past, and I wondered vaguely if anyone had bothered to show those poor Pandavs where the dining hall was. I hoped one of the maids had done so.

Bhishma opened the door and stood back for me to enter first. I did not head to my usual chair, though. I was too anxious.

Closing the door behind us, Bhishma came to stand in front of me. We were both silent for a moment, but I felt the familiar sensation of comfort as I looked into his eyes. Bhishma still had the power to stare into my soul and mend me. What a figure he was!

'What do you think happened there?' he said finally.

I shrugged. This seemed so obvious.

'Duryodhana was extremely rude to his cousin. Never mind that Yudhishthir is the future king, it is just not the way to treat a guest, especially after, after … all they have been through.'

Bhishma's expression gave nothing away of what he was thinking and he spoke in his usual measured tone.

'Do you really think Yudhishthir should inherit the throne?'

I caught my breath. What a strange question. What was I missing?

'He is older than Duryodhana,' I said, doing my best not to sound impatient. 'That is how it works.'

'Does it?'

My head was spinning now. Bhishma was not reproachful, yet he clearly did not agree.

'Perhaps we must look at in another way.'

'Another way?'

'Merit is important too. In fact, more important. If it were not for his blindness, Dhritarashtra would have been king right from the start and Pandu would never have sat on the throne. Therefore, Dhritarashtra's son would have rightfully always been expected to be the next in line.'

Just for the merest second, the world seemed to stop spinning. How had I not seen this? I had always simply assumed that Pandu's son would follow in his footsteps and be the king.

'Simply assuming Yudhishthir would inherit the throne is a mistake. There are many other factors to consider,' Bhishma said quietly. 'It is a mistake that, if repeated, will have grave implications, both now and in the future.'

My face burnt with shame and I bowed my head because I did not want Bhishma to see me this way. I had got this so very wrong. Was it my age? Had I reached a stage where I was no longer of use to Hastinapur? Unlike Bhishma, I did not have godly powers to sustain me. I had made the mistake of ignoring Dhritarashtra before and swore I would rectify it. But I had done it again. Worse still, I had carried my carelessness to the next generation.

Bhishma said nothing, but even though I looked at the ground, I knew he was watching me as I worked it all through. Duryodhana had behaved terribly, but I understood why now. If I continued in this way and allowed the son to be overlooked in the same way as his father, I would ensure that this child would be as bitter and angry as my eldest grandson.

'I need ...'

I got no further before being interrupted by the sound of the door opening behind us. Swinging around, I gasped in shock. Standing there, with a lengthy white beard and flowing orange robes, was Sage Vyasa. My son. He had an aura of calm radiance and his skin was weathered, as one might expect from a noble sage who spent much of his life in meditation and spiritual contemplation, but it seemed to glow too. His eyes, deep and penetrating, shone with wisdom.

'Sage Vyasa,' were the only words I could manage as he bent to kiss my feet.

'Mother,' he said, rising up.

'My good sage,' Bhishma said, greeting our guest with a bow. 'You honour us.'

'It is I who is honoured,' my son smiled.

Everything within me wanted to ask what he was doing there. While I always yearned to see him, I had only ever met him twice as an adult. It was, therefore, almost certain there was a purpose to his visit. Sage Vyasa was not the type to turn up on an impulse.

'I have come to speak with you, Mother,' he began. 'I have something important to say.'

Tears sprung to my eyes. Whatever it was, I already sensed it was serious. Bhishma's expression was impassive. *He knew already.*

'It is time for you to go,' the sage said quietly.

'Go? Go where?'

My son clasped his palms together in front of him, his eyes never once leaving mine.

'You cannot bear witness to fate. What happens next is for others to see.'

'And me?' Bhishma said. 'Shall I accompany my mother?'

The sage shook his head.

'You story is not over,' he said. 'It has not even reached the halfway point. There is much to do in Hastinapur.'

By now, tears were streaming down my face. A jumble of words swirled around my brain. Go? Witness to fate? What happens next? Was I to be alone now?

Did they not understand? Hastinapur needed me now, more than ever. We were about to lurch into another crisis, and I needed to be there, alongside Bhishma, to steer us out of it. That was my sworn duty. It had always been my sworn duty.

I glanced at Bhishma and felt a powerful wave of love for the man who had given up everything to be my son. I could see it in his face, though; this was his wish too. My time had come.

How could I blame them? They were right, of course. I was an old lady now and so very different from that young girl who had arrived at the palace with nothing but a secret and an unwavering desire to right the wrong that had brought me there. I had fought and fought and fought, but each battle had seemed to lead to the next. I was exhausted, and my judgement was clearly off-key now. First, I had got it so very wrong with Dhritarashtra and then repeated the mistake with his son, Duryodhana. Bhishma was so much more qualified than I was, in every way. Perhaps I had kidded myself all along that I had something useful to give.

'You mustn't do yourself a disservice,' Bhishma said, looking at me intently. 'Things would have been very different if you were not here. You have got us this far, but as the good sage says, what happens next is in the hands of others.'

Bhishma was right. He always was. Besides, I had no fight left. It was time to go. There was no point arguing with such powerful men.

'Thank you. Please, if you would both excuse me, I will make my preparations.'

As I left the room, I did not look back. I felt my heart would break.

It took a few days to finalise the arrangements. I chose Pandu's house in the forest as a place to live. Somehow, I felt it would give me some comfort in my old age. His spirit would be there to guide me and keep me safe. While the conclusion of his time in the forest had been tragic, he was always surrounded by an aura of happiness. If just a little of that marked my retirement, I would be a very lucky woman. To my relief, Ambika and Ambalika requested to accompany me, and Bhishma had agreed this was a good idea. I enjoyed their company, and we had been so close over the years. They were like my daughters.

By far, the most time in my preparations was spent in saying my goodbyes. It was a wrench to leave the Pandavs. I'd waited so long to meet them, and now I was leaving, having barely got to know them. Dhritarashtra was characteristically aloof, but Gandhari was warm and supportive, as always. The most affectionate farewells, aside from each of my one hundred great-grandchildren, were from Kunti. The two of us understood one another, and I was hopeful that she would take on some of my role, making sure that the people of the court thought beyond the here and now and considered the future of our once-great kingdom.

I knew the hardest farewell of them all would be with Bhishma, and I left that task until the very last moment. He was waiting for me out in the yard, alongside Sarathee and my chariot.

I had rehearsed in my head over and over what I might say to the demigod. Each time, though, I would blush with embarrassment at my words. How could I ever say what I really wanted to say and thank him for all he had done? I was a foolish mortal and he was a great, great man. By becoming his mother, I had robbed him of everything.

What could I have done differently, I thought, as I crossed the courtyard towards Bhishma? I had sworn to protect Hastinapur, yet had I really made a difference? So many of the decisions I had made had only seemed to make things worse. My heart mourned for what I left behind, and for my sons Chitrangada and Vichitravirya, for Shantanu and, of course, Pandu. I had lost so many people that I loved so deeply. I was also devastated that I would never truly know what would happen next. This story, the one that had begun at the river in my little boat, was only just beginning. I was certain of that. Yet, my part in it was done.

I stopped beside the chariot and Bhishma turned to face me. Neither of us wanted to be the first to speak. I had to say something, though. If I did not speak now, it would be too late.

'I am so sorry,' I said, breathing hard. 'Everything I did was to make up for … what you did for your father and me. I tried to …'

Words failed me for a moment.

'… tried to take responsibility and right the wrongs, but everything I did only made things worse. I just …'

Bhishma shook his head.

'That is not how it was. Not how I saw it. Not ever.'

He reached forward to gently brush the tears away from my cheeks.

'But I have given you a lifetime of pain,' I pressed.

Bhishma smiled. 'I was always destined to suffer every moment I spent on this earth,' he said softly. 'That was always Prabhasa's destiny.'

I looked at him uncomprehendingly, but he did not pause.

'It was preordained from the moment my father, your beloved Shantanu, stopped my mother, the goddess Ganga, from drowning me. She would have released me from a lifetime of torment in the same way as she helped my seven brothers.'

This still made no sense. Perhaps it never would. Bhishma was not going to explain, though. He indicated the conversation was over by holding out his hand to help me onto the chariot.

As Sarathee flicked the reins and the chariot moved away, I looked over my shoulder. Bhishma had not moved from where he was standing, and regret clung to me like a shadow. Fate had thrown us together, and I had hoped that time and destiny would weave a different narrative for us. I feared for the future of Hastinapur. I doubted that fear would ever go away. Equally, though, I yearned to be of at least some use to Bhishma through whatever came next. Whatever it was, though, he would have to face it alone.

JAICO PUBLISHING HOUSE

Elevate Your Life. Transform Your World.

ESTABLISHED IN 1946, Jaico Publishing House is home to world-transforming authors such as Robin Sharma, Sadhguru, Osho, the Dalai Lama, Deepak Chopra, Eknath Easwaran, Paramhansa Yogananda, Devdutt Pattanaik, Radhakrishnan Pillai, Morgan Housel, Napoleon Hill, John Maxwell, Brian Tracy, and Stephen Hawking.

Our late founder Mr. Jaman Shah first established Jaico as a book distribution company. Sensing that independence was around the corner, he aptly named his company Jaico ('Jai' means victory in Hindi). In order to service the significant demand for affordable books in a developing nation, Mr. Shah initiated Jaico's own publications. Jaico was India's first publisher of paperback books in the English language.

While self-help; religion and philosophy; mind, body and spirit; and business titles form the cornerstone of our non-fiction list, we publish an exciting range of current affairs, history, biography, art and architecture, travel, and popular science books as well. Our renewed focus on popular fiction is evident in our new titles by a host of fresh young talent from India and abroad.

Jaico's translations division publishes select bestselling titles in over 10 regional languages including Gujarati, Hindi, Kannada, Malayalam, Marathi, Tamil, and Telugu. These include titles from renowned national and international authors like Sudha Murthy, Gaur Gopal Das, Swami Mukundananda, Jay Shetty, Simon Sinek, Ankur Warikoo and Jeff Keller.

Visit our Website

Boasting one of India's largest book distribution networks, Jaico has its headquarters in Mumbai, with branches in Ahmedabad, Bangalore, Chennai, Delhi, Hyderabad, and Kolkata. This network ensures that our books reach all parts of the country, both urban and rural.